And the Killer Is . . .

Books by G.A. McKevett

SAVANNAH REID MYSTERIES

Just Desserts
Bitter Sweets
Killer Calories
Cooked Goose
Sugar and Spite
Sour Grapes
Peaches and Screams
Death By Chocolate
Cereal Killer
Murder à la Mode
Corpse Suzette
Fat Free and Fatal
Poisoned Tarts
A Body to Die For
Wicked Craving
A Decadent Way to Die
Buried in Buttercream
Killer Honeymoon
Killer Physique
Killer Gourmet
Killer Reunion
Every Body on Deck
Hide and Sneak
Bitter Brew
And the Killer Is . . .

GRANNY REID MYSTERIES

Murder in Her Stocking
Murder in the Corn Maze

Published by Kensington Publishing Corporation

G.A. McKevett

And the Killer Is . . .

A SAVANNAH REID MYSTERY

KENSINGTON BOOKS
www.kensingtonbooks.com

KENSINGTON BOOKS are published by

Kensington Publishing Corp.
119 West 40th Street
New York, NY 10018

All Kensington titles, imprints and distributed lines are available at special quantity discounts for bulk purchases for sales promotion, premiums, fundraising, educational or institutional use. Special book excerpts or customized printings can also be created to fit specific needs. For details, write or phone the office of the Kensington Special Sales Manager: Kensington Publishing Corp., 119 West 40th Street, New York, NY, 10018. Attn. Special Sales Department. Phone: 1-800-221-2647.

Library of Congress Card Catalogue Number: 2019953559

Kensington and the K logo Reg. U.S. Pat. & TM Off.

ISBN-13: 978-1-4967-2013-9
ISBN-10: 1-4967-2013-X
First Kensington Hardcover Edition: May 2020

ISBN-13: 978-1-4967-2015-3 (e-book)
ISBN-10: 1-4967-2015-6 (e-book)

10 9 8 7 6 5 4 3 2 1

Printed in the United States of America

For Tracie,
the sister my heart adopted

Acknowledgments

Thank you, Leslie Connell, my dear friend and faithful copy editor, who read my stories before *anyone* else and set my mind at ease, telling me that they were good and getting better all the time. You will never know how much that meant to me.

I wish to thank all the fans who write to me, sharing their thoughts and offering endless encouragement. Your stories touch my heart, and I enjoy your letters more than you know. I can be reached at:

sonja@sonjamassie.com
and
facebook.com/gwendolynnarden.mckevett

And the Killer Is . . .

Chapter 1

"**H**ey! What the bloody hell do you think you're doin' there, woman?"

Savannah Reid turned to her enraged husband, sitting next to her in the driver's seat of his old Buick, and thought she had seen happier expressions on felons' faces who had just received a sentence of fifty years to life.

"Bloody hell?" she asked calmly. "Since when do you say 'bloody hell'?"

Detective Sergeant Dirk Coulter thought it over a moment, looked a tad sheepish, and admitted, "Okay. I dropped by Ryan and John's restaurant and had a pint with John earlier. That British accent thing of his is almost as bad as your southern drawl. Rubs off on you. I'm around him ten minutes, and I start talking about dodgy weather and how knackered I was after givin' some nutter a bollockin'."

"Do you drop by ReJuvene regularly?"

"Naw. Maybe five or six times a week."

"These pints you're downing—they're free, no doubt, considering Ryan's and John's generous natures."

"Of course they're free. You wouldn't expect me to drop into a swanky establishment like theirs and plunk down my hard-earned cash for a beer, wouldja?"

"No, darlin'. Never crossed my mind that you would do such a thing as pay for a drink you could get for free."

"Good." He looked relieved for a moment, then seemed to remember his former complaint. "But don't think you're distracting me. I still got a beef with you, gal."

She glanced around, trying to determine what faux pas she might have committed. After all, she was doing him the enormous favor of keeping him company on an afternoon stakeout that was as exciting as eating a mashed potato and white bread sandwich, followed by vanilla pudding.

The locale wasn't anything to quicken the pulse either. They were parked on a nearly deserted residential street in one of the few unattractive and unsavory neighborhoods of sunny little San Carmelita—otherwise known as "the picturesque seaside village where native Southern Californians themselves go to relax and play."

Instead of sunlit beaches, boutiques, gift shops, and upscale restaurants, this part of town had ramshackle buildings, barred windows, signs warning of fierce dogs who could run faster than any trespasser, graffiti-smeared cement block walls, and burned-out streetlights. From what Savannah could tell, this section of San Carmelita possessed no virtues whatsoever, except those held by the souls who lived there—strength, courage, pride, and determination born of desperation.

Over the years, Savannah had seen more than one glorious flower bloom on this side of town, thriving in poverty's mud and squalor. But there were still a lot of places she'd prefer to be and things she'd rather be doing.

Considering the price she was paying to keep her bored cop

hubby company, she couldn't imagine how she had managed to offend him.

She wasn't painting her fingernails—an activity he despised, claiming he was deathly allergic to the odor.

She had brought a tin of fresh-from-the-oven chocolate chip and macadamia nut cookies and had been considerate enough not to eat more than her rightful half of them.

She had allowed him to choose the music on the radio and, as a result, she had spent the last hour listening to Johnny Cash.

In truth, she liked Johnny quite a lot, but there was no point in letting Dirk know that. At the end of this tour, she wanted him to feel sufficiently indebted to her to take her out for a nice dinner. Otherwise, he would assume he could buy her off with day-old donuts and stale coffee . . . which he would also manage to finagle for free.

"Sorry, sweetcheeks," she said, her down-in-Dixie drawl a bit slower and softer than usual. "I don't know what sort of sins I've committed to get you all in a dither."

He nodded toward the dash, where she had set her empty soda can.

"Yeah?" she said, genuinely confused. "It's not going to spill, if that's what you're frettin' about. It's empty."

"You better make sure," he told her in a tone that was uncharacteristically bossy for him.

Over the years, she had trained him well.

He knew better.

She figured it must be mighty important to him, for him to risk riling her. So, she snatched the can off the dash, then began to roll down the window.

"What do you think you're doing?" he snapped.

"I'm gonna see if I can squeeze a drop or two of Coke out of this here can that you've got your willy all tied up in a Windsor knot about."

"You go pouring it out like that, some could splash on the outside of the door and ruin the paint job."

For a few seconds, she stared at him, calculating how much energy she would have to expend to cram a soda can into a highly annoying husband's right ear.

She figured, in the end, she could get the job done, but Dirk wasn't one to quietly submit to having items inserted into his orifices without offering resistance, and she was tired, so she abandoned the plan.

Instead, she rolled the window back up, opened the door, leaned out, bent down, and shook the three remaining drops of soda onto the curb.

Then, with much pomp and circumstance, she shut the door and handed him the can. "There you go. Feel free to shove this . . . wherever you're putting your garbage, now that you no longer hurl it over your right shoulder and onto the floorboard, the way you did for years and—"

"Until your brother restored this car to cherry condition!" he snapped, grabbing the can from her hand. "After all the work Waycross did on my baby, do you think I'm gonna let her get all dirty again? No way. You could do brain surgery back there on my rear floorboard now."

"Unsettling thought, but possibly necessary if this conversation continues," she muttered.

"You could lick ice cream off these seats."

"Knowing you, if you dropped your cone, you probably would," she whispered.

"What?"

"Nothing. I'm glad you're so proud of how clean your car is now, after years of slovenliness."

"Thank you. I guess." He crushed the can flat with his

hands, reached behind her, and lovingly placed it into the fancy-dandy auto litter receptacle attached to her headrest, hanging behind the passenger's seat.

The bin was lined with a deodorized plastic bag, and Savannah was pretty sure she could detect the scent of bleach.

Her baby brother, Waycross, had restored Dirk's old Buick after it had been all but totaled in a severe accident. Before, the car had been pretty much a trash heap on wheels.

But since Waycross had surprised Dirk with the perfect "resurrection model" of his formerly deceased vehicle, Dirk was treating the car even better than Savannah babied her red 1965 Mustang. That was saying quite a lot, since she sometimes used dental floss to clean its wire-spoked wheel covers.

While she was glad to see Dirk finally give a dang for a change, embrace a passion, and abandon his former lifestyle— a study in untidy apathy—she found his new obsessive cleanliness annoying, to say the least.

"Be careful what you wish for," she murmured. "Lord help you if you happen to get it." Under her breath she added, "Maybe I could get Waycross to remodel the area around my toilet."

"What?"

"Nothing."

Twenty minutes and several cookies later, both Savannah's and Dirk's banter had turned to silence born of acute boredom. Not even Johnny's rousing rendition of "Folsom Prison Blues," recorded in the infamous jailhouse itself, was enough to keep Dirk from nodding off.

"I could be home right now, you know," she told him, confident that he was sound asleep and wouldn't hear a word. "I could be watching TV or reading my new romance novel."

Surveilling a drug house was seldom a joyous occasion, and

the one they were observing was even less exciting than most. They weren't even sure the occupants inside were selling drugs. Dirk had received a tip that they were a high volume, well-fortified operation. But the informant had a reputation for being less than honest, especially when offering information to avoid arrest.

Dirk's objective was simple: determine whether the tip was legitimate before going to the trouble and expense of sending an undercover cop into the house to score.

So far, other than a pizza delivery, no one had come in or out of the place, and it looked like any other run-down bungalow in the neighborhood. Quiet and reasonably law abiding.

To the point of boring.

"Yeah. I could be relaxing in my comfy chair, petting my kitties and shoving raspberry truffles in my face," she continued, berating the sleeping man. "Instead, I'm sitting here, my butt numb, listening to you snore like a warthog with a head cold and . . ."

Her complaint faded away as an old van with battered fenders and rust-encrusted paint pulled in front of the house in question. After jumping the curb, driving onto the grass for a moment, then down, the vehicle managed to park.

A woman exited the driver's door, nearly falling on her face in the process. Even from where Savannah sat and without any sort of sobriety test, she could tell the gal was strongly under the influence of something.

Savannah grabbed her binoculars off the dash and took a closer look at her. She paid special attention to the woman's haggard, anxious expression, her drug-ravaged body and shaky, fidgety movements.

She was painfully thin and dressed to reveal as much skin as possible in a teeny bikini top and short shorts that suggested the goods she was displaying were for sale—or at least for short-term rental.

"As Granny would say," Savannah whispered, "you can see all the way to Christmas and—glory be!—New Year's Eve, too."

When the woman walked around the rear of the van, on her way to the sidewalk, she paused to bang her fist on the back window several times. She yelled, "You stay put! Set one foot outside this van and I swear to gawd, I'll whup your tail good when I get back."

A rusty old bell clanged deep inside Savannah's personal memories. For a moment she was a twelve-year-old child, sitting in the open bed of an ancient pickup truck filled with her younger siblings, watching their mother stumble across a dark alley and enter a tavern's rear entrance. She felt the chill of the night air, the ache of hunger in her belly, and the crushing weight of responsibility, knowing that she alone would be responsible for keeping them all safe for the next four or five hours.

Warm, fed, or entertained . . . those were impossible luxuries.

Safety would be the only gift she might be able to afford.

But even that could prove difficult, considering the drunken patrons coming and going through the bar's back door. Not to mention the older children's propensity to ignore her orders, climb out of the truck, and play in the unlit parking area strewn with broken glass, discarded hypodermic needles, and used condoms.

Adjusting the binoculars' focus, Savannah saw a small face appear at the van's rear window for a second, then duck back down.

Deep inside her, among the dark memories, a presence stirred—a being that had been born long ago in that lonely, dangerous alley. A child with a woman's fierce maternal instincts, who carried a sword that she named Justice and a shield that was wide enough to protect not only herself, but any and all innocents she could gather behind it.

"Don't worry, darlin'," she whispered to the little one with the frightened face she had seen in the window. "Tonight . . . your life changes for the better. I promise."

Chapter 2

Savannah nudged the sleeping Dirk. "Wake up, sugar," she told him. "Your nap's over. Time to get to work. You don't want to miss the show."

Dirk stirred, glanced around with sleepy eyes, then managed to focus on the retreating woman's backside as she walked away from them, stumbling up the sidewalk toward the house they were surveilling.

"Eh," he said with a dismissive shrug. "I've seen way better butts than that—like this morning, when you bent over to take the biscuits outta the oven."

Ordinarily, Savannah would have been flattered and happy to receive the compliment. Of Dirk's numerous, endearing qualities, one of her favorites was his attitude that "more is more" when it came to feminine curvature.

But under the present circumstances, considering the child in the van and the fact that the woman entering the drug house could barely walk, let alone drive safely, Savannah had other things to think about than her husband's unabashed enthusiasm for his wife's ample backside.

"Is that her van?" Dirk asked, nodding toward the decrepit vehicle.

"Yes," Savannah replied.

"Was she drivin' it?"

"Rather badly, but yes."

"Good. When she comes out, we'll let her drive a couple of blocks—far enough away that the dealers in the house won't see. We don't wanna tip them off just yet that we're watching them. We'll get her on a DUI along with the junk, assuming she scores some."

"That would be nice, if only it was that simple," Savannah said with a tired sigh.

"Whaddaya mean? Maybe I can get 'er to talk. If I withhold her goods for a few hours, she'll flip."

Savannah watched as the woman tripped over her own feet, entering the house. "She looks like a flipper all right. Five minutes with you in the sweat box, she'll fold like a shy oyster."

"Exactly. Instead of messing with setting up an undercover buyer, we'll use her statement, and maybe a couple of others to get a warrant and come back next week with a full team to roust the house good and proper. No problem."

"She's got a child there in the van. From what I could see, a little one."

Savannah watched as the reality of the situation dawned on her husband, along with its implications.

"Damn," he said.

"Yeah. We can't let her drive away with a youngster in the van and her drunk as Cooter Brown. Not even a few blocks."

"But if we remove the kid she'll notice he or she is gone, throw a fit, and alert the house that we're out here. They'll figure out that they're being watched."

"Exactly."

She could tell from his grimace that Dirk's brain was spinning as fast as hers, trying to form a plan.

Reaching a conclusion at the exact same moment, they said in unison, "Call Jake."

Dirk reached for his phone, punched in a number, and waited for his fellow detective, Jake McMurtry, to answer.

Since she was only a few feet away and Dirk always had the volume up on his phone, Savannah could hear Jake's drowsy tone when he said, "Yeah, Coulter. What's happenin'?"

Her husband wasn't the only one who nodded off on stakeouts. It was an occupational hazard. One that could cost a cop their job . . . or worse.

"You still sittin' on that house in the projects?" Dirk asked him.

"Yeah. Nothing's going on here. I think I'll pack it in."

"I'm at the house on Lester with Savannah. Turns out we may have to bust them now. Get over here as quick as you can."

"Call for backup."

"I will. Move!"

As soon as Dirk had placed the second call for reinforcements, Savannah said, "We have to get that young'un out of that van now. I'll bring the kid back here to the car and babysit till y'all are done doing what you gotta do."

"Yeah. Okay."

Both bailed out of the Buick and hurried up the sidewalk to the van, trying to stay behind the vehicles as much as possible in case someone in the house was looking out the window at that moment.

"Where did you see 'em?" Dirk asked. "Front or back?"

"Looking out the rear window. I'll try the back door, and you open the driver's side. I didn't see the mother lock it."

"Watch yourself," he said. "There might be someone else, another adult, in the back with the kid."

"I already thought of that. But thank you."

"Maybe I should take the rear."

As she had many times, Savannah reminded herself that Dirk hadn't done the protective male thing years ago, when they had been partners on the force. Back in "the day" he had treated her as an equal.

He still did. For the most part. But she had been shot and nearly died in his arms.

Near tragedies like that changed everything.

It had certainly changed him . . . her . . . them.

Eventually, skin, muscle, and bone healed. But the scars left by fear on the human psyche—those were forever.

"I got it, darlin'," she told him, her southern drawl soft but confident. "If there's a problem, you'll come scrambling between those bucket seats, into the back, and save me."

"Well, okay. But don't open the door till I give the word."

"All right. But not your usual one. It needs to be G rated for the kiddo."

He chuckled, a bit nervously. "Yeah. Gotcha."

They ducked as they scurried to the back of the van, keeping wary eyes on both the vehicle and the house.

Once Savannah was crouched at the rear door with her head beneath the window, her fingers around the handle, Dirk rushed to the driver's side.

A few seconds later, she heard his authoritative but, thankfully, suitable for all ages command, "Go!"

She twisted the handle, yanked hard, and the door came open with some difficulty and a loud, creaking sound, like an ancient, partially buried, dirt-encrusted casket opening in an old horror movie.

Peering inside the dark, cluttered interior, she saw nothing at first. But her eyes quickly adjusted, and she could see a small, frightened child with heartbreaking, large, frightened eyes staring at her.

"It's okay, sugar," she said, holding up both of her hands in a surrender pose. "Everything's all right."

The little head whipped around to watch Dirk as he climbed into the driver's seat and turned to face them.

"She's right. You're okay. We're just here to help you," Dirk said, using his "soft, sweet" voice. It was the one he usually reserved for his three favorite creatures on earth—Cleo, the gentler of their two cats at home, Vanna Rose, their red-haired, toddler niece, and of course, Savannah . . . when they weren't quarreling.

As Savannah climbed into the rear of the van, she could see the child better and realized it was a boy, about six years old.

Even in the dim light she could tell that he was underfed and barely clothed in only a pair of dirty shorts and flip-flops. He was in dire need of a good bath, a shampoo, and a haircut.

"My name is Savannah," she told him, holding out her hand to him. "What's yours?"

The boy hesitated and glanced down at her outstretched hand. Then without accepting the handshake, he looked her square in the eyes and said in a strong, confrontational tone and a southern accent even stronger than her own, "I'm Mr. Brody Greyson. But I'm not supposed to talk to strangers, especially ones that's just broke into my momma's van."

Something about the boy's squared, bony shoulders touched Savannah's heart, not to mention his Southern twang. His thin arms were crossed over his chest and his chin lifted defiantly. But she could see he was trembling.

She glanced out the side window of the van toward the house. The path was clear. No sign of Mom. At least, not yet.

"That's good advice your momma gave you about not talking to strangers, but in this case—"

"It weren't my momma that said it. My teacher tells us that."

"Then good for your teacher," she told him, "but in this case, it's okay, because that fella there is my husband, Detective Sergeant Coulter, and he's a policeman."

Dirk pulled his badge from his pocket and held it up for the child's inspection.

But instead of being impressed and comforted, Brody Greyson whirled on Dirk with a vengeance and shouted, "A cop? You're a stinkin' cop? Then you'd better get your smelly butt outta here right now, before my mom comes back! If she catches you in her van, she'll whup you up one side and down the other! She's mean as mean can be, and she *hates* cops! She says you're nothin' but a rotten, stinkin', lousy bunch of—"

"Now, now, Mr. Brody Greyson," Savannah said. "If you make a habit of speaking to police officers in that disrespectful manner, your life's bound to get complicated real fast. You could find yourself in a whirlwind of trouble, even at your age!"

"I don't give a hoot! You clear outta here, before I knock you into next week myself! My momma left me in charge of her van, and if she finds out I let you in here, she'll thrash me with her belt. I'd a heap rather *you* get a whuppin' from *me* than *I* get one from *her*!"

"How about if nobody gets any whuppin' at all?" Savannah said, placing her hand gently on the boy's shoulder. "There's no call for anybody to get hurt. We're just going to talk and sort out some problems, all nice and peaceful. Would you like that? Would that be okay with you?"

She glanced over at Dirk and saw the sadness she was feeling in his eyes.

Something told her that a woman who had raised her son to be this aggressive and opposed to peace officers wasn't likely to be taken into custody gracefully.

"If you try to talk to my momma 'bout anything, it ain't gonna be nice *or* peaceful, I guarantee you," the child stated with deep conviction, echoing Savannah's thoughts. "She ain't known for 'peaceful,' and she's not all that nice either, even to people she likes, and she hates cops more than anything in the world. 'Cept maybe preachers."

"But if Detective Coulter treats her with respect—"

"Won't make a bit of difference. She says she'd be happy to skin every cop in the world alive and roast 'em all for dinner."

Savannah winced, then faked a laugh. "There's a lot of police officers in the world. If she tried to roast them all, she'd find herself busier than a one-eyed cat watching nine mouse holes."

"She's got a lot of energy, my momma," Brody said, nodding solemnly. "She'd get 'er done."

Savannah looked at Dirk and noticed he was watching the front door of the drug house intently. She wasn't surprised. The woman had been inside for several minutes now. Certainly long enough to do a quick drug deal. Most likely, she'd be coming out at any moment.

Behind Dirk, through the windshield, Savannah saw two police cruisers coming down the street toward them, their lights off. They pulled to the curb and parked, half a block away.

"Backup's ten-twenty-three," she told him.

"What've we got?"

"Two units."

His cell phone dinged. He glanced at the text message. "Jake too," he told her.

He didn't have to tell her that the time for conversation with young, but old for his age, Mr. Brody Greyson was coming to an end.

"Listen, son," Dirk told him, "I'm going to have to ask you

to go with this lady and do everything she tells you to do. We've got some important business to tend to here at this house, and it would be best for everybody if you go with her until it's all over with."

"I ain't goin' nowhere!" the boy said, shoving Savannah's hand off his shoulder and scrambling to the other side of the van, away from her and Dirk. "I know what you're fixin' to do. You're gonna bust my momma and her friends and lock 'em up."

Savannah's brain tried to process what she was hearing. How could a child possess such street smarts at this "tender" age? She decided to be honest with him. There was no point in trying to sweeten this bitter cup of coffee.

"How this goes down," she began, "pretty much depends on your mother, what she's done, and what she decides to do in the future. If she cooperates with—"

"She doesn't cooperate with nobody," he said. "Ever. 'Bout nothin'."

For a moment, Savannah could see the sadness, the vulnerability in the boy's eyes. Briefly, she saw the fragile child behind the hard exterior.

"I'm sorry to hear that," she told him.

"It's gonna be bad," he whispered.

"Then come with me. I'll take you to a safe, quiet place. At least, then it won't have to be bad for *you*. Something tells me you've had enough of the bad stuff already. Right?"

She saw the nod, faint as it was. Quickly, she moved toward the boy, took his hand, and coaxed him toward the rear of the van.

She jumped out herself, then lifted him down and closed the door.

"I could've done that myself," he said. "I get out all the time without any help. Been doin' that since I was a baby."

She looked back at Dirk, who had also exited the vehicle and closed the driver's door. He gave her a slight, sad smile and a thumbs-up. Then he glanced over at the house. The door had opened, and Brody's mother was coming out.

"Come along, young sir," Savannah said, grasping Brody's hand tightly and rushing him down the sidewalk toward the Buick.

"I think I should stay here and help my mom," he said, his voice quivering as he resisted and tried to pull his hand free.

"You can't, darlin'," Savannah told him, her own tone shaky as her throat tightened. "Adults have to take care of themselves, make their own decisions, sink or swim."

"She's bound to sink. I know her. She always sinks . . . 'specially when it comes to cops."

He tried to stop, to pull his wrist from her tight hand, but she held him fast and rushed him along.

"If she does, then it's on her, sugar," she told him. "Not you."

They had arrived at the Buick. When she reached for the rear door handle, he tried even harder to wriggle away. "This ain't no cop car!" he yelled. "Are you sure he's a cop? Are y'all just tryin' to kidnap me?"

She glanced behind her and saw that Dirk was standing on the sidewalk next to the van, talking to the boy's mother. All seemed to be going okay.

Two houses away and out of sight of the surveilled house, Jake and four uniforms watched from behind a neighbor's thick shrubs, waiting to see if they might be needed.

Everyone would try to remain low-key for as long as possible, rather than alert the house there was a problem outside.

Okay, so far, so good, Savannah thought. There was no need to grab the kid up and toss him into the car, further exacerbating his fears, if she could just talk him into going peacefully.

Sinking to one knee, to be at his eye level, she said, "No, Brody. We're not going to kidnap you or hurt you in any way. Detective Coulter is a real cop, a good cop. I swear. I used to be a police officer, too. All we want is for you to be safe. If we're lucky, maybe we can get your momma some help, too. Then you could be both safe *and* happy. Now, wouldn't that be a fine thing?"

Outside the dark van, Brody's small face was clearly visible, and Savannah could see with heartbreaking clarity the child was a mess.

His hair was long and badly matted, and his gaunt cheeks were smudged with far more grime than a child would normally accumulate during a single afternoon of roughhouse play.

Savannah didn't want to think about how long it would take to get a pair of shorts that filthy.

Even through the dirt, she could see copious bruises in various stages of healing on his legs and arms, not to mention a dismaying array of untended cuts, scrapes, and scratches.

But it was his eyes that held her and her heart captive.

Throughout her career with the San Carmelita Police Department, she had seen a lot of sad, neglected, abused children, but she never got over the pain of it. She was sure she never would.

Years ago, she had been a sad, neglected, abused child. Back in the tiny rural town of McGill, Georgia, another policeman—brave and strong, with a heart that hurt when he saw sad children—had rescued her and her siblings from a situation much like this child's.

She knew exactly how Brody Greyson felt. She could see the same pain in his big eyes . . . eyes filled with innocence, hope, and grim, worldly knowledge far beyond what any child should have to carry.

"Hop inside the car, Brody," she said softly. "Take a chance. Brave guys like you get rewards for their courage."

"What kinda rewards?" he wanted to know.

"They get better lives."

For a couple of seconds, he smiled at her, and Savannah was struck by the otherworldly beauty of the boy's face. Beneath the pain, the dirt, the poverty, the anger, and the fear, he had a cherubic quality that belied the harsh statements he had spoken and the quarrelsome attitude he had displayed earlier.

In that moment, Savannah believed—based on Granny Reid's religious instruction—that she was seeing what Brody Greyson's Creator had lovingly designed . . . before the child had been reshaped by his troubled environment.

"Come with me, sugar," she said. "You'll be so glad you did."

"Okay," he said softly. "Let's go."

"Atta boy." Savannah pulled the door open and motioned for him to get inside.

"Just hop in there and get buckled up, so we can—"

At that moment, they heard a scream, like that of a screech owl with its tailfeathers caught in a fox's mouth. The sound was so loud it literally caused Savannah's ears to ache. But it had a far more devastating effect on Brody.

"Momma!" he screamed as he broke away from Savannah and raced toward the van. His mother and Dirk had somehow gone from what appeared to have been a civil conversation to an all-out, no-holds-barred, wrestling match on the sidewalk next to the vehicle.

Savannah ran after Brody, but he was a spry little fellow and managed to arrive at the scene of the vigorous action before she, Jake, or the uniforms could intercept him.

Dirk had gotten the upper hand and was kneeling astride the wayward mom, who was displaying an impressive amount of strength for so tiny a woman as she flailed and kicked, screamed and cursed with an impressive vocabulary—even if it was mostly four-letter words.

On the sidewalk was a ragged backpack, its flap open and

contents strewn across the concrete—sandwich bags filled with pills of every color, packets of white powder and crystals.

Even with Savannah's prior experience, which included a stint in Narcotics, she was impressed by the magnitude of the haul. It was obviously far too much for a personal stash. Momma Greyson had to be dealing, as well as using, and during her brief visit inside the house she had scored, big time!

For all the good it was going to do her.

At that moment, it appeared Dirk might be able to accomplish the task of flipping her over and onto her stomach, maybe even cuffing her. But the situation took a dark turn when the enraged boy jumped onto his back, wrapped his skinny left arm tight around Dirk's neck, and began to pummel his face with his right fist.

Though shocked and horrified, Savannah couldn't help being impressed with the kid's ferocious fighting skills. Apparently, Mr. Brody Greyson wasn't a lad to be trifled with, and it appeared "trifling" included attempting to arrest his mother.

"Let go of my momma!" he yelled at Dirk. "Get off her, you lousy, pig-nose, skunk butt!"

"Tear his face clean off, Brody!" Momma screeched. "Tear it off and shove it so far up his—"

"That's enough!" Savannah shouted as she grabbed the boy by his shoulders and, with considerable effort, peeled him off Dirk's back. She lifted him off his feet and pulled him close, his back against her chest in a tight bear hug. With his arms pinned to his sides, all he could do was struggle—and, unfortunately, administer some well-aimed kicks to her legs.

"Stop, Brody," she whispered in his ear. "Just stop. Take a deep breath and calm yourself, darlin'. Make the good choice. Swim. Don't sink."

After what seemed like forever to her and her shins, he ceased to struggle. She lowered him, so he could stand on his own feet, then turned him to face her, so that he wouldn't see what was happening behind him with his mother.

Jake and the uniformed cops had joined Dirk in the effort to place the woman under arrest. Even with enforcements, the scrimmage had become a battle that law enforcement appeared, at least for the moment, to be losing.

Savannah suspected that Dirk was holding back in his efforts, treating his suspect far more gently than he would have a male perp whose child wasn't nearby.

She had seen him take a gentler approach before when there were youngsters present. His generosity was often to his detriment.

"Gentle" wasn't going to cut it with this gal.

She had elbowed one of the uniforms in the face. Hard. He was kneeling beside her, holding his hand over his right eye, rocking back and forth and moaning something about how he was "never gonna see again."

In her spare time, Ms. Greyson had managed to kick Jake squarely in the solar plexus. He was lying on his side in the road next to the curb, gasping like a salmon who had managed to swim the entire journey upstream to the spawning ground, only to be grabbed by a famished grizzly bear, intent on having him for lunch.

But worst of all, their would-be captive had a handful of Dirk's hair and was pulling it as hard as she could—a particularly egregious thing to do to a fellow who literally counted his front top hairs every morning to see if he'd lost any and how many.

Savannah debated whether to join them, to see if she could add anything worthwhile to the mix. But she didn't want to turn Brody loose, for fear of what he might do. The last thing she needed was to have to chase a frisky, frightened, angry child through a shady neighborhood with miscreants galore.

When Savannah saw one of the uniforms reaching down to his utility belt to retrieve his Taser, she knew it was time to get Brody out of the area. At any moment, his mother, who had graduated from slapping and kicking to clawing and biting, was likely to be flopping around in a manner that no child should witness.

Savannah glanced over at the house and saw that several faces were peeking from between drawn curtains at the windows, but no one appeared overly eager to rush outside and rescue their most recent customer.

Savannah had a feeling, based on experience, that the plumbing inside that building was being taxed at that moment by the number of drugs being flushed through its pipes.

Considering the quantity of pills and paraphernalia that had spilled out of Brody's mom's backpack, and since she hadn't been carrying the bag when she'd entered, Savannah knew that Dirk would have ample cause to, at the very least, knock on the door and have a serious conversation with the inhabitants before the evening was over.

He was going to have a busy night.

Not to mention the time and effort he would expend booking the reluctant Ms. Greyson.

It would be hours before Dirk would be coming home and seconds before Brody's mom was going to be zapped. Savannah decided it was the perfect time to leave.

"Come along, darlin'," she told Brody, grabbing him by the hand and dragging him back to the car. "We've got better things to do and nicer places to be than hanging around this mess."

"But, my momma . . ."

"I wouldn't fret about her none." Savannah glanced back just in time to see the woman on the ground kick the Taser gun so hard that it flew out of the cop's hand and hit Jake in the head, adding to his already considerable agony—and fury. "I think that little momma of yours can take care of herself just fine."

Once again, Savannah shoved him into Dirk's immaculate backseat and instructed him to buckle his seat belt.

She could tell by the awkwardness of his movements as he did so that he wasn't accustomed to even this, the simplest of safety practices.

She added that fact to the growing list in her head of serious reasons Ms. Greyson could be considered, at the very least, an inadequate parent.

Savannah and Brody were in the Buick and a block away when they heard a series of yelping shrieks that reminded Savannah of how her cat, Diamante, had reacted years ago when getting her tail caught beneath the back-porch rocking chair.

She looked in the rearview mirror at her passenger to see how alarmed the boy might be at knowing his mother was having a serious and personal encounter with a Taser.

To her surprise, he looked quite resigned to the fact. His voice was even calm when he said, "Guess she done made her decision, like you said, to sink or swim. When it comes to my momma, you can pretty much figure on her sinkin' ever' time. That's just how she rolls." He took a deep breath and sighed. "I wish I could say different, but . . ."

"I hear ya, sugar." She locked eyes with him in the mirror and gave him a weak smile. "Try not to feel too bad about it. She's not all that different from a lot of folks I've known in my day."

To her surprise, he smiled back—a mischievous little grin. "I'm feelin' okay. But if that's true, you must've had a pretty crummy life."

"You have no idea, puddin' head. Like we say in Georgia, it's been a tough row to hoe, and it's not showing any signs of letting up."

Chapter 3

"Wow! You live *here*? You must be rich!" Brody Greyson exclaimed when Savannah pulled her husband's Buick into the driveway of their small Spanish-style house with its white stucco walls and red-tiled roof.

She glanced around at the somewhat middle-to-lower-income neighborhood and wondered how bad Brody's home must be for him to be so impressed with hers.

"Rich?" she said, shaking her head. "Not so's you'd notice it, kiddo. My husband being a cop and me a private detective who's out of work most days, we do well to make ends meet somewhere in the middle."

Her denial did little to dampen the boy's enthusiasm as he pressed his face to the window, taking in every detail of the yard.

"But y'all got grass and flowers and stuff, and your house is white and clean as a hound's tooth."

Savannah chuckled, enjoying a bit of nostalgia at hearing the child's accent and terminology. Despite his scrape with Dirk and some of his too-adult language, the kid was positively oozing with charm, and his southern drawl was a bit of pecan and coconut frosting on the German chocolate cupcake.

Slowly, carefully she parked the Buick—heaven forbid she should get a scratch on that virgin paint!—next to Granny Reid's old Mercury panel truck. Until that moment, she had forgotten that her grandmother had asked permission to drop by this evening and use her kitchen to bake a coconut cake for the church picnic raffle.

Granny had never complained about living in the old mobile home that had once been Dirk's. Before moving in, she had tossed out his "furniture," which consisted of a school bus seat "sofa," TV tray "end tables," and "storage" units made of stacked plastic milk crates. Then she had set about decorating in earnest, adding enough floral fabrics, ruffles, and lace doilies to make her "castle" her own.

When Gran woke at dawn every morning, the first thing she did, even before having coffee, was say a prayer of thanksgiving that she now lived among the palm trees in a seaside town in California. It had been a lifelong dream of hers, to live by an ocean with a palm tree in sight, and she never got over the wonder of it all. . . .

Until it came time to bake something.

"That blamed trailer oven's got a lot of gall even claimin' to be one," she had told Savannah. "You can't put a mite-sized pan of brownies in that dinky thing, let alone one of my triple-layer coconut cakes. Mind if I come swing by and bake it in yours?" she had asked.

Since her grandmother was one of Savannah's favorite people on earth, she had quickly given her permission.

"Speaking of hounds' teeth," Savannah said as she turned off the car's ignition, "you're about to meet an honest-to-goodness hound dog by the name of Colonel Beauregard the third. But we just call him 'the Colonel.' "

"What kinda hound is he? There's all kinds, you know," Brody shot back with great authority. "Redbones and blue-ticks and basset hounds and beagles, too."

"Hey, you know a lot about hounds."

"I know a lot about dogs. I like dogs. Cats too. It's just people I don't like."

She chuckled as she got out of the car, opened his door, and helped him unbuckle his seat belt. "I can't argue with you there, kiddo," she told him. "I'm a bit partial to folks who wear fur coats and walk on four feet, like my two cats, Diamante and Cleopatra, and my granny's dog, the Colonel. He's an honest-to-goodness bloodhound."

"Really? Like they have in the movies that go chasin' people through swamps and stuff?"

"Sure as shootin'!"

"With long, floppy ears and one of them wrinkly faces?"

"Yes, and he can howl loud and long enough to curdle milk and send shivers up and down your spine."

Together, they walked up the sidewalk to the house. Savannah was surprised and pleased when he slipped his hand into hers. He seemed quite a different child from the one who had been pummeling her husband such a short time ago.

As they stepped onto the front porch, she noticed that he was particularly interested in the giant bougainvillea vines that grew from two large clay pots on either side of the door.

"How did you get them flowers to do that?" he asked, pointing to where they intertwined in a glorious crimson arch above the doorway.

"I planted them, and they grew. That twisting themselves together business—they just sort of did that on their own," she told him. "That's why I named them Bogey and Ilsa."

He gave her a look of total confusion.

Chuckling, she said, "Maybe someday, you'll watch a fine old movie named *Casablanca* and then you'll understand."

After thinking that over for a moment, he scowled, shook his head, and said, "Naw, I don't think so. If it's about plants getting tangled up together, it's probably a mushy movie. I ain't big on them."

"No, I don't suppose you are." She unlocked the door and ushered him inside. "At your age, I reckon it's ugly monsters out to destroy the world and superheroes trying to stop them."

"Well, yeah. Duh."

Once inside the foyer, she called out, "Gran! I'm home, and I brought company."

"Hey, darlin'! In the kitchen. I'll be out in a minute," was the cheerful reply from the rear of the house.

Still standing in the foyer, next to the coat closet door, Savannah hesitated a moment, then said to Brody, "You go on into the living room, while I put away my purse," she said. "Look around and see if you can find a black cat or two."

"You've got lotsa pets! You're lucky!"

"I certainly am," Savannah said as she watched the child scurry into the living room, in search of furry faces.

Once he was out of sight, she opened the closet door, shoved some coats aside, and punched in the number combination on the small wall safe's pad. With one more glance over her shoulder to make sure he wasn't watching, she opened the door, removed her Beretta pistol from her purse, and put it inside the safe.

In the olden days, when it had just been her living in the house and with only a few adult visitors, Savannah had simply placed her weapon on the closet's top shelf, far back in the corner. But her quiet little house had become far busier in the past few years, and children had been added to the mix. With two firearms in the family, she and Dirk had decided to install a safe and use it faithfully.

With a child like Brody visiting, she was glad they had done so.

Both she and Dirk had witnessed the tragic aftereffects of careless, unsafe gun storage practices.

With so much at stake, there was no point in taking chances.

Her weapon locked away and her purse on the top shelf, she closed the closet door and walked into the living room.

Not for the first time, she was surprised when she saw what Brody was doing. He had found one of her two black mini-panthers lying on the windowsill cat perch. The cat was soaking up the last bit of afternoon sun as the boy leaned over her, scratching behind her right ear, whispering sweet nothings to her.

Savannah was shocked to realize it was Diamante, the less friendly, far more aloof of the two sister kitties.

Strangers simply did *not* pet Diamante. It was unthinkable. She just didn't allow such things.

Cleopatra was affectionate to a fault, usually making a nuisance of herself by begging for pets, belly rubs, and ear scratches.

Diamante, on the other hand, deigned to allow Savannah, and *only* Savannah, to pet her. When absolutely necessary. For short periods of time. *If* she was in the mood.

This new turn of events was even more miraculous because Diamante had an ear infection and, as a result, was even grumpier than usual.

"Oh, watch out!" Savannah warned him, rushing to the window perch, ready to rescue her juvenile guest, if necessary. "Her ear's been bothering her lately, so she's not—"

"I know, I know," he said calmly, still stroking the cat. "But the right one's the sore one. That's why I'm just touching the other one."

Once again, Savannah was surprised. "How did you know that?"

"When I walked in, she was scratching the right one. Then she shook her head hard, like they do when they've got a bum ear."

He bent down and peered into the ear in question. "I don't see no mites. That ain't the problem."

"No. It isn't mites. The vet decided she had an allergic reaction to some new food I bought them at—"

"A food they never ate before?"

"Yes. I had a coupon and—"

"Yeah. Food allergy. That's what I woulda said, too. No mites and both ears are nice and clean. A change of food . . . that could do it."

Savannah could barely suppress a snicker at his somber little face and oh-so-grave tone. A prestigious cardio surgeon couldn't have been more serious or confident when diagnosing a complex artery disease.

"Did your vet give you some stuff to smear inside there?" he asked.

"Um, yes, as a matter of fact. An antibiotic cream. But she—"

"Hates it. Yeah, I know, and you probably have to put it in there a couple times a day."

"Yes. Twice."

"Next time she needs it, you just tell me, and I'll do it for ya, okay? I'm real good at it."

"No way! She'd claw your eyes out." Savannah reached down and pulled up one sleeve to reveal fresh scratch marks on her arm. "This is what I wound up with, and that was just because she saw the tube in my hand."

"Then I won't let her see the tube. I got a system. Really."

"Who's your new friend, Savannah girl?"

Savannah turned to see her grandmother standing behind her. She was wearing an old-fashioned apron over her bright tropical-print caftan. Her cloud of soft silver hair was tied back from her face with an equally colorful scarf, twisted into a headband.

A smudge of flour on her nose and a dusting across her cheeks suggested she had been cooking—along with the amazing aroma of fresh-baked goods scenting the air.

Her bright blue eyes sparkled with good-natured humor as she smiled at the boy and held out her hand. "I'm Stella Reid, but everybody I know calls me Granny, so you might as well, too," she told him.

The child accepted her hand and gave it a hearty shake. "I'm Mister Brody Greyson. Glad to make your acquaintance, Miz Reid," he replied with all the mannered graciousness of a well-bred southern gentleman.

"And yours, young man," Granny replied. Turning to Savannah, she said, "He's a real whiz with cats, it 'pears. Could've saved you a vet bill, if only you'd known."

Again, Savannah watched as Granny's sharp eyes swept over the boy, from head to toe. This time, Savannah could tell she was noting his soiled, worn, inadequate clothes. It took more than a pair of shorts and flip-flops to keep a child warm on a cool beach day. Then there were the unattended scrapes and cuts, not to mention the lack of basic sanitation.

Savannah watched her grandmother's smile fade into something more akin to sadness, tinged with anger. Gran harbored strong feelings for innocent children who were neglected—and toward those who should have been caring for them.

"How do you know so much about animals and their ailments?" Savannah asked Brody, as he continued his ear rubbing on the purring and highly contented Diamante.

"One of my friends is a vet. She helps me with my animals," he replied matter-of-factly.

"I thought you said you didn't have any pets."

"I don't have pets. But I take care of the cats and dogs out in the alley behind a motel we stay at when we've got the money. If they're hurt, I take 'em to Dr. Carolyn, and she fixes 'em up for me. I pay her back by helpin' her there at her clinic. I clean up after the animals and sometimes I help her hold them still while she works on 'em."

"No wonder you know so much about ear infections and the like."

"Yeah. I told her I'm gonna be a vet, too, when I grow up, so she's givin' me a head start."

"She sounds like a fine person," Granny said, "as are you, for helpin' out them poor alley cats and stray dogs."

Brody shrugged his bony shoulders. "It ain't as good as havin' pets of your own, but we can't."

"Why's that?" Granny asked.

"'Cause sometimes, when my momma can't pay the motel, we get kicked outta our room on our ears. Then we gotta sleep in our car on the beach. Can't have your own honest-to-goodness pets with that happenin' all the time."

"No, I reckon not," Granny said. "Animals need stability. Children too," she added softly.

Instantly, Brody bristled. "My momma ain't bad. She does the best she can!"

"I've no doubt that she does, son," Granny replied. Looking down at his skinned knees, she added, "But once in a while, life gets extra hard and folks need a helpin' hand."

A hard, cold look came over his otherwise sweet face. It occurred to Savannah that it was an expression seldom seen on one so young and usually observed on street-hardened criminals.

The thought also crossed her mind that, unless someone intervened soon, this boy, whose heart was tender toward animals and who wanted to be a veterinarian when he grew up, would probably never fulfill his dream. Unless his present path was drastically altered, he would probably be wearing that bitter expression behind bars.

The very thought broke her heart.

"As much as both you and that cat are enjoying that petting," Savannah told him, "I promised you an introduction to a real-live bloodhound."

Instantly, he brightened, and she was grateful for the change.

He abandoned Diamante and rushed around the room, looking up the staircase, behind the living room furniture, and then into the kitchen. "I forgot about the hound dog! Where is he?"

"He's out in the backyard," Granny said. "With Diamante feelin' poorly, her ear hurtin' and all, I didn't have the heart to lock the kitty cats upstairs all by their lonesome so's he could run around loose downstairs here."

"They don't play good together?" Brody asked.

"No," Savannah assured him. "Years ago, when the Colonel was just a pup back in Georgia, our neighbor's mean old cat darned near beat the tar out of him, and he never got over it."

"Hates cats?"

"Despises them."

"Can't be around 'em?"

"Not for a second."

Brody shook his head solemnly. "Then we wouldn't want them to run into each other. If he killed one of them . . ."

Savannah chuckled. "Oh, they've fought a few battles over the years, and the cats' lives were never in any danger. The Colonel's, maybe. It's his safety we're worried about."

"His snout and eyes?"

"Exactly." She reached over, placed a hand on the boy's shoulder, and guided him toward the kitchen and the back door. "You skedaddle on out there and introduce yourself to him."

"He won't bite me, what with me bein' a stranger in his yard?"

"Naw," Granny replied. "He ain't gonna chow down on you. You're a young'un, and the Colonel loves little'uns. He thinks they're all puppies for him to play with. He'll be tickled to have yer company. You'll see."

"I'll go out and introduce you, if you like," Savannah offered.

He considered it, then straightened his shoulders and, looking both doubtful and eager, said, "That's okay. I got this. I can handle a hound dog any day and twice on Christmas."

With that, he hurried toward the back of the house and out the rear door, slamming it closed behind him.

Savannah and Granny rushed to the kitchen window to watch the meeting.

It went as Granny had predicted. The Colonel met Brody halfway across the yard, jumped up, put his massive feet on the child's shoulders, and gave him an enthusiastic, wet slurp across his cheek.

Laughing, Brody wiped off the canine slobber with the back of his hand, and the women heard him say, "You cut that out, Colonel What's-Your-Name, or I'll lick you right back."

"That dog's 'bout as tall as that child is," Granny said, laughing. "But lookie there. The boy stands right up to him and tells him what's what."

"Oh, Mr. Brody got grit in his craw to spare. I had to pull him off Dirk earlier. That boy was, as we say, 'stompin' a mudhole' in my husband and 'walkin' it dry'!"

The normally calm and cool octogenarian gasped and turned to her granddaughter with a genuinely shocked expression on her face. "You had to rescue your big, burly policeman husband from a scrawny, underfed young'un like that?" she said.

"I'm dead serious. I swear. He was on Dirk's back, riding

him like he was a rodeo cowboy and Dirk was a Brahma bull, and the boy was socking him in the face the whole time he was on him. I had to peel him off him like he was an overly sticky bandage on a hairy leg."

Granny looked out the window again at the child, who was now rolling around on the grass with the bloodhound. He was laughing, the Colonel was howling, and all appeared right with the world—or, at least, in Savannah's backyard.

"Hard to imagine such a thing," Gran said. "What brought *that* on?"

"Dirk arresting his momma, who'd just walked out of a drug house with more pills in a backpack than your average pharmacy's got on their shelves."

Granny nodded somberly. "That'll do 'er. Dirk don't look kindly on such goings-on."

"None of us do. Especially now," Savannah added, her voice heavy with sadness.

She stole a quick sideways glance at her grandmother and saw the same sorrow reflected on the older woman's face. Savannah wished she hadn't said it. The last thing either of them needed was to be reminded of her brother's struggle with drug addiction. At the moment, Waycross was doing well, attending meetings and staying clean. But they all lived in fear that he might relapse.

They knew, all too well, that addiction was a monster who could never be buried in a grave and forgotten. It had a terrible habit of resurrecting itself when its victims least expected it. One could never consider the battle won and relax. The disease was incurable. Though, thankfully, in some cases, manageable.

With the help and support of his loved ones, Waycross seemed to be managing.

That was enough. For today.

One day at a time.

"Is that why you brung the child home with ya?" Granny asked, nodding toward Brody, who was running around the yard, trying to hide from the dog with no success whatsoever. The Colonel was, after all, a bloodhound. "Was it because his momma's in jail?"

"I brought him home because when I took him to CPS, the intake gal there told me she didn't have a foster home for him to go to. She was fixing to stick him in juvie hall, so I asked her if Dirk and I could just take him for the night. Maybe something would open up for him tomorrow. It took some convincing, but I finally talked her into it."

"Good for you . . . and for him."

They watched and laughed as the hound grabbed a mouthful of the back of the boy's baggy shorts and took him to the ground, where he playfully mauled him like a stuffed toy, Brody squealing with delight the whole time.

"I'm going to have to get him some clothes right away," Savannah said. "He can't run around all over Kingdom Come in those filthy shorts."

"Looks like he has been. For a long time, too."

"I know, and we're putting a stop to that. Like you always told us, 'No matter how poor a body is, there's no excuse for dirtiness.'"

"That's for sure," Granny replied. "He desperately needs an introduction to Mr. Soap and Miss Bath Water before he's much older."

"I hate to interrupt his good time though," Savannah said, watching the boy try to teach the dog to retrieve the stick he had thrown. The Colonel was great at chasing any thrown object and picking it up with his massive mouth, but he was loath to return his prize to the pitcher. Instead, he pranced around the yard, stick in mouth, head high, showing off his treasure.

"Yeah, if the child had a tussle with the law earlier today, he's probably in need of some rest and relaxation."

"Not to mention a good meal. I've got some leftover fried chicken and potato salad in the fridge. I'll ply him with that."

Granny glanced away, looking a bit guilty. "I must admit, you ain't got quite as much as you had when you left the house earlier today."

Savannah laughed. "That's okay. I knew I was taking a risk when I left you alone with it. Us Reid women can't resist left-over chicken."

"I'll make it up to you though. I baked two of them coconut cakes. Had you in mind for the second one."

Savannah thought it over a few moments, weighing the pros and cons. "Let's see now . . . A drumstick in exchange for one of Granny Reid's prizewinning coconut cakes. I'd say I came out ahead in that deal."

"A drumstick *and* a thigh. I was plumb starved to death."

"Still a bargain." Savannah headed for the refrigerator. "Let me get that food on the table, and then I'll call him in to wash up and—"

Her cell phone rang, just as she entered the kitchen, and she didn't recognize the chime as any of her "regulars."

For a moment, the thought occurred to her that the intake official might have found a foster home for Brody, and she had to admit that she was a bit disappointed to think that was the case.

To her surprise, she was actually looking forward to having the boy around for the evening, feeding him a good meal, getting him cleaned up, finding some decent clothes for him, "treating" him to some of the simple pleasures of life that, sadly, might be luxuries for him.

That would be a more fun and worthwhile way to spend an evening than reading a few more chapters of her romance novel. Surely, Lady Wellington and her new coachman hottie could wait yet another day to consummate their torrid love affair in the hayloft.

She pulled the phone out of her pants pocket and instantly felt better when she saw the name. In fact, she felt a bit of a thrill that, she had to admit, was a tad more exciting than a married woman should get when answering a call from a man who hadn't given her the diamond ring on her finger.

But she quickly consoled herself with the thought that literally millions of women would have been thrilled to death to receive a call from this particular man.

Ethan Malloy—Academy Award–winning movie star, heart-throb, leading man in the fantasies of lust-besotted fans worldwide—had once been Savannah's client and was now her treasured friend.

Just before clicking the on button to receive the call, Savannah turned to Granny and mouthed the single word, "Ethan."

The gleam that lit Granny's eyes in an instant was testimony to the appeal the actor held for all ages. No one, young or old, could resist the charms of Ethan Malloy.

"Hello, Ethan. So nice to hear from you," Savannah said, suddenly conscious of the fact that she had just put on her sexiest phone voice . . . and sounded pretty darned silly in the process. She wondered if he heard that sort of thing a lot and considered her and her "type" ridiculous.

No, Ethan was much too kind for that.

Long ago, Savannah had decided that his gifts, which included standing at least six inches taller than the average male, a voice a full octave deeper than most, and pale blue eyes that reached into the soul of every person they studied, hadn't ruined him. This Texas boy, son of a moderately successful rancher, seemed to have no clue about his effect on women. His modesty, along with his calm, soothing, deep voice, might have been his greatest charm.

But he didn't sound calm or soothing when he said, "I'm sorry, Savannah. This isn't a social call. Something bad—" She heard his voice break and he struggled to speak. "Very bad, has happened. I need help."

Again? she thought. *No, please, not again!*

The last time he had spoken words like that was upon the occasion of their first meeting. Ethan's wife and young son had gone missing, and he feared they were victims of foul play.

"Not Beth and Freddy," she said, almost afraid to even think it, let alone say it. For days she had searched for the two, afraid that, when and if she found them, she might be too late.

Fortunately, that hadn't been the case. She had located and rescued them, but not before blood had been shed. It was a case that would haunt her forever.

"No," he said. "Freddy's okay, and Beth. Well, you know we aren't together anymore."

"Yes. I know. I'm so sorry."

How could she not know? Everyone in the world knew, thanks to the tabloid magazines that had splashed the gory destruction of their personal lives across the covers of newspapers and gossip rags from one side of the globe to the other.

It wasn't surprising to her. The marriage had been in trouble even before the tragic kidnapping. Few couples would have survived their ordeal and managed to stay together.

"What's wrong, Ethan," she said, "and how can I help?"

"I thought maybe you'd heard already. What with your husband being a detective. We called the police, of course. I was the one who found her."

"Found who, Ethan?" she asked, her heart pounding. "What's happened?"

"It's Lucinda Faraday."

Savannah searched her memory banks and recalled a woman with platinum blond hair, bobbed short and wavy. Big, doe-like eyes and thin, arched eyebrows. A silver-screen star from the late forties and early fifties. In particular, Savannah recalled a famous picture of her, lolling on a satin chaise lounge in a provocative pose, dressed in a peekaboo chiffon negligee with marabou feather trim, smoking with an opera-length cigarette holder.

There had been a scandal of some sort attached to her name, but at the moment, Savannah couldn't recall it.

"Yes," she said. "I remember her. The old movie star?"

"Yes. She was an accomplished actress. She was also a wonderful person. My friend."

"She *was*?"

"Yes. She's . . . she's dead."

"How?"

"Murdered, I think. It was me who, who . . . I found her. About a half an hour ago."

Savannah could tell he was crying. Her heart ached to think of this kind, gentle man in the midst of yet another tragedy of some sort.

Some people just never seemed to get a break. Not even those who appeared to be good, law-abiding folks.

"Where's the body?" she asked.

"In her home."

"Her home. Oh, yes. I remember. It's that old mansion out in Twin Oaks, right? With a funny name I can't pronounce."

"Yes. Qamar Damun. It's a beautiful old place. Used to be anyway. She's lived here for years."

"*Here?* You're there now?"

"Yes. Like I said, I found her. We called the police already, but I'd appreciate it so much if you'd come out here. You know a lot more about . . . this kind of thing than I do. I'd feel a lot better if you were here."

Savannah looked out the window at Brody, who was still wrestling his new canine friend. How could she leave this child, so in need of simple, basic care? And yet, this friend of hers was hurting and frightened. . . .

"Ethan, I'd like to help you," she said, "but . . . can you please hold on for just a moment?"

"Yes, of course," he replied.

"Go," Granny said quietly. "If that young man needs help, you go help him."

"But—"

"No 'buts' 'bout it. If there's anything I'm still perfectly capable of doin', it's takin' care of a young'un. Go do whatcha gotta do."

"Are you sure?"

Granny propped her hands on her hips, squared her shoulders, and lifted her chin. "Do I look sure?"

Savannah couldn't help grinning, despite the circumstances. "Okay. Thank you, Granny."

"It sounds like you're busy, Savannah," she heard Ethan saying. "I'm sorry. If it isn't a convenient time, I can—"

"That's the thing about murder, Ethan," Savannah said, her tone nearly as sad as his. "There's never a convenient time for evil like that."

She drew a deep breath and shifted mental gears from a stand-in mom for a night to a private detective and former policewoman. "I have to explain the situation to a young fella, and then I'll head right out there. I'll arrive inside half an hour."

"Thank you, Savannah!" He sounded so relieved. "You have no idea how much I appreciate this."

She knew exactly how much. She could hear the heart-deep gratitude in his voice, see the confidence in her grandmother's kindly smile, and she knew she'd made the right decision.

"I know you do, Ethan. Now listen to me carefully. Do you have any reason to believe that the killer might still be there on the property?"

"No. I don't think so. She looks like—" She heard him make a gagging sound. "—like she's been . . . gone . . . awhile."

"Okay. You said 'we' called the police. Who's there with you?"

"Mary Mahoney. She's Lucinda's housekeeper. More like a companion, really."

"That's it? Just the two of you?"

"Yes. Just us."

"Then don't touch anything. Neither one of you. In fact, you two just go outside. Is your car there?"

"Yes."

"Good. Then sit in your car and wait for either me or the cops, whoever arrives first. Okay?"

"Okay."

"I'll get there as quick as I can."

"I know you will. Thank you."

"You're welcome, sugar. Try not to worry. Everything's going to be okay."

There was a long, awkward silence on the other end. Finally, she heard him say, "Except that my friend is dead."

Savannah felt like a jerk. Platitudes, so ineptly uttered, were worse than worthless under such dire circumstances. When would she learn not to let them just fly out of her mouth like bats out of a cave at sundown?

"Yes, I'm sorry, darlin'," she said, as softly as she could. "You're right. Nothing can ever make that okay. Or even close to all right."

Chapter 4

As Savannah drove Dirk's precious Buick through the quiet little beach town, then into the canyon leading eastward and away from the ocean, she could feel the tension in her body. It was a nasty and unwelcome presence that tightened her muscles, strained her nerves, and caused her heart to beat faster than it needed to.

In her twenties, Savannah hadn't noticed such things. Or if she had, she had chalked such symptoms up to "excitement."

In her thirties, she had noticed, but not minded so much. Again, a heightened pulse was a small price to pay for a life fueled by adrenaline. Challenge, conflict, and even the occasional life-threatening drama seemed acceptable, if that's what was required to follow one's passion.

But now, well into her forties, Savannah found that she didn't recuperate as quickly as she had before from these tussles with her fellow human beings. The sore muscles, frayed nerves, and resulting exhaustion tended to linger for days afterward, causing her to wonder if, perhaps, she might have accomplished the same ends with more peaceful methods.

Peace.

With each passing year, she realized the value of that rare commodity and found new ways to pursue it, embrace it, and enjoy its rewards.

As she crossed the city limits and entered the canyon, Savannah rolled down the driver's window and slowly, deeply, breathed in the fragrance of the countryside. The beloved, familiar scents of the desert—the dry smell of the dust, the pungency of wild sage, and the rich perfume of eucalyptus—filled her lungs and calmed her soul.

The trauma of the arrest and her concern about leaving a troubled child in the care of her elderly grandmother began to fade away with each exhalation.

Savannah reminded herself that Brody Greyson's mother wasn't a problem that she could fix. The woman herself was the only person with the power to do that, and something told Savannah that even she might not be able to save herself at this point.

Although Granny Reid had taught her grandchildren to never give up on anyone, that no one was beyond redemption, Savannah had seen far too many people who had traveled their dark, rocky roads so far and so long that only a miracle would bring them into the light.

Miracles happened, of course. Every day. But, having seen the worst of humanity, Savannah didn't hold her breath waiting for them.

She just whispered a prayer for the person in need of divine intervention and kept moving.

Peace.

It had a lot to do with figuring out what you could fix and what you couldn't.

As she wound deeper into the canyon, leaving most of civilization behind, she allowed the serenity of the place, unspoiled by humanity, to seep into her soul. She also released the fear and guilt of leaving Brody with Granny. Her grandmother had laughed at her when she'd asked if she thought she could handle the boy.

"If there's one thing I'm durn good at—other than bakin' goodies, that is—it's handlin' young'uns," she'd told her.

"But Brody's not your average kid," Savannah had started to explain, "and—"

"*No* child is average. Plus, remember, I managed to raise your sister, Marietta, and both of us lived to tell the tale."

"True," Savannah had admitted. Surely, anyone who had managed to rear a child like Marietta Reid and keep her out of jail and the graveyard could handle the likes of Brody Greyson. Especially with some help from an overly energetic bloodhound.

Savannah took another relaxing, deep breath and released her concern about Brody and Granny. That was just needless worrying, and surely, she could find something more pressing to worry about.

Like a murdered movie star.

As she approached the outskirts of the tiny town of Twin Oaks, Dirk's car phone rang. As she answered it, she silently thanked her brother, Waycross, for at least the hundredth time for this additional, loving gift. Last Christmas he had installed hands-free phones in both of their vintage vehicles, making their lives easier and considerably safer.

Her little brother was one of Savannah's dearest blessings. Every time she thought of him, which was many times a day, she was grateful for his love and that he, himself, had found his way back to a life of sobriety. She would be forever thankful that her little brother was one of those rare miracles.

She glanced at the caller ID and smiled. "Hey, you," she said. "Did you get her booked in and locked down?"

"Finally," Dirk said, sounding tired and grouchy. Even a bit more than his usual degrees of haggard and disgruntled. "I've arrested rabid grizzly bears that were more cooperative."

"Did you have to go to the ER and get patched up? Gashes stitched, bones set, brain scan done?"

"Ha, ha. Aren't you funny. No, but I've got a serious shiner from that ankle-biter kid of hers. Did you get him settled in with CPS?"

"Um. Not exactly."

"What happened?"

"Let's just say, we have company tonight. Maybe for a few nights, until they find a foster home to take him in."

"Ah. That's why your grandma said she was busy and couldn't talk when I called the house."

Savannah gulped. "Uh-oh. Did she sound okay?"

"She sounded fine, laughing her head off. But I could hear the Colonel howling like a hyena in the background."

See there, Savannah told herself. *You were fretting over nothing. No wonder you're sprouting new gray hairs every day.*

"She did have time to tell me that you're on your way to Twin Oaks," he said. "A homicide?"

"Yes. Ethan called me and asked if I'd come up here. The victim's a friend of his. I just got into town, passed that big fruit stand that sells apple cider. Where are you?"

"Right behind you."

She glanced at the rearview mirror and saw a police cruiser rapidly approaching, its blue lights flashing.

She laughed and said, "Let me guess. You caught the case."

"Yep. So much for our quiet, romantic evening together at home. Huh, darlin'?"

Savannah momentarily considered what a "romantic evening" with Dirk entailed. Plenty of salty snacks and cold beverages to wash them down, served by the lady of the house. Then some form of baked goods, also conjured into being by the on-premises chef, and all the while, a boxing match on cable TV.

"*Romantic*," *indeed*, she thought.

But she decided to be kind. Pointing out the obvious wasn't always the best way to assure domestic tranquility.

"I figured they'd give it to you," she told him. "That's why I drove the Buick out here instead of the pony. Reckoned you'd show up and prefer to have your own car to drive home."

"How considerate of you. Wouldn't be that you actually enjoy driving her, now that she's all cherried out."

"Oh, right. I'd choose a boring Buick Skylark over my smokin' hot Mustang. Get real. This was an act of true love. Pure self-sacrifice. Nothing else."

The heavy silence on the other end of the phone told her she'd gone too far. The day might come when Dirk could take a bit of teasing over his beloved, returned from the grave ride.

Apparently, it had not yet arrived.

She decided to return to the former topic. "Yeah, no romantic, stay-at-home evening for us," she said. "Considering all the rumpus and commotion you heard that's going on back there, a simple murder scene might be more peaceful."

More silence on the other end.

She hated it when he threw her olive branches into the wood chipper, as he was inclined to do.

But she soon realized he had more on his mind than just pouting, as he quickly pulled alongside her, then shot past her, leaving her figuratively "in his dust."

She heard him chuckling as he said, "See ya later. When you finally get there. What's your ETA? An hour? Two?"

"Yeah, yeah. You've got lights, a siren, and a police cruiser. While I'm pedaling this crummy, *boring* old Buick."

"Hey, you'd better watch what's comin' outta your mouth there! That's *my girl* you're talking smack about!"

"I thought *I* was your girl!" she shot back.

But he didn't hear her.

Detective Sergeant Dirk Coulter had already ended the call. He and his cruiser with its powerful engine and flashing blue lights were far down the road, then around a sharp curve and well out of sight.

He'll beat me to the crime scene with a minute and a half to spare. Woo hoo, she thought, grinning and shaking her head. *The dude's easily impressed. With himself.*

Chapter 5

Even with his lights and siren, Dirk hadn't beaten her to the mansion by much, Savannah realized when she reached the end of the long driveway and saw him climbing out of the cruiser.

Of course, he would still count it as a win. Like horseshoes and dynamite, "close" was enough.

But all thoughts of their little competition left her mind the instant she turned her attention to the home itself. Certainly, she had heard of Qamar Damun, the art deco mansion whose Arabic name meant "Blood Moon." It had been built in the 1920s and, over the course of the past century, had been inhabited by some of Hollywood's brightest luminaries.

The Moroccan-style castle set high upon a secluded mountaintop enjoyed quite a history. It had a colorful reputation and not only for its brilliant stained glass windows, complex brick and stone work, and massive arched entryway.

Usually, when the estate was discussed, it was with hushed tones, and the stories were of decadent, violent parties, attended by movie stars, mobsters, highly influential politicians, and wealthy adventure seekers.

The mansion's darkest crimes had occurred during its first thirteen years, in the era of Prohibition. But over the past hundred years, it was widely believed that every one of the basic Ten Commandments had been broken, some more than once, within its marble walls with embossed bronze friezes.

The phone call Savannah had received earlier caused her to consider the idea that Qamar Damun might have returned to its evil ways. Or at least, someone within its walls had.

Savannah parked behind Dirk's cruiser and saw that he was walking toward her, a jaunty swagger to his steps, a grin on his face.

For a guy who had gotten his butt whipped only a short time ago by a kid who was knee-high to a duck, he was acting far too frisky in her opinion.

But he didn't have time to do much bragging, because before he could reach her, Ethan Malloy had climbed out of a GMC Sierra Denali parked nearby and was hurrying over to greet them.

Normally, on any given occasion, when Savannah first laid eyes on the world-renowned movie star, she was taken aback by his good looks and innate charisma.

But the stricken look on his handsome face and the sadness in his famously blue eyes caused Savannah to remember the first time she had met Ethan Malloy.

Once again, Ethan's fame, fortune, and the adoration of millions had not protected him or those he loved from life's harshest realities.

She hurried to meet him halfway and folded him into a hearty embrace, which he returned. For a moment, she could feel him melting into the strength and compassion she was offering. Not for the first time, it occurred to her that for all the fan adoration, Ethan Malloy was a terribly lonely man.

"I'm so sorry," she told him. "You were the one who actually found her?"

He nodded. "Yes. Mary called me and told me she was missing. I came right over, and we looked for a long time. You'll see why, once you're inside the house, and I was the one who first saw her."

He shuddered, and for a moment his face turned so pale that she thought he might faint.

She couldn't blame him. There were scenes in her memory that still haunted her, causing her to feel the same way when she made the mistake of recalling them.

Dirk approached them and shook Ethan's hand. "I just heard you say, 'We' were looking for her. Who's 'we'?" Dirk asked, wearing his most officious detective expression.

"Mary Mahoney and myself."

"Who's that?"

"Lucinda's housekeeper, though she's more like a companion—as you'll also see when you go inside."

"Where's she now, this Mary gal?" Dirk wanted to know.

Ethan passed a shaking hand over his face. "In her quarters. She's a mess. I told her what you said, Savannah, about staying out of the house, but she was crying so hard that she could barely walk. She just wanted to lie down on her own bed, and I didn't have the heart to force her to—"

"No, of course not. I understand. As long as she isn't anywhere near the body."

"Not even close. Lucinda's in the ballroom," Ethan told her. "The servants' quarters are on the opposite side of the house, in the rear."

"When exactly did Mary call you?" Savannah asked.

"A couple of hours ago. She said she hadn't been able to find her all day. I came right over. We've been looking the whole time. It wasn't easy. You'll understand why when you go inside."

"When did Mary last see her?" Dirk asked.

"I think last night, when they both went to bed. She said when she took her breakfast to her, she couldn't find her."

Savannah noticed he was shivering, even though he was wearing long sleeves and the night was fairly warm.

"We were afraid something like this might happen," he said, "what with her being so old and in poor health, and the house being so . . ."

Dirk craned his head, looking up at the massive, four-story high brick and marble facade with its ornate geometric bands of patterns. "This *is* a big place," he said. "I can see how somebody'd get lost in a joint like that. You'd have to carry a sandwich in your pocket if you decided to go from one side of it to the other. By the time you got there, it'd be time to eat again."

Savannah could see that Ethan was spending far more time and effort trying to figure out what Dirk had just said than the comment deserved—especially under the circumstances.

"Why don't you show us where the . . . she . . . is, if you're up to it," she said, slipping her arm through his. "Or, if you don't want to have to see her again, you can just point us in the right direction, and we'll find her."

"No, you won't. Not without help." He looked up at the massive arched entrance and the sick expression came over his face once again. "You'll never find her on your own. I'm surprised that I was able to."

* * *

53

As they approached the doorway, Savannah quickly became aware of what they were going to find on the other side of the eight-feet-tall carved and inlaid doors, even before Ethan opened the one on the right and waved them inside.

There was no mistaking that smell. To her knowledge, there was only one thing that stank like this combination of terrible odors: garbage, decaying food, dust, mothballs, rotting wood, mildewed cloth, moldy plaster, as well as copious other unidentifiable, toxic substances.

A hoard.

Thankfully, this particular blend lacked the added horrors of urine and feces. But it was especially strong, dense, and overpowering, as though the door and windows hadn't been opened and no amount of fresh air or sunlight had entered in many years.

Once they passed through the door, the enormity of the mess inside was all too apparent.

They were unable to take three steps inside without having to walk upon a layer, at least six inches deep, of accumulated garbage.

Although the giant foyer was as large as that of a glorious old theater, they had to make their way along a narrow path, barely wide enough to accommodate them, walking single-file, between towering piles of assorted boxes, furniture, clothing, rotting household items, and miscellaneous trash.

Savannah's claustrophobia rose with each halting step she took, as she tried to follow Ethan and not fall behind.

A dozen comments sprang to her mind, but she kept them to herself, recalling that this was the home of someone who had been Ethan's dear friend.

As Granny would say, "If you can't say something nice . . ."

Ethan was grieving. He didn't need anyone to state the obvious, horrible as it might be.

"Ho-leeeshee-it!" Dirk exclaimed, following close behind her. "What sorta nut job lives in a trash heap like this?"

Okay. So much for discretion and sensitivity, she thought, shooting him a warning look over her shoulder.

Ethan stopped, turned around, and gave Dirk a look that was neither threatening nor angry, but his voice was decidedly firm when he said, "In this case, it was a beautiful, loving lady, who battled depression for many years and lost the war. Lucinda suffered many devastating losses in her life. Eventually, they took their toll."

"Not every ship can weather every storm," Savannah added.

"Sorry," Dirk mumbled with more humility than Savannah would have expected. "She's your friend. I shouldn't've said anything."

Ethan gave him a half smile. "I understand. For the record, I didn't know until today that she was living like this. I'd never been inside this house. No surprise that I was never invited. I was as shocked and horrified as you must be. Probably more."

He turned and continued to lead them along the narrow path through the clutter and grime of Lucinda Faraday's life.

It reminded Savannah of the tunnels that ants created to navigate through their hills. In places, the piles of junk were well over their heads, seven or eight feet high. She couldn't help but wonder how on earth anyone could even reach up that far to stack it.

"This isn't just gross. It's downright dangerous," Dirk said, obviously still unable to grasp the importance of delicacy and diplomacy. "This mess could've caved in on her and mashed or suffocated her. Are you sure that's not what happened? Maybe it wasn't a homicide after all, but more like an avalanche of—"

"Murder," Ethan snapped back angrily. "She was murdered! Okay?"

"Yeah. Yeah. Okay. Sorry."

Dirk gave Savannah a sheepish look. It told her that Mr. Sensitivity finally realized he needed to shut up. At least until they saw their victim.

Ethan led them from the foyer into an enormous room that Savannah decided must be the ballroom. Like the entry, clutter obscured most of the floor. Although there appeared to be more pathways through the mess, and the piles on either side were mostly only waist high.

Here and there, Savannah could actually see a patch of worn, filthy parquet.

The only evidence that it had once been a glorious room was the coffered ceiling with intricate panels decorated with plaster vines, leaves, and roses. The graceful design spiraled toward the center of the ceiling, to a magnificent crystal chandelier, almost completely covered with dust and cobwebs.

"She's over here," Ethan said as he headed toward a far corner. "I searched this room, and all rooms on the first two floors, three times before I finally found her."

"Any particular reason you only looked on the lower floors?" Savannah asked.

"Mary told me that Lucinda hadn't been on the third and fourth floors for years." He paused, looked uncomfortable, then added, "Apparently, the two uppermost floors are even worse than these."

Savannah couldn't imagine such a thing, but she kept it to herself. Ethan seemed to be not only grieving but embarrassed on behalf of his deceased friend.

Suddenly, he stopped and stepped as far to the side as the narrow walkway would allow. "I don't want to see her again if I don't have to," he told them. "Setting eyes on something like that once in a lifetime is more than enough. I don't know how you people can stand to do that sort of thing for a living."

56

"I'm sure it helps if the bodies aren't someone you knew and loved," Savannah said as she and Dirk maneuvered around him, then headed deeper into the corner, where he had pointed.

Dirk pushed ahead, working his way through the piles of clothing. Some garments were filthy and crusty with mold and mildew, while others still had tags and were in their original designer packaging.

After coming to the end of the trail, facing a wall, he said, "I don't see a body back here." He turned to Ethan. "Are you sure you—"

"Under that pink satin comforter thing," Ethan replied.

A warning bell went off in Savannah's head. "Is that how you found her, Ethan?" she asked as she spotted the gaudy flamingo pink throw. "Was she covered up like that, or did you . . ."

"I covered her," he said. "I had to. I couldn't just leave her like, well, you'll see."

She saw another violent shudder go through him, and for a moment, she was again concerned that he might pass out. She decided he was in too fragile a state for her to lecture him about how unwise it was to tamper with a crime scene in any way at all. Even to modestly cover the body of a woman you held in high esteem.

Why make him feel any worse than he already did?

"Don't *ever* mess with a crime scene, man," Dirk barked. "Especially a murder. At a time like this, catching who did it is a lot more important than guarding a woman's modesty. It ain't like she's gonna mind at a time like this, huh?"

Savannah cringed. In all the years she had spent with Dirk, she had yet to impress upon him the value of civility. He considered "tact" a waste of time at best, and at worst, evidence of a weak, sneaky character who didn't possess the courage to speak their mind.

No, Dirk Coulter was a manly man who had never entertained an unspoken thought. No filter whatsoever. No pesky childhood training like Granny's "If you can't say something nice, say nothing at all" to cramp his style or burden him with the nuisance of forethought or the onus of empathy.

But you always knew where you stood with Dirk.

Whether you wanted to know or not.

Savannah moved closer to the covered body as Dirk took a couple of pictures of it and the surrounding areas with his cell phone.

She noticed that one foot was sticking out from beneath the duvet. From the skin texture and the condition of some of the toenails, it was obviously the foot of an older woman. But the nails were meticulously painted in a crimson polish, and the high-heeled slipper was a black satin mule, accented across the top with marabou feathers.

A long-forgotten image stirred in Savannah's memory. The red toenails. The glamorous black footwear. But before the full picture could form in her mind, she was distracted by Dirk pulling some surgical gloves from his inside jacket pocket and handing a pair of them to her.

"Don't touch anything if you don't have to," he grumbled. "The scene's been interfered with enough already."

She glanced over her shoulder at Ethan and saw him wince. The verbal dart had found its mark, to be sure.

"I think enough's been said about that already," she whispered to her husband. "If it hadn't been for Ethan, you'd probably be searching through this hoard by yourself, looking for the missing woman. What a grand, fun time that'd be, huh?"

"Yeah, well, whatever," was the lackluster reply.

"I'm going to step away now, if that's all right with you guys," Ethan said. "Like I said, I really don't want to have to see her again."

"No problem," Savannah said. "You can wait for us outside if you prefer."

"Or better yet," Dirk added, "you could go get that gal, Mary, and tell her I'll meet her out front in a few minutes. I'm gonna have to ask her some questions, whether she feels like talkin' or not."

"Okay. I'll do what I can."

Ethan disappeared in an instant, and Savannah couldn't blame him—on so many levels.

She turned back to Dirk, a couple of choice statements on the tip of her tongue. But she quickly swallowed them, because he had uncovered the body.

It was a sight that she would never forget. A vision that she was quite certain would reappear in nightmares for a long time. Maybe for the rest of her life.

Chapter 6

"It's the pose," Savannah said, studying the body sprawled atop the garbage on the floor. "Her famous calendar girl shot."

"I ain't got a clue what you're talking about. How famous could it be?" Dirk said as he tossed the hot-pink satin duvet that had covered Lucinda Faraday onto a pile of clothes next to her body.

Savannah took her phone from her jeans pocket and began an Internet search. A moment later, she shoved it beneath Dirk's nose. "That one," she said. "It was taken back in the forties."

"Oh, yeah. I remember seeing that," Dirk replied, squinting at the small screen. "I think I heard a lot of the Second World War GIs had it on their lockers or whatever. Pretty racy stuff for back then."

Savannah took the phone back and read the caption beneath it. "Says here they found out later that she was underage when she posed for it. Barely sixteen."

"She sure didn't look sixteen."

"No, but she certainly looks like she does here, pose-wise anyway." Savannah pointed at the body, which had been placed in the same suggestive position as the old photo.

Savannah could better understand why Ethan had felt the need to cover his friend. The overtly sexual positioning had been considered inappropriate by many censors in its day. But the same pose on a ninety-year-old gave the impression that the killer had arranged the corpse that way to dishonor the woman, to insult her memory.

Savannah hated to think what the papers would do with this information if it leaked . . . and it was bound to. Such salacious details almost always came to light sooner or later, especially if they involved a celebrity.

"She's even holding the long cigarette holder," Savannah said, comparing the picture with the smoking tool in the body's hand.

"The killer obviously wanted to make a point of some sort."

"They wanted to embarrass her."

"Embarrass her? She's dead. How can you embarrass a corpse?"

"Spoken like a true guy. We women have the ability to be mortified about our appearance and a lot of other things long after death. Believe me."

He shrugged. "Okay. If you say so."

She put her phone away and turned her attention to the body. The negligee's chiffon had some holes in it and the lace edge was ragged. The feathers on the slippers were sparse and limp. The carved ivory opera-length cigarette holder was stained from years of smoke.

"Her clothes," she said. "They're old, like antiques. If I didn't know better, I'd say they're the exact same ones she wore in the picture."

"She saved them all these years?"

"Probably. You've been wearing that same Harley-Davidson T-shirt since I met you."

"I'll have you know I replaced that first one ten years ago." He pointed to the logo on his chest. "*This* is a *second* edition!"

"Oh, okay. I stand corrected."

She tried to move closer to the body, but the limited space and a large wire bird cage stuffed with Christmas decorations prevented her from getting a good look at the head and face area. All she had was a vague impression of a blond wig, sitting askew, maybe even backward, atop the victim's own gray hair and some garish red lipstick and turquoise eyeshadow, smeared around the mouth and lids.

"Any obvious cause of death?" she asked him. "Blood maybe?"

"No blood, but it's not hard to figure out the cause of death."

Carefully, he stepped into a plastic milk crate containing a dozen or more assorted ashtrays to make room for her to move forward.

Shining the flashlight from his phone onto the head and neck area, he said, "I'll take a wild guess and say it was strangulation."

She gasped when she saw what he was illuminating for her benefit. A stocking was wrapped around the victim's neck, then knotted. It had been tied so tightly that, in places, the cloth was actually embedded in the flesh and invisible.

"Wow. I'd say whoever did that relished the task, if you know what I mean," she said.

"It was personal, that's for sure," Dirk replied. "Nasty. Also, the killer was strong."

"Or at least, quite revved up at the time."

Savannah turned on her own phone's light and looked closer. "That's an old stocking, too," she said. "Silk, not nylon."

He bent beside her and looked closer. "How can you tell?"

"It's seamed, a matte look, not shiny like nylon. I'd say . . . silk crepe, extra fine forty-five gauge with a dull luster. Color, Toffee Apple."

"Seriously?"

"Absolutely."

"Wow, you know your stockings. I'm impressed."

"Don't be. That's all written on the bottom of the foot."

She stood up, turned off her light. "Like I keep telling you, boy, you gotta download that magnifier/light app. In your line of work, it'd come in handy."

"Yeah, yeah. Whatever." He began to punch in a number on his phone. "Might as well call Dr. Liu. Get 'er over here."

"She's not going to be happy that you moved the duvet. How many times has she told you not to—"

"—move the body or anything over it, under it, or around it?"

"Yes. That. She gives you the same speech every time you get to a scene before she does."

"Goes to show, you can't make that gal happy. If she gets her liver in a quiver over a little thing like that, it's on her."

"O-o-kay." Savannah clucked her tongue and shook her head. "But I've gotta question the wisdom of getting on the bad side of an ill-tempered woman who makes her living by cutting up bodies with a scalpel."

"Good point."

When Savannah and Dirk finally made their way through the maze of mess and out the mansion's front door, they found Ethan sitting on the bottom porch step.

A woman sat close beside him. He had one arm around her shoulders and was holding her hand in his. She had short salt and pepper hair, and was a slender woman, possibly in her late sixties. She wore a crisp white blouse and black slacks with sharp creases. It occurred to Savannah that the garments had been carefully ironed and had the look of a manager's uniform.

Ethan said something to her in a low, comforting tone, and she responded by laying her head on his shoulder.

But when Ethan heard them close the door and step onto the porch, he immediately released her, stood, and turned to them.

His eyes searched Savannah's, then Dirk's. "Did you get what you needed?" he asked. "Did you see what I saw? Why I knew it wasn't an accident?"

"Yeah," Dirk replied. "I've called the county medical examiner. She and the CSU are on their way."

Ethan looked relieved. "Oh, good," he said. "I guess they'll take Lucinda, I mean her body, to . . . wherever. . . ."

"To the morgue for the postmortem," Savannah offered. "Then, after that, they'll send her to a mortuary to be prepared for burial or for cremation, as she preferred."

The woman, who was still sitting on the porch, her back to them, stirred a bit. Ethan seemed to remember she was there.

"Oh," he said, turning to her, "I'm sorry. Mary. These are friends of mine, Savannah Reid and her husband, Detective Sergeant Dirk Coulter. Savannah and Dirk, this is Ms. Mary Mahoney. She's, um, *was* Lucinda's housekeeper and companion."

"Companion," Mary said. "As I'm sure you can tell, there was no housekeeper for years. Not since I gave up trying."

Mary struggled to stand until Ethan reached down, placed his hands on her waist, and lifted her onto her feet.

Savannah watched her closely and noted that she grimaced, as though she was in terrible pain, even from such a mundane action. Her hunched shoulders, the way she moved, all indicated that her muscles and tendons might be tight, her bones and cartilage brittle, resisting even the smallest shift in position.

Savannah knew better than to offer her a handshake. Having met too many people suffering from severe arthritis, she knew the friendly gesture could cost the woman dearly in pain.

"How do you do, Miss Mahoney?" Savannah said instead. "I'm so sorry for your loss. A terrible thing to happen, and right here in your home."

"Oh, I don't live there!" she said as though she had just been accused of a terrible crime. "I have my own apartment in the back of the house. It has a separate entrance and everything." Her already florid face flushed even darker. "I would never. I could never live like—"

"I understand," Savannah said, feeling sorry for the woman, who was obviously embarrassed by her mistress's lifestyle. "I'm sure your apartment is nice and tidy."

"Not like the rest of this dump heap," Dirk chimed in.

A heavy, awkward silence descended on the porch. As Savannah waited, what seemed like years, for it to end, she thought how many times her husband had created such an unnatural vacuum.

Too many to count.

It was just part of the wonder that was Dirk.

He wasn't a cruel man. Quite the contrary, in fact. But he had never felt the need to weigh words before spitting them into a room, or across the front porch of an art deco mansion with the hoard from hell and a murdered woman inside. Who would have thought such circumstances required delicacy?

Certainly not my *husband*, she thought. *Nope. Not ol' Blurt-It-Now-and-Think-About-It-Later-If-At-All-Dirk.*

"How long has the place been like that?" he continued. Obviously, still not thinking.

"For years," Mary whispered.

65

"Well, yeah." Dirk nodded solemnly. "I mean, you sure couldn't accomplish something like that in one day!"

"I used to try to keep it clean. But the last twenty years or so, she got worse and worse. Finally, she wouldn't let me throw anything away. Nothing. Not even real garbage."

Suddenly, Mary was overcome with a coughing fit that turned her face from red to a deep purple. Savannah was alarmed. It wasn't a normal, mundane chest cold or the hacking brought on by allergies. It sounded like the deep, strangling lung spasms that would come out of someone who wasn't long for the world.

"Are you okay, Mary?" Ethan asked her, seemingly as alarmed as Savannah.

Mary nodded, unable to speak.

"We can drive you to the hospital, if you need to go," Savannah offered. "You should probably have that looked at."

Finally, Mary recovered and said weakly, "I'm okay. I've been to the doctor about it. Not much they could do, what with me living here, you know, in that."

"What'd you keep workin' here for?" Dirk asked. "If breathin' that mess was causin' me to hack up a lung, I'd be movin' on."

Tears flooded Mary's eyes. She crossed her arms over her chest and grabbed her upper arms tightly, as though giving herself a badly needed long, hard hug.

"I don't have any place to go," she admitted, "and after all the years I'd spent taking care of Miss Lucinda, I couldn't leave her. She wouldn't have made it this long without me. She doesn't have a lot of friends or family."

"Yeah, I was gonna ask you about that," Dirk said. "We'll need to inform the next of kin. Who is it?"

Both Mary's and Ethan's faces darkened at the question. Savannah knew it wasn't going to be a cheerful reply.

66

"She had a great-grandson," Ethan said. "But the way she spoke about him, I didn't get the idea they were close."

"He's still around, and they weren't at all close," Mary added. "Far from it. In fact, they hated each other."

"Any particular reason?" Savannah asked.

"Yes." A look of intense anger crossed Mary's face. "Because he's a horrible excuse for a human being. That's why. She disowned him years ago, and I don't blame her one bit. He gave her no choice."

"All right," Dirk replied, watching her intently. "I'll keep that in mind when I inform him of his loss. Anyone else that she was close to?"

Ethan thought for a moment, then shrugged. "Not that I know of. She and I did a movie together about three years ago. That's how we met. It was her last role, a cameo appearance. She was amazing. Took me under her wing and taught me everything she knew. But I didn't get the idea she had a lot of friends or family."

"She had nobody," Mary said. "She either chased them away, or they ran off on their own steam for their own reasons. Lucinda was alone and lonely. Had been for years."

"That's sad," Savannah observed, thinking of the picture of the vulnerable fifteen-year-old, exploited for her exceptional beauty, her innocence robbed, her life forced down an unsavory, dangerous path before it had even begun.

Savannah recalled seeing headlines that proclaimed Lucinda Faraday the most beautiful woman in the world. "Every man wants her! Every woman wants to be her!"—or so said the publicists, as they scrambled to sell her to adoring throngs.

Seeing Lucinda Faraday back then, at the height of her beauty, who would have thought she would end up like that? Savannah wondered. *Murdered and thrown onto the refuse heap that had come to define her life?*

Savannah could see a convoy of white vehicles turning from the highway and heading toward the mansion. The vans' sides bore the county's official seal and the letters *CSU*.

Dr. Liu and her crime scene unit had arrived.

Savannah didn't envy the medical examiner and her crew the job that lay before them. Trying to gather evidence at the scene of any homicide was difficult, no matter what the circumstances.

But, considering what lay inside the walls of Qamar Damun—the strange, formerly beautiful house with its dark past and exotic name—their task was unenviable at best. Savannah was afraid that their search for the truth of Lucinda Faraday's violent death might prove all but impossible.

Chapter 7

"Okay," Dirk said, "we inform this dude that his great-grandma's dead, and then we go home and to bed. That sound okay to you?"

Sitting next to him in the Buick's passenger seat, Savannah nodded. She could feel the fatigue and the stress of the day weighing heavily on her. Ten years ago, she wouldn't even have noticed. It would've taken a week's worth of rotten days to slow her down.

Now, well into her forties, a ten-minute encounter with a quarrelsome, druggy mother, while trying to keep her son from witnessing that quarrel, had left Savannah drained and in need of her comfy chair, a steamy romance novel, and some serious kitty purring and petting.

Add a homicide—like the maraschino cherry on the melted sundae—and Savannah felt twice her age.

"Good idea," she said. "I was hoping to get back in time to tuck Brody in and tell him good night." She glanced at her watch and realized it was 9:10. "No doubt Gran's already put him down. She's always been dead serious about getting kids to bed on time. Says it stunts their growth if they don't get enough sleep."

Dirk laughed, but there was no mirth in it. By the lights of the dashboard, Savannah could see his grim expression when he said, "Didn't seem to affect my growth none. I did well to get four hours' sleep on a good night there in the orphanage."

As usual, when Dirk mentioned his childhood, Savannah felt a pang of sadness. In all the years she had known him and the countless personal things they had shared, she could count on her fingers the times he had said anything at all about his upbringing.

Dirk Coulter was a man with a well-established reputation for complaining constantly about everything—that his free coffee was stale, that he had to wait longer than five seconds in a grocery line, that it was raining or not raining as he desired. So, the fact that he had so little to say about being raised in a no-frills, poorly regulated orphanage told Savannah a lot.

She was almost afraid to ask. But, as usual with her, nosiness won over courtesy. "Why weren't you able to sleep?" she wanted to know.

"I could've. But you close your eyes, you take your chances."

"Of what?"

"At least, gettin' your junk stole."

"And at worst?"

"Gettin' jumped."

"At night? When you were in bed?"

"That was the best time to settle whatever happened earlier in the day. No adults around to put a stop to it. If they could be bothered. If they weren't too busy, gabbing with each other or sneakin' off for a smoke."

"Important stuff like that."

"Yeah. Right."

They rode on a few more blocks in silence. Then he continued, "At night, the lights are off. The other kid's got his eyes closed, not on guard. If he's all the way asleep, you could get three or four licks in before he'd even know you were on 'im."

"Wow," she said quietly, shaking her head. "You sound like an expert there."

He grunted and shrugged. "I gave as good as I got. Usually better."

She didn't hear any pride or satisfaction in his words. Just a flat, matter-of-fact delivery of the facts as he saw them.

Reaching over, she placed her hand on his thigh and patted it. "I'm sorry you went through that, sugar," she said. "No kid should've had to grow up that way. It wasn't fair."

He turned and gave her a sweet smile. "Yeah, well, you and me both know that 'fair's' got nothin' to do with nothin'."

"True."

"Grown-ups, they've got a lot to say to kids about how important it is to be fair. But then, you notice that they aren't fair even half the time, and life itself is even less fair. Good things happen to rotten people. Rotten things happen to good people. That's just the way it is. Nothin's fair about nothin'."

"I like to think that, in the end, everything works out. The good people get rewarded, and folks who hurt others get their comeuppance, sooner or later."

"That's because you got them rose-colored glasses on, Van. From what I've seen, there ain't a lot of justice in this world. What little there is comes later, a lot later, rather than sooner."

"But it does come."

"If you say so."

"Granny would say so, too."

"She would. That's true. You and your grandma are two special women. Both of you went through hell and back when you were growing up. There's no denying that. But I figure the suffering you and her went through, it's what made you who you are—the two best people I've ever known in my life."

He reached down, lifted her hand from his leg, and tenderly kissed it.

Savannah could feel her throat tightening and some tears wetting her eyelids. Leave it to him to get all mushy when she was extra tired. It was a dangerous combination—romance and exhaustion. If she didn't watch out, she'd be reduced to a blubbering ninny in the next five seconds.

That wouldn't do because they were approaching the house where Lucinda Faraday's great-grandson lived with his fiancée. Making a notification was tough enough without arriving in tears because your hubby had said something sweet a minute before.

As Dirk pulled the Buick up to the curb in front of the tiny Spanish-style house with its beige stucco walls and clay tile roof, Savannah was a bit surprised to see that Lucinda Faraday's heir lived in a place that was even smaller than hers, not to mention that it was in worse shape.

Savannah had repainted hers and had some missing tiles replaced within the past few years. Even with only the fading light of the setting sun to illuminate the house, one look at the old structure told Savannah that no one had done any improvements since it had been built, decades before.

The yard was equally neglected, as was a rusty old SUV sitting in the driveway.

"That thing's seen better days," Dirk said.

"A few decades ago," Savannah added. "Like the house."

"From the looks of this place, it was back when the old lady and her great-grandson had their falling out. When she cut off the money."

"If she ever gave him any in the first place," Savannah

added. "Just because folks are rich, that doesn't mean they pass it down."

"Not till they're dead and got no use for it anymore."

"Something to consider, since he's the sole heir, huh?"

"Yeah. We'll have to keep an eagle eye on him when he gets the bad news. See if he takes it hard, gets weepy and all that."

"Or refrains from dancing a jig."

"Exactly."

They got out of the car and headed for the house. It was dark inside, except for the glow of a television coming from the living room window.

"Looks like somebody's home," he said. "I hope so. I don't wanna have to go running around town lookin' for the guy in bars and pool halls."

Savannah grinned and thought, not for the first time, that Dirk had never noticed that San Carmelita's last official pool hall had closed over twenty years ago. Now the town's miscreant juveniles tended to while away their idle hours in the food court at the local mall. Much to the distress of shoppers and the mall security team.

As they were about to step onto the porch, Savannah glanced around to the side of the house and saw something that stood out in sharp contrast to the rest of the property. A shiny new black Porsche, whose price tag would have exceeded the value of the house and land combined.

"Hey, hey, hey," she said. "Nice ride."

Dirk sniffed. "If you like those fancy foreign jobs. I'm partial to American-made myself."

"Made in America back when the buffalo and the dinosaurs roamed."

"Yeah. Like your Mustang."

"Shush about my Mustang. I noticed you were happy to

leave the cruiser with one of the uniforms back at the Faraday place, so's you could drive your Buick home."

"Yeah, well. Can't have *you* drivin' it everywhere."

"Might spill a drop of Coke on the dash."

"I know! I break out in a cold sweat just thinkin' about it."

He knocked on the door—a bit more softly than his usual cop-pounding barrage. The nearby windows didn't rattle, and he didn't shout, "Police! Open up!"

Savannah was proud. Who said a husband couldn't be taught a bit of civility by a highly determined wife?

He had to knock twice more before someone finally opened it a crack and looked out.

"Yes?" answered a meek voice. A woman's voice.

"Yeah, hi," he replied, pulling his badge from his jacket pocket and holding it up to her eye level. "I'm Detective Sergeant Dirk Coulter with the San Carmelita Police Department." He nodded toward Savannah. "This is Savannah Reid. Can we come in for a minute?"

"Why? What do you want?" she asked, her voice almost squeaky with timidity.

"To talk to Geoffrey Faraday," Dirk told her. "Is he here?"

"Um." She glanced back over her shoulder. "Yes. But he's busy."

"Then tell him to get un-busy and come to the door."

Savannah noticed that Dirk had dropped his nice-guy tone and was about to go flat out Aggravated Cop. From experience, Savannah knew that wouldn't bode well for Miss Squeaky Voice behind the door.

Savannah stepped forward and in her most "down home" Dixie tone said, "Please, ma'am. This is important. Detective Coulter has a matter of serious family business to discuss with Mr. Faraday. Something he needs to hear."

When the woman hesitated a moment too long to suit Dirk, he called out, "Faraday! Come to the door! Now!"

Sooner than Savannah expected, Dirk's new tactic worked. Almost instantly, the door opened halfway, fully revealing the timid lady of the house, who was standing there in a pair of pink pajamas with cartoon teddy bears on them. She appeared to be in her late twenties and in desperate need of a shampoo. Her dark hair hung in limp, greasy strands nearly to her waist. Other than a smudge of mascara beneath both eyes, she wore no makeup. Just a frightened, nervous look.

Next to her stood a guy, maybe ten years older than she was. He was as overly dressed and meticulously groomed as the lady of the house was slovenly. His thick strawberry-blond hair was so heavily gelled that Savannah was sure not a strand of it would budge, even in an EF5 tornado. He was wearing a charcoal suit that, even to her relatively untrained eye, appeared to be of the highest quality with a contemporary, physique-flattering cut. A crisp white shirt and designer tie completed his ensemble. She was sure she could have paid off her mortgage several times over for the price of his platinum, diamond-accented watch.

He flashed them a smile as gaudy as his jewelry and said in an oily smooth voice, "Good evening, Detective Coulter, Ms. Reid. I'm Geoffrey Faraday." He waved a casual hand toward the woman standing beside him. "This is my fiancée, Brooklynn Marsh. How can we help you?"

Instinctively, Savannah knew he had been standing right behind the door the entire time. That and her instincts caused her to distrust and dislike him instantly. Most law-abiding people, if visited by a representative of law enforcement, were curious, concerned, and open. Not guarded, nervous, and scared, as Brooklynn appeared to be, or fake-friendly and suspicious like Geoffrey.

People with nothing to hide didn't hide behind doors.

"We need to come inside and speak to you, Mr. Faraday," Dirk was saying, even as he put his hand on the door and pushed it farther open. "It won't take long."

"Good, because I'm going out for the evening," Faraday said, adjusting his gold cuff links in such a way as to give them both a good, long look at them.

"Maybe you are, and maybe you aren't," Dirk told him, not bothering to hide his annoyance. "That depends on how our little talk goes."

Savannah shot Dirk a warning look. After all, this man was about to hear that a member of his family had been murdered. Since they had no evidence to the contrary, they had to assume he knew nothing about it and would probably be devastated.

"Could we all sit down, sir?" Savannah asked.

Faraday glanced behind him at the cluttered living room, then gave his fiancée an angry look. "I guess you could," he said, "if there was somewhere to sit in this place."

Instantly, Brooklynn sprang into action, scurrying around the room, grabbing dirty clothes, magazines, and a pizza box off the sofa and tossing it all behind a recliner. "There," she said. "All clear. Sit down."

Faraday picked up a bra from a nearby chair, gingerly, with thumb and forefinger, and tossed it behind the recliner with the rest. Then he took a seat on the edge of the chair and waved Savannah and Dirk to do the same on the sofa.

They did. Though Savannah made a mental note to toss her slacks into the washing machine the moment she arrived home. The place stank of urine, which she hoped was from unseen pets and on the carpet, not the furniture.

"What's this all about?" Faraday asked as Brooklynn sat down, cross-legged, on the floor at his feet.

Dirk cleared his throat and then plunged in. When forced to do something he hated, he didn't waste time. "I'm sorry, Mr. Faraday, but you must prepare yourself. I'm afraid I have some bad news for you."

Faraday didn't seem particularly alarmed, or even all that curious, Savannah noted as she watched his face, taking in every nuance of expression, as he said, "Oh? What news?"

"It's about your great-grandmother. Mrs. Lucinda Faraday."

"Okay. Let's hear it."

Hardly the normal response, Savannah thought. Most folks were frozen in terror by this point in such a conversation.

"I'm afraid she's passed away," Dirk said with more compassion than she thought him capable of mustering under such strange circumstances.

Brooklynn gasped and clamped her hand over her mouth.

Faraday, on the other hand, sat quite stoically until Dirk clarified his former statement. "She's gone, sir. I'm sorry, but she was found dead in her home a few hours ago."

"I guess it had to happen sooner or later. Great Granny was old. Old as dirt, as they say," Faraday stated quite matter-of-factly. "It's not like we weren't expecting it."

"Yeah, okay." Dirk leaned forward, his elbows on his knees, unabashedly staring at the not-particularly-bereaved great-grandson. "But were you expecting her to expire due to foul play?" he asked.

Again, his fiancée on the floor at his feet made a small, choking sound, while Faraday registered hardly any reaction at all.

"Foul play?" she said with a half sob. "Do you mean, like someone . . . hurt her?"

"Yes, very much so. Someone killed her, ma'am," Dirk said. "I'm sorry. I'm sure that makes the news much harder to hear."

She nodded, then covered her face with her hands. "It's horrible!" she said, beginning to cry in earnest. "She was a difficult person, but for someone to actually . . . Oh, it's just awful! Who would do such a terrible thing?"

"That's what we need to find out," Dirk said, studying Geoffrey Faraday like an owl eyeing a rat he was contemplating having for dinner. "We will. But first, we need to know if your great-grandmother had any enemies that you're aware of, sir."

"Enemies?" Faraday gave an unpleasant little snort. "Yes, she had enemies."

"Who?" Dirk asked, reaching into his jacket and taking out a small notebook and pen.

"Who *wasn't* her enemy?" Faraday replied with a shrug. "I don't think I ever heard her say a kind word to anybody. She was ill-tempered, conceited, opinionated, and ruthless when it came to getting her way. Which she always did."

Brooklynn looked up at him, her mouth open in shock. "Geoff! Don't say that about your great-grandmother! Miss Lucinda could be nice . . . when she wanted to be."

"When it served her purpose, you mean," he replied. "She managed to anger, insult, and alienate everybody from her housekeeper, to the guy who delivered her newspaper, to her local congresswoman." He paused to take a deep breath, then added, "Let's just say, she's not going to be missed. Quite the contrary, in fact."

Savannah turned to Dirk. She could see his mental wheels spinning, taking in all of this, trying to make sense of it.

Geoffrey Faraday didn't appear at first glance to be a stupid man. Yet, with every word he was uttering, he was making himself look, more and more, like their number one suspect.

"Okay," Dirk said. "Nobody's going to grieve her passing? Everyone she knew could have wanted her dead?"

"Absolutely. Most people will probably be relieved."

"That's a horrible thing to say, Geoff," Brooklynn said with a sniff, twisting a strand of her long dark hair around her finger. "I'm not happy she's gone. Now it's too late for us to ever make peace with her. I'm sad it had to end like this."

There was a long, awkward silence in the room as Geoffrey glared down at his fiancée.

Finally, Dirk said, "Okay. Was there anyone in particular you can think of who might have had a worse-than-average grudge against her? Anyone she had a confrontation with recently? Anybody who might've threatened to do her harm?"

"Nope. Afraid not." Faraday gave Dirk a little smile that set off alarm bells in Savannah's head. It was a mocking grin, almost as though he was daring Dirk to challenge him.

Not smart, Savannah thought. *Not when my man's tired and hungry.*

Dirk was almost always one or the other. Often both.

Suddenly, Dirk snapped his notebook closed and shoved it, far more forcefully than necessary, into his jacket pocket. He stood and said, "Okay, Mr. Faraday. If you don't want to help me figure out who killed your great-grandmother, I'll take it from here myself. The first person on my suspect list is going to be the one who has the most to gain from her passing."

Faraday looked up at Dirk blankly, his mocking grin gone. He didn't reply.

Savannah stood and followed Dirk to the door. But before they left, Dirk turned back to Geoffrey and said, "Oh, yeah. I understand you're Lucinda Faraday's sole heir. That makes you number one on my list. Congratulations!"

As they left the house and Geoffrey Faraday with an unhappy look on his formerly prissy face, Savannah couldn't help thinking how glad she was that she'd married a policeman, instead of a certain banker's son she'd fancied herself in love with, years ago.

She had nothing against bankers or their sons, of course. No doubt many of them were exciting, fun guys. But she was pretty sure her own life was more interesting, hanging out with her favorite cop.

Chapter 8

Nearly an hour later, when Savannah and Dirk arrived back at their house and pulled into the driveway, she saw the living room lights were on.

"Granny's still awake," she said, feeling a tug of guilt to have kept her grandmother up past her bedtime.

"Of course she is," Dirk said as he parked the car and shut it off. "When did you ever come home, after being out late, and find your grandma snoozing?"

"It happened. But I could probably count the times on one hand. She used to say, 'A mama hen cain't close her eyes to sleep till all her chickees are safe and sound in the nest.'"

As they got out of the car and walked to the front door, Dirk draped his arm over her shoulders and pulled her against his side. "I just hope that little ankle-biter didn't give her a hard time tonight. If he did, him and me's gonna tangle."

Savannah laughed, slipped her arm around his waist, and gave him a squeeze. "I hope not, too. It purely traumatized me, watching my beloved husband get the stuffin' beat out of him by a squirt that doesn't weigh as much as his thigh."

Dirk sniffed. "I had my hands full with his wild hyena of a mother. I've taken down bikers on PCP who gave me less hassle than that woman. I'll be happy if the only time I ever have to see her again is from the witness stand at her trial."

"You think she's going away?" Savannah asked, as the harsh truth of the boy's situation hit her.

"Oh, she's goin' away for sure. No doubt about it. That gal's rap sheet's longer than my"—he gave her a quick, suggestive grin—"my right arm."

She snickered. "Well, as long as it's your right arm and not your third leg."

"That's for sure. If that was the case, she'd be goin' away for life."

He unlocked the front door, opened it, and stood aside to allow her to walk through before him.

That was one thing she deeply appreciated about her West Coast boy. He might not be a son of the old South, but he had good ol' boy manners when it came to how to treat a lady.

Best of all—after the many years they had been together, first as partners on the force, then best friends, then husband and wife . . . after all the intimate knowledge they had of each other, gleaned from circumstances that were anywhere from deeply romantic interludes to dealing with the effects of bad chili cheese dogs—he still considered her a lady.

His lady.

The fact that he treated her as such, even when performing the simple act of going through a doorway, was one of his more endearing qualities.

She was also pleased that, without her even asking, he immediately took the precaution of putting his own weapon into the closet safe, rather than placing it on the top shelf.

When it came to kids, Dirk took no chances. Not even with ones who had given him a shiner earlier in the evening.

As they walked into the living room, Savannah glanced to the left, expecting to see her grandmother sitting in the most comfortable chair in the house, Savannah's infamous "comfy chair."

Like most of the Reid women who sat in it, the chair was soft, pretty, feminine, and overstuffed. The large, cushy foot-stool, also covered in the same rose floral chintz, was usually inhabited by one or both of her sister cats, Diamante and Cleopatra. Like bookends covered with silky black fur, they provided comfort and love in the form of purring foot warmers.

But, to Savannah's surprise, the chair was empty.

For half a second, she thought something might be wrong. Perhaps she shouldn't have left her elderly grandmother in the company of a juvenile delinquent, whom she had known for only a couple of hours.

But one glance toward the sofa put her mind at ease.

Granny sat in the middle, an open, well-read copy of *Peter Pan* in her lap. To her right was Cleo, curled in a ball against her thigh.

To her left sat Brody, his head on her shoulder, his eyes closed.

He looked like a different kid from the one Savannah had left in her grandmother's care earlier. This kid was clean. Shockingly clean. His dirty blond hair was now three shades lighter, definitively blond without a speck of the dirt. Sun-bleached, no doubt from spending a lot of time outdoors, his long hair was now fluffy and curly instead of straight and greasy.

Brody Greyson was the poster kid for Southern California Surfer Boy.

He was wearing Savannah's Mickey Mouse T-shirt, one of her many souvenirs from Disneyland. It was far too large for him, hanging down to his knees.

Savannah could see only a bit of his shorts beneath the shirt. But like the boy's hair and the rest of his body, the shorts had undergone a transformation in Granny's expert hands and were far cleaner than Savannah would have guessed they could ever be.

On the boy's lap was Diamante, curled into a contented, purring, snoozing circle of ebony fur, like her sister. Although the boy appeared to be asleep, too, his fingers were lightly stroking the cat's neck.

Granny was still reading the book, her voice soft and low. She glanced up at Savannah and smiled, the personification of peace.

"Hi," Savannah whispered. "I see you have everything under control, as expected."

Granny quietly closed the book and set it aside. "Nothin' needed controllin' 'round here tonight," she said. "The child was good as gold. Not a cross word or a disrespectful action outta 'im. He wanted to bring the Colonel indoors with him once it got dark. But I explained how that could result in a hound dog with no nose on his face." She nodded toward the cats. "He dropped the subject, we put the hound in the utility room on his bed, and we sailed through the rest of the evenin' with nary a problem."

"Then you did better than me," Dirk said, taking off his tennis shoes and kicking them under the coffee table.

Granny looked up at him and squinted, trying to see him clearly in the dim lamplight. "Mercy sakes alive, boy. Is that a black eye you're sportin' there?"

Dirk nodded. "About as black as it's ever been, I hate to admit," he told her. "Don't let that angelic look there fool ya. That little runt can be a tear-cat when he wants to be."

"I ain't asleep, you know," Brody said, his southern accent

thick and drowsy. He opened his eyes halfway. "I can hear everythin' you're saying. I ain't no runt, and I ain't a tear-cat neither, 'less you're puttin' a whoopin' on my momma."

"Yeah, and I'm an officer of the law," Dirk shot back, "not a lousy, pig-nose skunk butt neither. Your momma was resistin' arrest and encouraging her boy to rip my face off, which I might remind you, you were tryin' your best to do."

Granny cleared her throat and looked down at the child next to her, a frown on her face and a distinct twinkle in her eye. "Brody Greyson, tell me the truth, 'cause I don't abide no lyin'. Did you call Detective Coulter a pig-nose skunk butt?"

"I did."

Brody didn't appear embarrassed. Not even a little. Savannah didn't know whether to be amused or concerned.

She decided she was both.

Granny continued, "Okay, thank you for your truthfulness. Did you lay your hands upon him in a violent manner, intendin' to do him bodily harm?"

Brody thought it over for a minute, then said, "I jumped on his back and started whalin' on him for all I was worth, intendin' to rip his face off and shove it where the sun don't shine—just like my momma was tellin' me to do."

He looked up at Granny with eyes that were filled with more innocence than might have been expected from someone who had just delivered such a damning confession. "Is that what you mean by 'bodily harm'?" he asked.

"Yessiree bob. That there's exactly what I meant." In one practiced move, Granny reached for the child, grabbed him by the shoulders, and spun him around until they were eye to eye.

The awakened and unhappy Diamante jumped off his lap and joined her sister on Granny's right side.

Granny looked deeply into the boy's eyes and said in a gentle but firm voice, "Young man, you and me gotta get somethin' straight right now. Detective Coulter there is a policeman, and in this household, we hold police officers in high regard."

The boy bristled. "Well, me and my momma don't like 'em. They're mean, nasty, monkey—"

"Stop! We don't allow no name-callin' in this house!" Granny took a deep breath, then having gathered a modicum of calmness, she continued. "You may have met some mean police in your young life. I'll grant you that. There's no-goods in any group of people. You line up a bunch of plumbers, teachers, even preachers, you'll find a dud or two among 'em. Cops ain't no different that way. But the vast majority risk their lives ever' day to keep us all safe, and we won't have nobody bad-mouthin' 'em in this house, let alone raisin' their hand to 'em. You hear me?"

With his nose only a few inches from hers, Brody continued to glare at Granny for what seemed to Savannah an eternity. But the older woman's steady, gentle gaze finally wore him down. He nodded and looked away.

Granny smoothed his hair back away from his eyes and placed a quick kiss on his forehead. "Detective Coulter is part of my family, Brody," she said. "A precious part. He's like a son to me. If you and me's gonna be friends, you'll have to treat him with respect. Understand?"

Savannah glanced over at Dirk and thought she saw a tear in his eye. She couldn't be sure because the black one was bloodshot and swollen. But she could tell that Gran's words had found their way to his heart.

As she had countless times already in her life, Savannah felt infinitely grateful to have a grandmother like hers.

So what if her childhood, her parents, hadn't been all they

should have? She wouldn't trade her own upbringing for anyone's. Not if it meant losing Gran.

Savannah walked over to the sofa and held out her hand to Brody. "I think it's about bedtime, young man," she said. "I know it is for us old folks."

"That's for sure," Dirk grumbled. "But I've gotta eat something first. I'm about to starve. Is there any of that coconut cake left?" he asked Granny.

"It's in the icebox," she told him. "We saved you both big slices. Why don't you two eat 'em whilst I put our youngest to bed upstairs in the guest room?"

Surprised, Savannah looked at her grandmother. "No, no," Savannah told her. "The guest room is for you, like always, when it's late and you stay over. I'll make up a bed for Mr. Brody here on the couch."

"But . . . but he's the guest of honor tonight," Granny argued.

"Yes, he is," Savannah agreed. "As a gentleman, he would be honored to give you, his elder and a lady, the best bed while he holds down the couch and keeps it from floating away."

Savannah gave Brody a wink and a grin. "He's tough, aren't you, darlin'?"

Instantly, the boy gave her a broad smile. "I sure am. Tough as they come. I'm used to sleepin' on the floor in the back of my momma's van. Sleepin' on a couch ain't no big deal to the likes o' me."

Granny stood and whispered in Savannah's ear, "Are you sure? I don't mind bein' down here on the—"

"Sh-h-h. We won't hear of it," Savannah told her. "I had a feeling you'd be staying the night when I left earlier. I put fresh sheets on the futon, so the guest room's all ready for you."

The two women embraced and kissed each other good night. Granny hugged Dirk tightly, gave Brody a peck on his cheek, then disappeared up the stairs.

Savannah began to take the back cushions off the sofa and set them aside to make more room for the boy to sleep.

Dirk walked into the kitchen, and Savannah assumed he was headed to the refrigerator and the coconut cake. But a moment later he returned with his arms full of bedclothes from the utility room closet.

He waited until Savannah had removed the last cushion, then he spread the sheet and tucked it in.

"Lay down there, kid, and be quick about it," he told Brody with gruff playfulness.

The child grinned and scrambled to do as he was told.

As Savannah spread the second sheet and a blanket over his legs, she couldn't help thinking what an improvement that was over his and Dirk's earlier exchange.

"There's just one thing I'd really like to have," Brody said as he sat on his newly made "bed," his arms crossed over his chest.

"Whaddaya want now?" Dirk asked. "Oh, I know. A pillow fight!" He smacked the boy soundly with the pillow, knocking him onto his back. "Oops! Fight's over," Dirk told him. "I won."

Brody roared with laughter, grabbing the pillow away from Dirk and shoving it under his head.

Then the child turned to Savannah, his eyes filled with a longing that went straight to her heart.

"What is it?" she asked. "You want a glass of milk to help you sleep or—"

Brody shook his head. "No. Your grandma gave me so much

to eat, I don't think I'll ever be hungry again. What I'd really like is . . . Do you think I could sleep with the kitties?"

Savannah and Dirk looked at each other for a moment, then Dirk said, "Actually, they're *our* bed partners. I sleep with Cleo, and Savannah cuddles up with Diamante."

The boy looked crushed, but he busied himself fluffing his pillow. "That's okay. I understand," he said. "They're used to sleeping with you guys. They'd probably be scared if we changed things up."

Savannah reached down and scooped up the still-pouting Diamante from the floor, where she had been placed when they had started making the bed. "Oh, I don't think Di would be scared to sleep with you. She likes you a lot, after you paying so much attention to her hurt ear and giving her all those good pets earlier. We've got two cats, and we aren't stingy folks. I reckon we can share with you."

Brody Greyson's bright, grateful smile was the only reward Savannah needed for her sacrifice of a purring, furry bed warmer.

She handed Diamante over to the child and watched him cuddle the contented feline close to his chest. Then Savannah bent over and gave him a kiss on the forehead.

"See there," she told him. "I promised you earlier that you'd be rewarded for being brave and making the right choice. I told you your life was going to get better. Remember?"

He nodded solemnly. "I remember. I'm always gonna remember that. Forever and ever."

Dirk reached down and rubbed the kid's head with his knuckles, rustling his hair. Dirk nodded toward Savannah and said, "This gal here, I've known her a long time. When she makes you a promise, you can take it to the bank and cash it."

"Okay." Brody grinned, tucking Diamante's head under his chin, while being careful of her ear. "You two are married, right?" he said to Dirk.

Dirk laughed. "Figured that out all by yourself, didja? Maybe we'll make a detective outta you someday."

Brody snorted. "That'll be the day. My momma'd pitch a fit if I was to ever become a cop. She'd rather me be a bank robber."

Dirk opened his mouth to say something, shot a sideways look at Savannah, and mumbled, "No comment."

As he ambled off to the kitchen, no doubt in search of coconut cake, Savannah hurried over to the end table near Brody's head and switched off the lamp.

"Good night, sugar," she told him. "If you need anything at all, don't be afraid to come up and get me. Upstairs, down the hall, last door on the right. Next to the bathroom in case you need that, too."

"I'm fine," he said. "I don't get scared, and I'm used to holdin' it."

Savannah felt her heartstrings twang. "You're in *my* house now. Everybody here gets scared once in a while. It's nothing to be ashamed of, and when you're under my roof, you go when you need to. It's not healthy to . . . 'hold it.' Okay?"

"'Kay." He glanced toward the kitchen. They could hear knives, forks, and plates rattling. "That cake your grandma baked is the best I've ever ate. You better get in there quick, before he eats it all."

Savannah laughed. "How did you know?"

"He's the kinda guy you gotta watch your food around. Believe me, I can tell."

Savannah recalled something Dirk had told her once about literally having to fight for food back in the orphanage.

She looked down at her little guest with his gaunt cheeks and too-thin body. "You two boys have more in common than you probably think," she told him sadly.

"Me and him? Naw. We're nothing alike at all."

She gave him a final tuck in. Then, as she walked away, she whispered, "More than you might think, little man. In fact, more than you could ever imagine."

Chapter 9

"Your new boyfriend was lookin' pretty sharp this mornin'," Dirk told Savannah the next day as she drove him to the county morgue. "How much did all those new clothes set ya back?"

"More than you'd think," she replied. "Outfitting a young'un from head to toe with a week's worth of clothes—even a little kid—it's not cheap."

"Lemme know how much it was, and I'll pay it," he said, much to her shock. Since when did Ol' Stingy Pants fork over money without being asked nicely? Asked nicely while being prodded with a red-hot pitchfork or being hung upside down by his toenails.

"Seriously?" she asked, sure she had heard wrong.

"Yeah," he replied, moderately grumpy. "Most of the time I make more money than you. I don't mind pickin' it up this go around."

She thought her heart would burst with tenderness. He really could be a sweetie when he wanted to be.

"You don't have to," she said. "Ethan gave me a big retainer. But I appreciate the thought. A lot. Thank you."

"Sheez. Dodged that bullet," she heard him whisper.

"Yeah. You get credit for offering, but don't have to actually shell out any real cash."

"I know! Best of both worlds."

They rode on in silence awhile, leaving the picturesque residential area where they lived, passing the hospital and the junior college area.

"How hard was it to enroll him in school?" Dirk asked. "Did they give you a hard time about it?"

"Yes. They did. I had them call CPS, and by the time the gal there was done with them, they seemed pleased to have him."

"Was he okay when you left him? Was he happy to be there?"

"He's a kid whose mother's been letting him play hooky and hang out on the beaches for most of the school term. What do you think?"

"Did he say he misses the ol' gal?"

"No. He didn't mention her one single time."

"Good."

"I take it as a positive sign. Beats him crying his eyes out over her. Is she asking about him?"

"Not that I heard."

"Good."

Savannah turned off Sunset Avenue and headed toward the less touristy, more industrial part of town. There were hardly any palm trees in that area and no ocean views to speak of. Instead of quaint Spanish-style architecture, the buildings were enormous square boxes made of cement and steel with flat roofs, few windows, and loading docks.

Savannah hated that area. She considered it soulless. But

mostly she resented the fact that countless acres of orange and lemon groves had been destroyed in order to build these monstrosities.

Not once since the orchards had been ravaged had she driven into this area and not recalled the dismembered trees bulldozed into giant piles and burning, the black smoke staining the turquoise sky.

"You know how much I hate coming down here," she said, beginning her well-worn complaint.

The one Dirk had heard far too many times.

"Yes, I know. I know," he said. "You're still pissy about them cutting down the trees."

"Not pissy. You are minimizing my feelings there, boy. I'm bereaved. Bereft and bereaved."

"And bemoaning the fact ad nauseam," he mumbled, turning away to look out his window.

"What?"

"Sorry to hear that you're in pain, darlin'. Again." He sighed. "Next time, I'll drive, and you can wear a blindfold. Then you won't have to belabor the point that you're beset with bereavement."

She turned and shot him a withering look. "Keep that up and you might *be* smacked upside the head."

He grinned at her and winked. Obviously terrified by the threat. "What're we gonna have for dinner tonight?"

"Whatever the kid wants, I reckon," she said.

"How come *he* gets to choose?"

"'Cause *you'll* eat anything."

"True."

When Savannah pulled the Mustang into the morgue's parking lot, she steeled herself for the ordeal ahead.

It wasn't the prospect of seeing a dead body. She had certainly seen more than her share of those. So many, in fact, that if she didn't know them personally, it didn't bother her that much anymore.

Except for the smell.

That she couldn't handle. No amount of pungent mentholated ointment spread generously inside a surgical mask could cover the stench of decomposition. It was an odor that went through the nostrils, straight to the stomach, and caused many people who smelled it to need to purge. Instantly.

Savannah was sure that the sink near Dr. Liu's autopsy table had been used for that purpose more often than for washing hands and disinfecting instruments.

It was the main reason that, fascinated as Savannah was by the miraculous design of the human body and as intrigued as she might be by the amount of forensic evidence it might provide during an autopsy, she wouldn't have done Dr. Liu's job for a million dollars.

Per autopsy.

Even worse, there was the gruesome task of dealing with Officer Kenny Bates, who manned the front desk.

Since she had Dirk with her, she doubted that Kenny would turn the full force of his "charm" in her direction. Not long ago, Dirk had assured Kenny that, if he didn't leave Savannah alone and refrain from making lewd suggestions in her company, Dirk would rearrange his digestive system so thoroughly that he would have to sit on his plate to eat his lunch.

Considering that Dirk was a head taller, ten years younger, leaner and far meaner than Bates, good old Kenny had taken the threat to heart and behaved himself thereafter. As long as Dirk was present.

But as luck would have it, just as they were approaching the building together, Dirk received a call on his cell phone from the police chief.

"I wanna take this call first, before I go inside," he told her. "Are you gonna wait for me?"

Savannah smirked and shifted the plastic container filled with macadamia chocolate chip cookies under her arm. "Naw. I think I'll go ahead. I'll get Dr. Jen softened up for you. One bite of my cookies and she'll be putty in your hands."

"Yeah, right. In *your* hands, maybe. But *mine*? Never. Watch out for Bates."

"*He'd* better watch out for *me*."

She left Dirk to deal with the chief, glad that was no longer part of her job description, and walked through the front door of the county morgue.

As expected, Officer Kenneth Bates was wasting the taxpayers' money, making himself utterly useless at the front desk, watching some sort of television program on his computer screen while shoveling an enormous ice-cream sundae into his face.

His was a face that had been acquainted with far too much ice cream in its day, not to mention pizza, chips, dips, and doughnuts. Since he was not in the habit of changing and laundering his uniforms regularly, anyone with even minor detecting skills or a morbid curiosity could determine what he had eaten in the past week, simply by looking at his shirt front.

That, along with his askew, threadbare toupee, rendered Officer Bates totally resistible to most human beings. Especially females with a modicum of discernment and taste.

The bright smile that crossed his face the instant he saw her walk through the door might have been heartwarming, had it not been for the chocolate sauce running down his chin.

The thought of being held in such high esteem by one of her fellow humans might have proven at least a bit flattering in most circumstances. Over the years, Savannah had enjoyed more than her share of male attention. Although the fashion industry might have considered her to be overweight, men seemed to be attracted to, even fascinated by, her generously proportioned curves.

Then there was Kenny.

Kenny wasn't just attracted or fascinated by her.

Kenny was head over heels in lust with her. Deeply, hopelessly obsessed.

Even with a husband the size of Dirk threatening him, and in spite of the fact that Savannah had once beaten him soundly with his own rolled-up porn magazine, Kenny's ardor had not cooled one bit.

He wanted her, and he wasn't going to stop until he got her—or died in the process.

Savannah was hoping for the latter, as the former was unthinkable.

"Savannah!" He nearly dropped the tub of ice cream he was holding as he rushed to the reception counter. "I haven't seen you for so long!"

"Uh, yes," she said, reaching for the clipboard with its sign-in sheet and pen. "My luck was bound to run out, sooner or later."

"I was worried about you," he said, moving quickly into her personal space by leaning much too far over the counter. "I asked everybody about you, if something bad had happened to you, like a car wreck or something."

"Nothing quite as trauma-inducing as walking in here just now and laying eyes on you, Bates," she said in a silky smooth, semi-sexy tone meant to confuse him.

Confusing Kenny Bates was so easy it was hardly even worth the effort. But then, a gal had to take her entertainment where she could find it.

"I told a bunch of people, if they saw you, to give you my love," he said. "To tell you I was worried sick about you. Did they? Did anybody tell you I said that?"

"No. They didn't mention it." She picked up the pen, glanced at her watch, and jotted down her arrival time in the appropriate space. "They wouldn't dare."

He appeared puzzled, so she clarified. "A few years back, a patrolman told me that you'd asked after me. He made the mistake of repeating, in sordid, grotesque detail, what you said you'd like to do to me on a date."

"Oh yeah?" Ken brightened considerably. "What'd you tell him?"

"Nothing."

"Nothin' at all?"

He looked so disappointed. It was all she could do not to guffaw.

Donning her most solemn "Would-I-lie-to-you?" face, she told him, "Let's just say that by the time I finished with your little messenger, he was blind, deaf, lame, and unrecognizable to his loved ones."

"Oh. I guess that's not good."

"I reckon not. People talk, Bates. That sort of thing happens . . . word gets around. That might be why no one's willing to play Cupid for you anymore."

She glanced down at the sign-in sheet, paused to contemplate the possibilities, then scribbled the signature, "Et Durt AnDi."

For a moment, she thought she was finished with Kenny Bates. But no, Ken's deviant desires knew no bounds. He never seemed to know when he was ahead.

"That stuff the patrolman told you I wanted to do to you," he said, a hopeful gleam in his eye. "Didn't any of it sound fun? Like maybe you lickin' peanut butter offa my—Ow-w!"

She had shoved the clipboard at him just hard enough to knock the tub of half-melted hot fudge sundae all over the front of his already filthy uniform.

"You did that on purpose!" he shouted, looking down at the ruination of his snack, which was running down his legs into an unappetizing puddle on the floor.

Behind her, Savannah heard the front door open and close. She assumed and hoped that Dirk had entered just in time to witness the calamity.

He had.

"Nope," her husband assured her tormentor. "She didn't do it on purpose. If she had, your teeth would be down there on the floor next to the maraschino cherry."

Dirk walked up to Savannah, slipped his arm through hers, and gave her an admiring look. "Anything else you'd like me to do to him?" he asked her. "Just say the word."

Savannah thought it over, then shrugged and said, "No. I think I got it covered. But I appreciate the thought. You've always been my favorite backup."

They left Kenny Bates, standing in the melting mess of his destroyed dessert, bemoaning his loss . . . bereaved and bereft.

Chapter 10

Savannah and Dirk opened one of the two swinging doors at the end of the hall a crack and peeked inside the autopsy suite. As expected, they saw Dr. Liu exactly where they thought she would be, standing over the stainless-steel table that bore the remains of a star of the Golden Age of Hollywood.

But Lucinda Faraday didn't look like a glamorous star.

She barely even looked human.

It always hurt Savannah's heart to see someone's body on an autopsy table. It certainly wasn't the way anyone would want to be seen on their final day on earth, robbed of their dignity, their identity, their clothing, unique grooming and jewelry—all that had defined them in life.

But at least Dr. Liu had the sensitivity and decency to keep the private areas of her "patients" covered whenever possible. As a result, Lucinda Faraday had a snowy white cloth draped across her, concealing her body from neck to knees.

Savannah knew that, by now, Dr. Liu would have completed her examination. Therefore, the cloth also hid the large Y-shaped incision that had been made from shoulder to shoulder, and all the way down the chest and abdomen.

Normally, a person as old as Ms. Faraday, or anyone who had been sick and died from natural causes, would not have received a complete autopsy. But seemingly healthy people who might have left the world at the hands of another, or their own, were required to be examined as thoroughly as modern science allowed.

If there was a story of murder to be told, the Great State of California wanted to know every detail of their passing.

Morbid though the autopsy process might appear, Savannah had seen profound truths brought to light from one simple fact, uncovered during such an examination.

Savannah believed that most victims, if they had been alive and able to speak on their own behalf, would want the details of their murder known and their killer brought to account.

Even precious things like dignity and privacy seemed insignificant when compared to the need for justice.

"Let me go in first," Savannah whispered to Dirk, as they stood by the doors. "I'll butter her up for you with the cookies."

"Of course," Dirk grumbled. "How would I do my job without my wife and her famous cookies?"

Savannah elbowed him in the ribs and grinned. "Not nearly as well. That's how. You can repay me later."

"Repay you? I thought you were on Ethan Malloy's payroll now. You're not helping me. You're working for a client. I don't owe you squat."

"Hm. That's a shame." She gave him a naughty grin. "The payment I had in mind involved whipped cream."

He perked up considerably. "On apple pie?"

"Nope. On something you like even more than apple pie."

"Damn."

"Yeah. You missed out, big boy."

The grin he gave her suggested that he was less than bitterly disappointed. He knew her too well. Well enough to know that Hard to Get wasn't a game that she played with skill. Unfortunately, she was as fond of whipped cream as he was.

Looking through the crack between the doors, Savannah could see that the medical examiner was removing her gloves and the protective clothing she wore while performing the more gruesome duties that her job required.

The exotic beauty looked more like a model than a coroner. Tall and thin with a lovely face and figure, Dr. Liu didn't bother to hide her attractiveness. No, she celebrated it, wearing short skirts and stilettos that showed off her legs to perfection. Her long, glossy black hair was tied in a ponytail, out of her way, with a colorful silk scarf.

Savannah had seen how men, even her own man, watched Dr. Liu move across a room. While Dirk wasn't ill-mannered enough to ogle females in public, Savannah couldn't blame him for looking when it came to Dr. Liu. Even other women stared at Dr. Liu.

Like that moment, as they both watched her peel off her lab coat, revealing a cold shoulder blouse and snug, short pencil skirt.

Next, she pulled the scarf from her hair, letting it flow over her shoulders. Savannah heard Dirk catch his breath when she turned away from them and bent over to remove the paper protectors that covered her high-high heels.

"Okay, enough of this," Savannah whispered to Dirk. "Wish me luck," she added, pushing the door open.

"You don't need luck. You got cookies," he replied.

"True."

When Savannah walked inside, Dr. Liu turned, saw her, and

smiled warmly. "Good morning, girlfriend. Nice to see you. Especially since you come bearing gifts," she added when she saw the container.

"We figured it might be about time for your midmorning break. Thought you might need an infusion of chocolate to keep you bright eyed and bushy tailed."

The doctor's eyes sparkled for half a second at the mention of chocolate, then she scowled. "We?"

Savannah nodded, and Dirk stepped inside the suite.

"I couldn't let her come see my favorite M.E. without me tagging along," he said in his worst, least convincing kiss-up voice that Savannah never heard him use.

Or at least, not since the last time he had visited the cantankerous doctor whose findings were almost always critical to his cases.

Dirk had no problem dismissing most people who irritated him with a curt zinger. Unfortunately for him, Dr. Jennifer Liu seemed impervious to his zings, considering him little more than a nuisance to be dealt with as quickly and infrequently as possible.

Worse still, she didn't mind if he knew it.

As the doctor tossed her used, bloody gloves into a biohazard waste receptacle with a bit more vigor than the task required, she said, "No, of course you'd come along. Getting a bit of one-on-one time with a good friend and not having to share my cookies with a brazen glutton, that was clearly too much for me to hope for. Huh, Coulter?"

Dirk sighed and shook his head. "Sometimes I think you don't like me, Dr. Jen, and I just don't understand it. I'm always nice to you, but every time we meet up, you go outta your way to hurt my feelings." Savannah watched as Dirk painted a "deeply wounded" expression across his face. Of course, she knew it was fake. She had actually seen Dirk hurt a few times, but he was a tough guy, and it took a lot more than a sarcastic M.E. to get beneath his thick hide.

Unfortunately, Dr. Liu knew that, too.

"You most certainly are *not* always nice to me, Detective," she snapped back. "You pretend to be pleasant when you're trying to get something out of me. When you want me to put your examinations in front of other cases, when you want me to rush lab results, when you want me to tell you, 'Who done it?' in thirty seconds when I arrive at a scene."

"Yeah, well, that'd be nice once in a while," he said, dropping the Nice Guy facade. "But I ain't gonna hold my breath till it happens."

"Go ahead." Dr. Liu tossed her white lab coat into the bin with the dirty gloves. "Hold your breath right now. For ten minutes. I'll rule your cause of death 'Asphyxiation' and the manner of death 'Suicide by Temper Tantrum.' It'll only take me five seconds. Case closed."

Calmly, slowly, Savannah opened the container of cookies and offered one to the M.E. "How about we stop squabbling and get down to the serious business at hand—eating some of these?"

"Sounds good to me," Dirk said, peering into the box.

Dr. Liu grabbed the box and hugged it to her chest. "Me too."

"Finally!" Savannah exclaimed. "The two of you agree on something. It's a miracle!"

Later, Savannah, Dirk, and Dr. Liu were settled in the M.E.'s office, munching cookies and discussing the preliminary findings from Lucinda Faraday's autopsy.

Dr. Liu sat at her desk, Savannah and Dirk on nearby no-frills folding metal chairs.

The county had been in the midst of a budget crisis when

they had originally "decorated" the M.E.'s office. That had been decades ago. Medical examiners had come and gone. The first female M.E. had been appointed. Time had marched along, but the now-rusty, rickety metal chairs remained.

Savannah couldn't help noticing, as always, that once the conversation turned professional between her husband and the medical examiner, the bickering stopped.

"No big surprise that it was strangulation," Dirk said. "I figured that out as soon as I saw the stocking around her neck."

"Whoever put it there didn't intend for her to survive the ordeal," Savannah added.

"No kidding. The ligature was so tight it literally cut into the skin, several millimeters, here in the front of the neck." Dr. Liu tapped her glossy crimson nail on an eight-by-ten photo on her desk.

Savannah winced when she looked closely at the picture, the dark brown line, broken by a red incision where Dr. Liu was pointing.

"That much violence," Dirk said, "has to be personal."

"Or a pervert's frenzy," Savannah suggested. "Was she sexually violated?"

The doctor shook her head. "No."

"Are you sure?" Dirk asked.

"Absolutely certain. Not one mark or bit of evidence to indicate she was in any way."

"That's a relief," Savannah said, thinking how glad she would be to report that to Ethan. He would be grateful that his friend had been spared additional misery and indignity. "Considering the suggestive posing of the body, it seemed likely."

"It did," Liu agreed. "I fully expected to find she'd been raped. I was surprised to find the body unharmed. In that way, at least."

"How about other kinds of injuries?" Dirk asked.

"Other than the obvious strangling, I found nothing at all."

Savannah frowned, puzzled. "Not even defensive wounds?"

"Not a single one. There was a Band-Aid on her ankle. Beneath it was a mostly healed scrape of some sort. Definitely not perimortem. I'd say it was at least a week old. Probably older, considering how long it can take for someone her age to heal."

"She didn't fight even a little?" Dirk said. "That's unusual."

"It certainly is," Savannah agreed. "When someone's being strangled to death, they fight for their life. Violently."

"I know. Every strangulation victim I've examined had the bruises, scratches, you name it, to show they fought."

"They also inflict wounds of their own," Savannah added.

"Very true." The doctor reached for the last cookie in the container. "Many have their attacker's skin under their nails."

Dirk watched her bite into it with a look of deep sadness, then said, "One of the first things I do is check out a suspect's face, neck, chest, and shoulders for scratches. It's a dead giveaway."

"Why on earth didn't she fight?" Savannah said, more to herself than the others.

Dirk nodded. "It would have taken some time. What, Doc, fifteen seconds or so?"

"Depends on a lot of factors. It's hard to say for certain, but it wouldn't have been instant, for sure."

Savannah leaned back in her chair and folded her arms over her chest. Just thinking about Lucinda Faraday, or anyone, dying that way made her feel heartsick. "Even if, for some strange reason, Lucinda was willing to die, her natural instincts would have probably kicked in at some point, and she would have resisted."

"I agree," Dirk said. "Even if it was some sort of assisted

suicide, I can't imagine she or her accomplice would have chosen a nasty method like that. There's always pills."

Unpleasant memories flooded Savannah's mind, pictures that would haunt her forever of people who thought they were taking an "easy" way out by swallowing pills. They hadn't understood the body's determination to survive and what it did to save itself, even if its owner wanted to leave.

"I've seen a lot of dead folks in my day," she said sadly. "I have to admit, other than those who die of natural causes, I have yet to see a passing that appeared easy."

Both the doctor and Dirk nodded solemnly.

"But now that you mention pills," Liu said, "I'll remind you that we won't be getting the toxicology report for a couple of days. I half suspect there may have been some drugs in her system."

"You saw signs of addiction?" Dirk asked.

"No. Her liver showed that she drank quite a bit, but it was still healthy for her age."

Dirk looked puzzled. "Then why are you thinking drugs?"

"You think someone else might have given her drugs?" Savannah guessed. "Maybe sleeping pills?"

"It could account for the fact that she didn't fight her attacker," Liu replied. "If someone slipped her some sort of sedative, she might have been unconscious through the entire thing."

Savannah felt a shiver go through her. "That would indicate a clear case of premeditation on the killer's part. No spur of the moment, in the heat of an argument, provoked fit of rage, or whatever."

"True." Dirk picked up the photo from Dr. Liu's desk and studied it as he said, "That'd have to be a pretty cowardly murderer—to be so afraid of an old lady that he'd drug her first before killing her."

"A coward," Savannah said, "or maybe some sicko's idea of compassion?"

Dr. Liu picked up yet another photo off her desk and looked at it. Savannah could see it was a picture of Lucinda Faraday, lying on her bed of garbage, provocatively posed.

"We already know the killer is cruel," the doctor said. "If they drugged her before murdering her, I don't know what their motive was. That's for the two of you to figure out. But I can tell you one thing. . . . It most certainly wasn't an act of mercy."

Chapter 11

When Savannah and Dirk left the morgue, Savannah wanted to return to the Faraday mansion with him. But she couldn't.

"Why not?" he asked her. "If you wanna check out the crime scene with me, I'm happy to have you come along."

"I promised Ethan I'd meet him on the pier at noon and catch him up on what we've got," she said, trying to hide her disappointment.

"What we *ain't* got is more like it," Dirk said as he turned toward their neighborhood instead of the freeway that would take them to Qamar Damun.

"I know, but he's paying me well, so I owe him the nothing he's paying for."

"What?"

"Exactly. Then when I'm finished with him, I'm going to ask Tammy to meet me at the house. I can get her started on the background checks for Geoffrey, Brooklynn, and Mary."

"Good. She does a lot better job than that new gal we got at the station house. That dingbat couldn't find a Boeing 747 if it was parked in her driveway."

Savannah laughed. "I never thought I'd hear you compliment Tammy while calling someone else a dingbat. Have you gotten soft in your old age?"

"Naw. I ain't soft. She's gotten better. She probably *could* find a 747 in her driveway, if all four of its engines were running. But don't tell her I said that. Wouldn't want her to get a swelled head or nothin'."

"I'll resist the urge to share," she replied.

"You gonna pick up the rug rat from school at three o'clock? It's only a few blocks from our house. I'm sure he could find his way. The kid seems, uh, quite streetwise, to say the least."

"I know, and Gran offered to get him. But I wanted to, it being his first day and all. He was nervous this morning, when I left him. He didn't say so, but I could tell. He acted like he'd never been to school before."

"Maybe he hasn't."

"He said he went to kindergarten and first grade there in Georgia. Said his mom just hadn't gotten him enrolled here yet."

"She probably figured she'd get around to it. Once she got her drug situation sorted out. First things first, you know."

Savannah thought it over for a moment, then groaned. "He had no clothes but those shorts and flip-flops. He said they were living out of their car. He's obviously undernourished."

"But she had a bagful of drugs, plus several cartons of cigarettes and all kinds of booze in her van." He shook his head. "A lady with her priorities in order. Obviously."

"We don't even know for sure if he was in school in Georgia. When I was registering him, they were having a hard time locating his records." She felt a knot forming in her throat. "Poor kid. All the more reason why I want to be there to pick him up when school lets out. I'll take him for an ice-cream cone or whatever. See if he'll open up to me."

Dirk gave her a little smile as he pulled into their driveway. "You're a good woman, Savannah Reid," he said. "Did I ever tell you that?"

She leaned over and kissed his cheek. "You might've mentioned it once or twice."

"If I get off work early enough, I'll take him over to my barber and get him shorn."

"I think he looks kinda cute with his hair long. Like a little surfer dude."

"Then I'll tell my guy not to take off much, just spruce him up. We want him looking sharp over at that new school."

She gave him another kiss. Longer this time and on the lips.

"Thank you," she said. "I appreciate your help."

"Hey, as long as the squirt's under our roof, he's my problem, too. Plus, your granny seems keen to help."

"I know. Isn't she great with him?"

"She's awesome. But more than anything else, I'm just sayin'—it ain't all up to you, darlin'. Takes a village and all that."

Savannah sat there, looking at her husband. His scruffy beard that he shaved once a week, whether it needed it or not. The faded second generation Harley-Davidson T-shirt. The bomber jacket that looked like it had actually had a few bombs land on it in its long lifetime.

She was on her way to see Ethan Malloy, a man adored by millions of lust-besotted women, whose face had graced the world's best-known magazines, who had been named, more than once, the sexiest man living.

But she wouldn't have traded Ethan or any other guy for the one sitting next to her, the man who frequently told her she was the best person he had ever met.

Bulging biceps, broad shoulders, a perfect smile, a deep voice, and piercing blue eyes were all nice.

But as any woman with a degree of wisdom or insight was well aware, the sexiest feature any man could possess was loyalty.

As Savannah and Ethan walked the length of San Carmelita's beloved wooden pier, it occurred to her, not for the first time, what a pain in the butt celebrity must be.

Yes, Ethan's was one of the best-known faces in the world. His size alone set him apart from most of the people around them. It was impossible for such a large man to hide in a crowd when he was a head taller than most.

Even wearing sunglasses and a baseball cap, he was recognizable. At least half of the people they passed gasped when they saw him, then pointed him out to their friends and family.

Cell phones were lifted, and pictures taken—photos and videos that would, undoubtedly, appear within minutes on the Internet.

Those were the nice people.

The not-so-nice ones ran up to him, grabbed his arm, shook his hand, hugged, and even kissed him. Savannah quickly lost count of how many autographs and selfies he had granted before they had walked the fifteen-hundred-feet length of the pier.

"I don't know how you stand it," she told him. "I'd go plumb crazy if I had that many strangers snatching at me all the time."

In a tone of voice that sounded like exhausted resignation, he said, "It's part of the job. Goes with the territory and all that. If getting their picture taken with me or owning a piece of paper that I scribbled on means that much to them, who am I to say no?"

"A lot of celebrities do—say no, that is."

He shrugged. "That's their right. But it's not me. I can spend ten seconds and give somebody a memory that'll last them for a lifetime. That's an honor and blessing I'll always be grateful for."

At that moment, a couple of teenaged girls spotted him and came running over to greet him. One grabbed his arm in a death grip, while the other jumped up and down several times in front of him, trying to kiss him.

Savannah was about to reach out and smack her when Ethan bent down and turned his head, allowing her a quick peck on the cheek.

"Oh, Ethan! I just *love* you!" the smoocher said, when she finally managed to catch her breath. "I'm not just saying that. I mean, love! *Really, really love!* I watch your movies every single night before I go to sleep."

"Um, that's nice. Thank you," he replied, moving into position for the selfie the other one was trying to take.

Once the girl who had confessed her "really, really love" got her giggling fit under control, she stood, gazing up at him with adoration and something that looked to Savannah like pretend sadness. She was a bad actress. "I was so sorry to hear that you and Beth broke up," she told him. "I can't believe she'd be so stupid. To leave a man like *you*. Why on earth did she do such a stupid—?"

"Okay! Enough with the rude questions!" Savannah said, giving the girl a hearty push that would have landed her on her rear, had she not collided with her friend. "You got your hug, kiss, and picture. Scram."

The girl's face flushed red with anger. "Oh yeah? Who are you? His new girlfriend? I read everything they write about Ethan, and I don't remember anything about *you*!"

"I'm his bodyguard, and if you don't want your butt Tased, you'll get outta range. Pronto!"

Savannah made a big show of reaching into her purse, and in seconds, the teens were halfway down the pier, heading for the beach.

Savannah heard Ethan chuckle. She turned to see him watching her, a smirk on his face.

"You're my *bodyguard*?" he asked.

"Yeah. I throw that in with the private investigating."

"Good deal! Two for the price of one!" He glanced down at her purse. "Do you really carry a Taser in your pocketbook?"

"No. The most lethal thing I've got in there is a bottle of spray perfume." She pulled her jacket back a bit, revealing her holster strap. "I do, however, carry a Beretta here."

"Then, if I'm attacked by marauding, overly curious teenagers, you can obviously deal with the problem."

"You betcha. Relax, Mr. Malloy. You're in good hands."

"I never doubted it."

They continued walking toward the end of the pier, which was thankfully less crowded. The sun was hot, but it was a windy day. A stiff breeze was blowing cool ocean spray up onto the pier and wetting their faces as they stood, looking out at the horizon.

Savannah breathed in the smell of the sea and, as was her habit, thought how grateful she was to be living in a place of such beauty and restoration.

"Do you ever miss Texas?" she asked him.

"No," was his instant reply. "Do you miss Georgia?"

"No." She paused and reconsidered for a moment. "Well, some of the people. The peaches. The pecan pies. That's about it."

They shared a companionable chuckle, then the view for a while. Then it was time for business.

"I'm so glad to hear that Lucinda wasn't, you know, hurt. That way," Ethan said.

She found it endearing that this man of the world still possessed his Texas good ol' boy sensitivities and was uncomfortable discussing indelicate subjects with a lady.

"Yes, me too," she assured him. "It's hard to imagine anything that would make a murder 'better' somehow, but I guess that does. A bit."

He nodded. "After seeing her body, you know, like that, I figured she'd been violated, too. I was so hoping she hadn't suffered that fate. Again."

"Again?" Savannah gave him a quick sideways look.

"Yes. Again."

She gulped. "When?"

"Long ago. Back when she first arrived in Hollywood. She was just a kid."

"I'm sorry to hear that."

"More than once."

"Oh, no. Really?"

"I'm afraid so."

"If you don't mind me asking, how do you know this?"

He gave her a half smile, glanced in both directions, and said, "I don't mind you asking me questions, but I have this rabid bodyguard who—"

"Has spray perfume in her purse and a Beretta on her side? Yeah, yeah. She ain't that tough. I could take her."

Ethan smiled, but it quickly disappeared. He sighed, removed his baseball cap, and ran his fingers through his hair. "I told you that Lucinda and I did a movie together some time back. That was the first time I'd ever met her, though I'd admired her work for years. One night, they were taking a really long time setting up a particularly difficult shot, and she invited me back to her trailer. She said that, if I wouldn't be offended, she could give me a couple of pointers about how to play to the camera."

"How nice of her."

"You have no idea. We became friends that night, and I can't tell you how much she helped me, as an actor and a person."

"You must have become close, for her to share something with you as personal as a sexual assault."

"Like I said, she wasn't victimized only once. She was passed around like a piece of candy, from one high-powered jerk to another, while she was still just a kid. Studio heads, politicians, mobsters, you name it."

"She had no guardians to watch over her?"

"She had a mother who sold her to the highest bidder."

Savannah winced, thinking how many times she had seen that scenario play out on ordinary, mean streets. "Unfortunately," she said, "Hollywood doesn't have a corner on that market. Some folks who should be protecting their young sell their innocence all day long."

"True." He drew a deep breath. "I just wanted to say that I'm relieved her death didn't include that particular horror. It's bad enough that someone murdered her."

"It certainly is."

"Do you have any suspects?"

Savannah shook her head. "We've interviewed her great-grandson, Geoffrey, and his fiancée. He's Lucinda's sole heir, and I wouldn't give you two cents for him. But neither of those things mean he's a killer."

"Yeah, I heard about Geoffrey. Lucinda couldn't stand him, great-grandson or not," Ethan said. "We had a few long talks about him over some fine Irish whiskey." He smiled wistfully. "Lucinda did enjoy her Irish whiskey."

"Any particular reason that she didn't like him?"

"She said he was lazy, worthless. Then there was the illegal stuff."

"What kind of illegal stuff?"

"I don't know exactly, but she mentioned that he spent some time in prison. More than once, I believe. She bailed him out and paid for his lawyers a time or two. Then she gave up on him and disowned him."

"Disowned? How about disinherited?"

"Probably that, too. I don't know for sure. Lucinda was a generous person, but she was smart enough to watch who she gave to and who she didn't."

"Wasn't one to throw her pearls before swine, huh?"

"Not at all, and I'm pretty sure she considered her great-grandson an oinker."

Savannah thought she might be seeing a glimmer of light in a dark crawl space.

"I'll sic Tammy on him right away," she said. "Between her and Dirk, they'll find out why he served time and maybe some other times when he should have but didn't get convicted. Tamitha's great at uncovering skullduggery of the, shall we say, well-hidden variety."

"I have total faith in you and your team, Savannah." He looked down at her with a depth of affection that touched her heart. "I'll never forget what you and your people did for me."

She reached over and patted his hand, which was resting on the top rail. "I was so sorry to hear about you and Beth divorcing. Unlike that silly kid, I really mean it."

"Thank you." He turned to stare out at the ocean again. "We'll never get back together again. I'm sure of it. But we aren't bitter enemies. We've decided to stay friends, for Freddy's sake."

"I'm not surprised. You're both good people with kind hearts. You'll do the right thing."

"We try. I guess we succeed. Sometimes."

"I don't know if it helps to know this, but most marriages wouldn't survive what happened to your family."

He took off his sunglasses, passed his hand over his eyes, and turned to face her. "To be honest, Savannah, the marriage wasn't going to last anyway. It hadn't been working for a long time before . . . that . . . happened."

"I understand."

More tears took the place of the ones he'd wiped away, as he said, "Everybody and their cousin's dog thinks they want to be a celebrity, Savannah, a big star. They think fame and fortune is what it takes to be happy."

"Yes, that's the rumor going around, I hear."

"It's a lie. Along with the prestige and the expensive toys, fame and fortune bring a lot of misery. Rich, successful folks have every problem that everybody else has."

Savannah thought about the tough times she'd endured because of a lack of funds. She saw his point but couldn't fully agree.

Experience had taught her: money might not buy happiness, but poverty could sure cause a heap of suffering.

"But rich folks don't have money problems," she gently argued.

"You might be surprised," he told her. "They have bigger incomes, but most of the ones I know also have bigger bills and wonder sometimes how they're going to pay them. Besides, life's worst problems, the ones we all have, can't be fixed with money."

She ran down a quick list in her mind of what she considered life's worst problems to be. Sickness, betrayal, shattered marriages, aging parents, wayward children, natural disasters, guilt, regret, and fear of the unknown.

"I reckon that's true," she said. "Money helps some situations, but it can't make anybody immune."

"It sure doesn't. Or Lucinda Faraday would have lived a bit longer and died peacefully in her bed, surrounded by people who loved her, instead of . . ."

"I know." Savannah nodded and patted his hand again.

There was no need to state the obvious.

Chapter 12

Savannah intended to phone Tammy the moment she got home and ask her to drop by for what Tammy liked to call a "sleuth briefing." Never in her life had Savannah known anyone who used the word "sleuth" as frequently as her best friend and assistant, Tammy Hart-Reid. Nor had Savannah had the pleasure of anyone's company who was actually more obsessed with private investigating than she was.

Therefore, Savannah wasn't exactly shocked when she pulled up to her house and saw Tammy's hot pink Volkswagen bug parked in the driveway. No doubt, Tammy already knew more about the case than she did. Granny's panel truck, parked next to the bug, told Savannah that there had probably been a "sleuth briefing" already.

In the Reid family's hometown of McGill, Georgia, there was a saying regarding Granny: "If you want to pass a bit of juicy gossip around town, quick-like, there are three sure ways—telephone, telegram, or tell-a-Stella."

Granny was the soul of discretion, *if* you actually asked her to keep something to herself. Ancient Babylonian torture techniques couldn't have wrenched your secret from her. But if you failed to mention that it was a private matter and not for general consumption, you could expect to be questioned about it by everyone in town, from the mailman to the grocery store clerk, the very next day. They probably already knew more details about your personal business than you yourself.

As Savannah walked into her house, it occurred to her, not for the first time, that maybe giving a key to everyone she knew and inviting them to "Just drop by and make yourself at home anytime you've a mind to" wasn't the best life strategy.

On the other hand, Savannah was seldom lonely. At any given time, there were usually at least five human beings and three furry critters inside her walls.

Plus, they were always hungry, and Savannah was never happier than when she was creating good food and shoving it into the mouths of her grateful loved ones.

"Yoo-hoo," she called out as she tossed her purse onto the piecrust table and stowed her Beretta in the safe. "Who's here?"

"Me!" yelled a cheerful voice that could only be Tammy. Savannah would've never allowed anyone else to be that obnoxiously vivacious on her turf. At least, not in the morning.

"Me too," called Granny from the kitchen. "Y'all wash your hands and come sit down to the table. I've got dinner ready— or 'lunch' as you Yankees like to call it."

Savannah grinned. In Granny's estimation, unless you were born and raised south of the Mason-Dixon line, you were a "Yankee." To her, Alaskans and Hawaiians were Yankees, and therefore needed to be cut a lot of slack when it came to their questionable manners. Not having been "raised up proper," they couldn't help it. Bless their hearts.

Savannah walked into the living room and saw Tammy seated at the rolltop desk in the corner. The office computer was on, and she was flipping from one Web page to another with dizzying speed.

On her lap was one of Savannah's favorite creatures on earth, a tiny, copper-curled fairy-child named Vanna Rose. Savannah's namesake, niece, and very heart.

The baby had already heard her aunt and was struggling to get down from her mother's lap, giggling and waving her chubby arms wildly.

"Okay, okay," Tammy said, laughing as she slid her down to the floor. "Go on. Show Auntie what you've learned since you saw her last Thursday."

Savannah watched, spellbound, as the child stood, wobbling on her miniature feet. She had a look of intense concentration on her face, as she held her arms out to each side as though she was getting ready to take flight.

"No way!" Savannah said. "Don't tell me she's learned how to—"

"Okay. I won't tell you. You can see for yourself in a few seconds. You might want to stand a bit closer though and get ready to catch her."

Savannah did as Tammy suggested and watched, her heart filling to overflowing, as the baby lifted one chubby little foot and, as carefully and dramatically as a tightrope walker balancing a hundred feet above the circus arena, daintily placed it in front of the other. She wobbled for what seemed like forever, then seemed to realize she had "landed" it and let out a squeal of triumph.

Her own joyous cries were joined by Savannah's and those of Granny Reid, who had come to watch at the kitchen door.

Savannah hurried to her and scooped her into her arms. Planting kisses on the child's dimpled cheeks, she exclaimed,

"Lord've mercy! Did you see that? She's on her feet! Look out, world! There's no stopping her now!"

Savannah danced around the room with her niece and, for a moment, grim topics like murdered movie stars left her mind, releasing her, allowing her to enjoy a bit of light to balance the darkness.

Finally, Granny called a halt to the celebrating. "Okay, the beans are gettin' cold and the corn bread's gonna set up, hard as a brickbat. Skedaddle in here and stuff your faces."

As Tammy stood and turned off the computer, Savannah noticed that she had a twinkle in her eye that could only mean one thing.

"Gran filled you in on the case, and you've already found something, right?" Savannah asked her.

"I sure did. Wait till you hear it!"

"I 'sleuth briefed' her on all the important details," Gran said as she started to lift a large bowl of white beans, cooked in a savory broth with onions, carrots, celery, and tomatoes.

"I'm sure you did," Savannah replied, relieving her grand-mother of the heavy bowl and placing it in the center of the table.

Granny set a small cast iron skillet containing the corn bread on a trivet beside the beans, next to the butter dish. "Don't wait for me," she said. "I'll just get the sweet tea from the icebox."

Granny turned to Tammy, who was buckling her daughter into her high chair. "Don't worry," she told her, "I've got some lemons cut up in mineral water for you and the punkin', and I didn't stick no ham in the beans neither."

Savannah couldn't help smiling at the concession her grand-mother had made for their health-conscious vegetarian guest. Like Granny, Savannah held the opinion that any pot of beans without a few ham hocks thrown in for "seasonin'" was hardly worth cooking, let alone eating.

For the first few years of Granny's and Tammy's friendship, Gran had lived in dread that Tammy might fall over in a dead faint at any minute, considering how little "fat she had on her bones." It had taken a long time for Tammy to convince Gran that drinking unadulterated water instead of Georgia style sweet tea was a good idea.

But after watching their svelte, athletic friend run for miles every day—even after bringing a baby into the world—and perform every task known to modern womanhood with boundless energy, even Gran had to admit that "clean eating," as Tammy called it, might not prove fatal after all.

Once Vanna was settled in her chair, Tammy crumbled a bit of corn bread around the tray for her.

Granny laughed when she saw the child begin to cram the tiny pieces into her mouth as quickly as possible. "Boy, look at that! Don't ever get between a Reid woman and her corn bread. You might lose a finger or two!"

When they were all settled around the table and had begun their midday meal, Savannah decided she couldn't wait any longer. She turned to Tammy and said, "Well, what did you find out? Spill it."

Tammy grinned, obviously proud of herself, which gave Savannah hope. Without a doubt, Tammy was the most skilled and enthusiastic techno-researcher Savannah had ever seen, and every day, Savannah was grateful to have her as a member of her Moonlight Magnolia Detective Agency.

Especially since the height of Savannah's computer skills was her ability to cut and paste a block of text or copy an image.

If Tammy was wearing her self-satisfied smirk, Savannah knew she had something juicy.

"Okay." Tammy pulled her electronic tablet from the baby's diaper bag on the floor next to the high chair. "As soon as I heard who the victim was, a wealthy woman with a ton of assets, I checked out her heirs, you know, to find out who had the most to gain by her passing."

"She only has one," Savannah said.

"I know. Sometimes you get lucky."

"Dirk's running a background check on him right now."

"Then Dirk-o's probably getting pretty excited. Geoffrey Faraday's a bad boy. A serious record. Prison time and everything."

"Mercy!" Granny said, slathering butter on her corn bread square. "Whatever for?"

Tammy's pretty face grew serious. "He served five years for human trafficking."

"Wow!" Savannah recalled the annoying but impeccably dressed young man they had interviewed earlier. Somehow, it defied logic that a man wearing such a pretty suit would have committed such an ugly crime. She also took into account that her "logic" might be a bit fashion-biased. "I didn't see that coming. I was thinking bad checks or tax evasion maybe."

Granny shook her head solemnly. "That human trafficking, it's an awful business, to be sure. Evil like that is bound to darken a body's soul. Though some might say it's hard to imagine somebody having a soul and doing such a thing to another human being."

"That's for sure." Savannah turned back to Tammy. "Got any particulars on that?"

"I do. Apparently, he was in cahoots with some really bad guys who were bringing women in from Thailand to, supposedly, work in nail salons. But as it turned out, those parlors were fronts for prostitution. They were offering massages in cubicles in the back of the salons, areas they claimed were for waxing, etc."

Tammy shot a quick look at her daughter, who apparently couldn't care less about bad guys and their misdeeds, as long as she had plenty of corn bread crumbled in front of her.

"Let's just say," Tammy continued, "folks were getting more than their feet rubbed and their brows waxed in those private cubicles."

"I hate human traffickers," Savannah said, feeling a wave of fury, hot and turbulent, rising in her soul. "Back in their victims' native countries, they promise them palm trees and golden beaches and money flowing through their hands. Except, of course, they don't get to keep the money, let alone send it back home to their homeless, starving families."

"That's the main reason most of them leave home in the first place," Tammy interjected.

"True," Savannah agreed. "The minute they arrive, these jerks take their passports and shove them into a filthy apartment, ten to a room. The only time they get out of those horrible places is when they're herded into a windowless van and hauled somewhere to work a sixteen-hour day."

"I was reading about that," Tammy said, blinking away some tears. "The traffickers take their passports and any money they might have. Then they guard them every minute to make sure they don't run away."

"Wouldn't do 'em any good even if they did get away," Granny said. "Most of 'em probably don't speak English. They wouldn't even be able to tell somebody what they're going through or that they need help."

"They don't run to the police for assistance either," Savannah said. "In many of their countries the police are corrupt and cruel. They have no reason to think it's any different here.

It would never occur to them to risk their lives breaking free of their captors, then run to the authorities for help. For all they know, the cops would take them right back to their tormentors, who would beat them . . . or worse."

"Do you think that sort of wickedness goes on much?" Granny asked Savannah.

"More than you might think. It's a terrible thing that's hiding in plain sight all around us and getting worse all the time. Like I said, some of the nail salons, massage parlors, and even the restaurants we eat in. You'd be surprised how many of the people who serve your food or bus your table or wash your dishes or harvest the food you're eating are slaves in every sense of the word."

"What I don't understand," Tammy said, "is why there isn't more being done about it."

"Don't look at me," Savannah told her. "I don't understand it either. It's an outrage for a so-called civilized society to just overlook such a thing, we who claim to be so concerned about human rights and dignity. It defies explanation."

The women continued to eat their lunch in silence, but the celebratory mood that Granny's meal had provided was gone.

Savannah felt bad, mostly for Granny. But considering the topic they had just discussed, the people who were suffering in silence and fear, she decided that maybe having a bit of a damper thrown on their family gathering might be a small price to pay in exchange for a bit of heightened awareness.

Finally, she turned to Tammy and said, "Exactly what was Geoffrey Faraday convicted of? What part did he play in this mess?"

"He owned the crappy house where the women were being held captive. Once in a while he'd pop over there to, well—"

"Get his mustache waxed?" Granny said.

"Something like that," Tammy said. "He was convicted and given five years. He served a little over three before they let him out."

"Three years for a crime like that?" Savannah shook her head. "That's what I mean. He probably would've gotten a longer sentence for writing bad checks."

Savannah thought of Brooklynn Marsh and how she'd seemed more upset that Lucinda had died than Geoffrey. "I think I need to have a private talk with that guy's fiancée. From the little she said when Dirk and I informed them, I got the idea she might have a more sensitive conscience than ol' Geoff."

"Wouldn't take much," Granny said. "I reckon even the majority of scallywags behind prison bars right now would draw the line at slavery. They got mothers and sisters and wives. How'd they feel if they was treated like that?"

"If only society itself would draw the line," Savannah said. She sighed and pushed her half-eaten bowl of beans away.

It was one of those rare occasions when she lost her appetite in the presence of Granny's fine cooking.

Chapter 13

Eager to tell Dirk what Tammy had found out about Geoffrey, Savannah tracked him down at the Faraday estate.

She arrived to find one of the crime scene unit's vans parked in the driveway, the mansion's front door wide open, and CSU techs trudging in and out, carrying brown paper bags filled, no doubt, with evidence. Or at least what they hoped would prove to be meaningful.

They looked disgruntled, and Savannah could easily guess why. On a day like that, with such a difficult scene to process, she figured they were reconsidering their decisions to pursue forensic investigation as a career.

There were certainly plenty of days when she doubted her own choice and wished she had followed her childhood dream, married Little Joe Cartwright, and become a cowgirl.

But then, of course, if she had married Little Joe and lived on the Ponderosa, she would've missed being Detective Sergeant Dirk Coulter's wife.

As she walked through the front door of the mansion, she could hear her husband's deep, booming voice in the distance as he instructed his team, a true alpha male, using his manly-man authority to impart his extensive knowledge of all things concerning law enforcement.

"Come on, people! What the hell's going on here? Get the lead outta your boxers! This ain't no Sunday picnic for any of us, ya know!"

Yes, she thought, *that's my man, all right. Tactful and kind, strong but gentle, a truly inspiring leader.*

"I ain't got all day to hang around here and babysit you guys," he continued. "For now, just bag up all this crap and haul it back to the lab. Eileen can help you test it there."

For a moment Savannah imagined the look on Eileen Bradley's face when her crew returned to the laboratory with two hundred bags of garbage that Dirk wanted dusted for fingerprints. Eileen hated Dirk only slightly more than Dr. Jennifer Liu did. For the same reason. Like every other detective working on a case, Dirk wanted results from the morgue and the lab ten minutes before the crime had been committed. Unlike other detectives, he wasn't the least bit shy about making his expectations known, loudly and in no uncertain terms.

Fortunately for Dirk, both women could be bribed with homemade baked goods containing chocolate, and he had a wife who didn't mind providing the goodies and delivering them with a smile.

Lucky him.

On a good day, Savannah didn't mind either. It kept her in the action, which she'd missed since parting ways with the SCPD.

Once again, Savannah found her way through the hoard tunnel, fighting her claustrophobia as she did so. At one point she met one of the male techs in a tight spot. He was a large fellow, both tall and wide, and his arms were filled with evidence bags.

Savannah broke what appeared to be a hopeless impasse by climbing onto a pile of clothing. When her hand brushed something furry in the heap, she instantly decided that it was some luxury item of clothing made of fur.

It was either that or scream bloody murder, like a hysterical woman who had lost her wits, in front of and within earshot of the entire CSU team. She never would've lived it down.

Having a vivid and easily manipulated imagination could be a blessing, she decided, once the man had moved past, and she had scrambled down from the clothing pile. As she hurried away she could swear that she saw the garments she had just touched move a bit.

It's just that fur stole settling back into place, she told herself, as a shiver ran down her back.

Or, at least, she hoped it was a shiver.

Yeah, yeah. That fur stole's just getting comfortable again, said the anti-Pollyanna realist in her head—the gal who could be a sarcastic bitch when she wanted to be. *Be sure to use a ton of bleach and a steel wool scrubber on that hand, first chance you get.*

As she worked her way across the enormous room toward the far wall and the area where the body had been found, Savannah heard the occasional curse and a few yelps of terror and discomfort from the CSU team members who were trying to maneuver through the maze.

"Guess they found some fur stoles, too," she muttered. "God knows how many of them are scattered among this junk."

Finally, she saw the opening in the mess and the area where Lucinda's body had been. Dirk was there with a couple of the techs.

Instead of surgical gloves, they were wearing substantial leather work gloves to protect their hands.

They even had dust masks over their mouths and noses.

That was a first for her tough guy hubby. Although he would deign to wear the mandatory surgical gloves when handling things at a crime scene, she had never seen him put on a mask before.

She could certainly understand him wearing it. After her close encounter with whatever that fuzzy thing had been in the clothing pile, she'd vowed that, if she came in here again, it would be wearing a full head-to-toe hazmat suit.

Dirk was picking up handfuls of the debris that had been a makeshift "bed" for Lucinda's body and shoving the garbage into large, grocery-store-sized paper bags. He looked absolutely miserable, as did the others doing the same job around him.

"How much of this are we going to take, Sarge?" asked the young female squatting next to him. She looked around, her eyes wide with wonder and alarm. "There's just gotta be an end to it . . . at some point."

"Keep goin' till we get everything that woulda been under the body. Once you guys have processed that back at the lab, if you find something useful, good. If not, you'll be back here, bagging up more."

The tech groaned like a teenager who'd been asked to wax the family car and clean out the garage on her first day of summer vacation.

"Yeah," Dirk told her, "think about that when you're mowin' through this crap back at the lab. Don't miss nothin'!"

Out of the corner of his eye, Dirk saw movement behind him. He turned and barked, "Yeah? What?"

She knew the exact moment he recognized her, because his eyes softened in an instant.

That was a common occurrence. No matter how bad his day might be going, Dirk's mood always seemed to improve when his wife appeared.

Savannah loved that.

"Oh. Hi, Van," he said. "I thought you were one of these knuckleheads."

He waved a hand in the direction of the two closest techs and, once again, she marveled at how her husband managed to consistently endear himself to those around him.

The miracle was that no one had bumped him off some night in a dark alley. She was pretty sure that, if she had ever worked under him, she might have done so. Fortunately for her, Dirk was a far better husband than boss.

He stood up, groaning as he did so, and placed his gloved hand on his lower back. She could only imagine how long he had been in that position, squatting on that dirty floor, scavenging through the garbage.

But she had come prepared. She knew what it took to coax her husband out of a cranky mood and onto the sunny side of the street.

Unfortunately, it would violate several laws to do that sort of thing at a crime scene, so she had brought food instead—his second greatest passion in life.

She leaned close to him and whispered in his ear, "There's a double chili cheeseburger and a large fry waiting for you in my car out front, if you can manage to tear yourself away from this fascinating place."

He ripped off the mask, revealing the dazzling smile of a true glutton. "Coffee?"

"The giant thermos full."

"I adore you, woman," he said, seeming not to mind one bit if his underlings heard.

They did. Savannah heard them snicker and saw them exchange some seriously dramatic eyerolls.

They should be so lucky, she thought, as she and Dirk found their way out of the mess and into the sunlight. How many people could buy unadulterated adoration—for the price of a burger and fries?

Later, when the food and half of the coffee were only a fond and distant memory, Savannah said something to Dirk that caused his mood to plummet once again.

"What if she wasn't killed there in the spot where we found the body?"

He stared at her for a long time without answering. Finally, he said, "You know, if I want to get depressed again, I could just walk back into that garbage dump of a house. I don't need you to do it for me by saying something like that."

"Sorry. But it's true. You guys could be combing through that area, bagging up all that junk, and you don't even know for sure that's where the deed was done."

He groaned and rubbed his eyes. She had no doubt they were burning from the lack of sleep and the dust he had been sorting through. "I guess she coulda been killed somewhere else in the house and then dragged or carried to where we found her, like a secondary dump site in a regular murder."

"We should probably consider it."

"But why? What makes you think the killer did that?"

Savannah took a deep breath and tried to think of the simplest way to make her point. He was tired. She had discovered that tired men—and women for that matter—had problems understanding what was being said to them. Especially when what they were hearing might mean even more work for them.

"Because," she said, "the place where she was lying, it didn't look like a bed of any kind. Even people who live in the worst of hoards usually have a mattress or a chair or a pile of bed-clothes, or at least one blanket, where they tend to sleep. Something resembling a bed. There was nothing like that under her or anywhere in that area. It was just junk and garbage and the body."

"Okay. What makes you so sure she was murdered in the bedroom—or wherever she sleeps?"

"Dr. Liu said she believes Lucinda was given a sedative."

"Yeah, I remember. No defensive wounds and all that."

"Exactly. When would you be most likely to give someone a sedative?" she asked.

He nodded thoughtfully. "When they're going to sleep."

"Right. When they're retiring for the night or getting ready to take a nap."

"But either way, they'd probably be in their bed—or whatever passes for a bed."

"I should think so."

"But what would be the point in killing somebody in one place of a house and then dumping their body in another room?" he asked.

"I don't know for sure, but I'd think for the same reason as any killer uses a secondary location to dump the body."

"To keep us from investigating the actual murder scene."

"Yes. Because they're afraid we'll find something there that points to them."

Dirk slugged back the rest of the coffee in one gulp, then screwed the top back on the thermos. "Okay," he said. "Time to go back inside. First order of business, we find Lucinda's bedroom."

"Even if it's the dining room or the bathroom."

"What?"

"You know what I mean. Mary should be able to tell us."

They got out of the Mustang and, as they were walking up to the mansion's front door, they encountered a CSU tech coming out, her arms laden with evidence bags.

She gave Dirk a dirty look over the top of her mask as they passed.

He nudged Savannah in the ribs and said, "If I go missing, don't stop searching until you find me. I'll be somewhere in the heap."

"Why? You afraid it's going to collapse on top of you?"

"Yeah, about thirty seconds after I tell this team that we've been baggin' up all that stinkin' garbage—I mean, valuable evidence—from the wrong place."

Chapter 14

When Savannah and Dirk entered the mansion, they realized that, other than the foyer and the tunnel that led into the ballroom, they had no idea how the mansion was laid out.

"Mary said her apartment is in the back of the house," Savannah reminded him. "If we just work our way toward the rear . . ."

"Yeah, easier said than done. We need a map of all the tunnels, where they lead, and how to get out of them in an emergency."

"A GPS would be nice."

"Or Mary's cell phone number, so we could just call her and ask her to come get us."

They gave each other a look that was mixed with humor and disgust.

"We're pathetic," Savannah said. "Two seasoned detectives who can't find their way from one end of a house to another."

He nodded and took her hand. "You're right. This is ridiculous. Come on."

They looked around and found what appeared to be a path leading in the opposite direction from the ballroom.

As he headed that way, he squeezed her hand and said, "If we get stuck and starve to death, at least we'll die together, and my last meal was a pretty good one."

She chuckled. Leave it to Dirk to worry about food at a time like this, or at any time for that matter.

"Or," she said, "if we get attacked and eaten by a fur stole."

"What?"

"Never mind."

The new tunnel, narrow as it was, did appear to be leading somewhere that they hadn't been before. They passed through a graceful archway trimmed with decorative tiles in shades of tangerine, bright yellow, and cobalt blue.

On either side of the arch were sconces made of delicate metal filigree and stained glass of the same brilliant colors.

"What a shame," she said, "that this house is so badly neglected. It must've been glorious in its day."

"Yeah, weren't we all?" he grumbled.

"Seriously. Tammy told me that she did a little research on the mansion itself, after she dug up that dirt on Geoffrey. Super famous movie stars, rich folks, and even hard-core gangsters partied here back in the twenties, thirties, and forties. *Serious* partying, too. All sorts of illegal stuff."

"Was our victim part of that scene?"

"In the forties, she was. She bought it in the fifties, when her career started to slow down, and she didn't need to spend as much time in Hollywood."

Savannah paused for a moment and looked around at the items stacked on either side of them in this new area.

"Apparently, at one time, Lucinda was big on decorating for the holidays," she said, pointing out the boxes of Christmas ornaments and tinsel stacked on top of other boxes and containers with labels that read, "Easter" and "Halloween."

A lot of it appeared to be cheap junk, but Savannah saw a miniature train and snow-covered village with animated additions like a carousel and townsfolk skating on a frozen lake. She imagined what it must have been like when this magnificent house was fully decked out for the holidays. Decorated by someone who, obviously, enjoyed celebrating life and its special occasions.

"How," she asked, "does someone get from setting up beautiful little villages at Christmas time to . . . this?" She waved her arm wide, indicating the hoard.

Dirk looked around, thought it over for a moment, and said, "A little bit at a time, I guess. It probably sneaks up on you, and you don't notice until it's too late. Nobody in their right mind would just wake up one day in a clean, neat house and decide they wanted to live like this instead. It has to be some kind of illness that causes it."

"I agree. It must be miserable, living with the disorder like that. Most people can hide their problems for a long time. Things like alcohol and drug addiction, gambling, infidelities, obsessive-compulsive disorders—those can be hidden for years. But the only way to hide all this is to never invite anyone to your home. To lock yourself in your own prison of mess and disorder in total isolation."

Dirk nodded. "True, and if those closest to you find out, they probably just tell you that you're being stupid or lazy or whatever, living like that."

Savannah remembered Geoffrey Faraday's impeccable grooming. Apparently, appearances were very important to him. "Can you even imagine the conversations that must've passed between prissy Geoffrey and his great-grandmother?

They were probably brutal. He didn't strike me as a nice guy who would pull his punches in an argument."

"Or any other kind of fight, for that matter." Dirk gave a nasty little chuckle. "You know, before I became a married man and a bit more civilized, I would've looked for a reason to clean that guy's clock. Especially once I found out about the human-trafficking crap. He's probably good at bullying weaker, disenfranchised people. I'd like to teach him what it's like to tangle with somebody stronger than him for a change."

"Before this is all over, you might get your chance. Though I'm not recommending that, of course."

"No, of course not." He gave her an evil little grin. "Don't worry. I'll make sure I'm not in uniform at the time."

"Except for a couple of copper funerals, you haven't worn a uniform in ten years," she said, pointing out the obvious.

"See? Nothing to worry about."

Once they had passed through the arch, Savannah looked around and decided that, perhaps, they had entered a living room of some sort. Like the ballroom, it was large with a ceiling that was breathtaking, adorned with intricate plasterwork. But instead of a chandelier, this room had been lit with a series of Moroccan style lanterns, like the ones that lined the walls of the house and lit the exterior gardens.

The giant marble fireplace sat at the opposite end of the room. For a moment Savannah tried to imagine all of the junk gone, the place decorated for Christmas, and one hundred or more guests milling about in the vintage attire of yesteryear. Women in silk beaded gowns and men in black tuxedos with tails, crisp white shirts, and top hats.

What a sight they must have been to behold.

But at that moment a rustling sound over in the area of the

fireplace caught her attention and gave her a shiver. She could still feel that fur brushing her hand. She suspected she would feel it, at least in her vivid memory, for years to come.

"What's that?" Dirk asked. "Did you hear it?"

She lowered her voice to a whisper and said, "I heard it. I think it's over by the fireplace."

"I hope it's Mary," he said.

"I hope it's human."

"Huh?"

"Whatever. We still have to find out."

There was a turn in the path ahead, and since the pile on either side was head high, they couldn't see who or what was there.

They headed that direction, walking softly, trying not to make any sound as they went.

She wasn't exactly sure why they were trying to sneak up on whatever it was. If it was human, it was probably Mary, and they were looking for her anyway. If it was vermin, the last thing she wanted was a friendly meet-and-greet with a rat. Especially one that was large enough to be mistaken for a fur stole.

By the time they finally reached the crook in the path, the noise around the corner was much louder. It sounded like someone or something was rummaging around in a careless, maybe frantic, manner, looking for something and not finding it.

They turned the corner and saw Mary Mahoney, on her hands and knees, tearing through a stack of junk that looked mostly like papers and old photographs.

She hadn't seen Savannah and Dirk yet, and the look on her face was one that Savannah could only classify as desperation.

"Damn," they heard her whisper as she looked over a paper,

then tossed it onto the floor with a bunch of other discarded sheets.

Silently, with more than a little curiosity, they watched the frantic search. Mary seemed genuinely upset as well as frustrated as she picked up each page, looked it over, and dropped it onto the already sizable pile.

Savannah also took the opportunity to study the space itself where Mary was conducting her search. It appeared they had come upon Lucinda's "bedroom," after all.

Although it had been a living room—or a "parlor" in its earlier days—that particular nook had obviously been used for sleeping. There was the pile of bedclothes that Savannah had noticed missing in the ballroom.

Next to the makeshift bed were several boxes that contained neatly folded clothing. These particular garments appeared clean and in better condition than the ones in the hoard itself. They looked as though they had actually been worn and laundered recently, and the styles were more contemporary and fashionable than those discarded in the piles.

Savannah also noticed a dozen or so books near the bedding that were neatly stacked rather than thrown into heaps like the others she had seen.

As an avid reader who possessed a beloved To Be Read stash of her own, Savannah recognized the careful arrangement.

Assuming the assortment was Lucinda's, Savannah felt a bit closer to the victim than she had before. Book lovers considered themselves part of a massive, worldwide club, kindred spirits who understood the necessity of escaping regularly into other worlds through the pages of a book. The mark of a true book lover was a substantial, well-organized stash.

At that moment, Mary Mahoney noticed them . . . and that

they were watching her. She jumped and squealed in a tone that sounded both frightened and angry.

"Oh!" she said, dropping the papers from her hand. "What on earth? I didn't know you were . . . What are you doing?"

"We were looking for you," Dirk told her.

"We were also looking for Lucinda's bedroom," Savannah said. "Looks like we found both at the same time. This is where she slept, right?"

Savannah scrutinized Mary's face, her eyes, and could tell that the woman was considering what her answer should be. More importantly, Savannah could tell that Mary was deciding whether to tell them the truth or a lie.

All day long, as a police officer, Savannah had seen suspects weigh the pros of lying versus the cons of telling the truth. In the end, when they made their decisions, they had usually lied.

But the look of resignation that crossed Mary's face told Savannah she had decided to take her chances and tell the truth.

"Yes," she said. "This is where Lucinda wound up sleeping in the end. After she couldn't get into her bedroom anymore."

Savannah winced. "How sad."

"Oh, please. There are a thousand sad things about how Miss Lucinda lived. Eventually, she had to start using my bathroom. Her own toilets, tubs, and showers were, well . . ." She shrugged. "Let's just say they were unavailable to her."

Dirk grimaced. "As the housekeeper, you couldn't keep even one of hers clean enough to—"

"Stop! Don't you dare judge me!" Mary shot up off the floor with far more energy and nimbleness than Savannah had seen her exhibit before on the front porch with Ethan. Apparently, rage could override the disability of arthritis. At least for a moment, in Mary Mahoney's body.

Dirk held up his hands in surrender. "Sorry, Ms. Mahoney. I didn't mean to get on your bad side. It just seems like—"

"You know absolutely nothing about my life, Miss Lucinda, or this house, Detective," Mary told him. "I'm not interested in hearing how you think things seem."

"Okay. Heard and noted," he said.

But that wasn't enough for Mary Mahoney. Her otherwise pale complexion turned red, then purple as she continued to rant. "Unless you're the one who's put up with a miserable, cranky, nasty woman, who also happens to be one of the world's worst slobs, you have no idea what I went through with Miss Lucinda. I tried! God knows, I tried! And this"— she waved her hand, indicating the garbage-packed room— "this is the result. This is the reward for all my efforts."

Savannah stepped forward, and in a voice that was as calm as the other woman's was irate, she said, "That must have been almost unbearable for you. I'm sure you're a very clean, organized person yourself. To be responsible for keeping a beautiful mansion tidy and presentable to anyone at any time, that would have been an enormous responsibility."

"It was, but I didn't mind. I loved this house! Loved it like it was my own. I worked day and night for years trying to keep on top of what she was doing to it. But she'd go out to garage sales and flea markets like most people go to the grocery store. I'd walk into the house to find the room I'd just cleaned filled up with dirty, half-rotten junk she'd found by the road or in a dumpster somewhere."

"That must have been terribly upsetting."

"Of course it was. She wouldn't listen to reason when I tried to tell her the junk she was collecting was nothing but garbage. She wouldn't let me throw any of it away either. I tried, and she would have a fit! I was afraid she'd suffer a heart attack someday during one of those horrible tantrums of hers. Then I'd get blamed because I tried to throw out a moldy old pizza box that she said she was going to turn into a work of art."

Savannah gave Dirk a sideways glance to see if he was seeing what she was—an enraged, bitter woman who obviously harbored some very strong resentment toward her employer, the victim.

He returned Savannah's look with a quirk of his eyebrow. Yes, they were of the same opinion.

"I can't even imagine what you went through with her," Savannah said in her best big sister voice meant to console even the most distraught child. Or adult, if necessary. "Doing your best, working so hard, and yet, having people think it was your fault, since you were officially the housekeeper."

Mary burst into tears. From her extreme reaction, Savannah figured it might have been the first time anyone had said such a thing to her, and she was desperate to hear it, to receive some sort of understanding, even if it was from someone who hardly knew her.

"It was awful," Mary said through her sobs. "Nobody will ever know how bad."

"Plus, you had to live in this mess," Savannah said. "You, a professional housekeeper, who values cleanliness above all else, and—"

"Yes! You're right! That was miserable, too! Although I made her keep her junk out of my rooms, in the servants' quarters in the back. Anytime she brought anything in there, I'd toss it out one minute later. I didn't even care if she threw one of her temper tantrums. That was *my* home! *Mine!* The only time I'd even let her come in was when she needed to use the bathroom—to bathe or shower or, you know, do her business."

"I believe that was very generous of you, under the circumstances," Savannah told her.

"You do? Really?" Mary seemed afraid to believe her good fortune in finding this boundless source of sympathy.

"Absolutely!"

"I'm so glad you understand."

Savannah knew the empathy she was offering the woman was self-serving, and she felt a bit like a hypocrite for slathering it on so thickly. But she wasn't lying to her. She did understand the housekeeper's frustration and anger with all she had endured at her employer's hands.

But Savannah had also interviewed enough people in her day to know that a little compassion could pay handsome dividends in the long run. People felt comfortable with those who showed an interest in their tribulations, and they were more likely to share information with them than with someone like Dirk, who relied on intimidation.

Sometimes she felt Dirk's method, while less popular, was more honest. But when trying to expose a cold-blooded killer, she decided the end justified her means.

So, she continued to soft-soap Mary Mahoney, but figured it was time to add a few interrogation-type questions to all that consolation.

"I can't blame you a bit," she said, "for feeling the way you do about Ms. Faraday, may she rest in peace. But I'll bet you, if she was half as difficult as you say, and I'm sure she was, there were other people who weren't particularly fond of her."

"Oh, of course. Like I told you before, when you first came over and Mr. Malloy was here, she chased everyone away by being mean and insulting them. Plus, as you can imagine, people don't enjoy spending time in a place like this. The smell alone can make you sick."

"It sure can," Dirk replied. "Speaking of that, would you mind if we continued our talk in your nice, clean apartment instead of in here?"

Savannah watched Mary closely as the housekeeper's eyes scanned the area around them. Whatever she had been looking for earlier, she still wanted to find.

What could be that important? Savannah wondered.

Whatever it was, it had to be paper, or she wouldn't have been scanning and discarding one after the other.

"I believe you were looking for something before," Savannah said softly, knowing she was pushing her luck. "If you like, we could stay in here long enough to help you look for it one more time. We can help you, too."

"No, that's okay," was the abrupt reply.

"We don't mind," Dirk chimed in. "I think I caught a case of the Creeping Crud-itis from being in here already."

"No!" Mary turned and started down a path that they hadn't noticed; it appeared to lead even deeper into the house. "Let's go," she said. "I'll make us some tea. Miss Lucinda always liked her afternoon tea."

When Mary looked back over her shoulder, probably to make sure they were following her, Savannah was sure she'd seen some tears in her eyes.

Savannah decided to take a chance and see if Mary Mahoney had any mixed feelings at all about her mistress's passing.

"Did you have tea with her, Mary?" she asked. "Was that something that the two of you shared together every day?"

Just for a second, Savannah saw the agony of loss cross the

housekeeper's face. She nodded ever so slightly. "Yes. Every day. We did enjoy that."

Then, as though catching herself being sentimental when she didn't want to be, Mary sniffed and lifted her chin a couple of notches. "We had to have it in my apartment kitchen though," she said as they headed down the new path. "She hadn't been able to set foot in hers for years."

Chapter 15

Savannah and Dirk expected Mary to lead them on through the mansion toward the rear of the residence to her quarters. But instead, she took them back out the front way, and the three of them walked around the house, and through neglected gardens that flower-loving Savannah could tell had once been beautiful.

"The back of the house is worse than the front half," Mary explained, shamefaced.

"Do you mean to tell me the hoard is more dense in the rest of the place than what we've seen already?" Savannah asked, unable to believe it.

Mary nodded. "She started upstairs, worked her way down, filled up the back of the first floor, and then finished with the front part, where you were."

"Where on earth do you even get that much stuff?" Dirk asked. "I can't believe that one little woman was able to fill up that huge house like that!"

Mary gave a dry chuckle and shook her head. "You didn't know Lucinda. She was a real fireball in her day, had more energy than anybody I ever knew. She lived ninety years—nearly a century. When you're determined, you can get a lot done in that much time."

"I guess so," Savannah agreed. "My own granny's been alive almost that long, and she's moved mountains in her day."

She decided not to point out the obvious—that Granny had raised children and grandchildren and made an enormous, positive difference in many people's lives.

As they continued to walk around the huge mansion, it occurred to Savannah that the ninety-year-old Lucinda had made this trip every time she wanted to use a bathroom.

"It must be terrible, having a hoarding disorder," she said. "It impacts a person's life so negatively in so many ways. Surely, Lucinda would have stopped if she could have."

"I don't know about that," Mary said. "I can understand how you'd think that. But I spent a large part of my life trying to help her get out of this trap she was in. I can't even tell you how tightly she clung to her lifestyle. She refused to do anything at all to change, even tiny steps."

"Eh, people are weird," Dirk said. "Who knows why anybody does anything?"

Ten minutes later, Savannah and Dirk were sitting in Mary's cozy kitchen, sipping tea from delicate antique china cups.

"Lucinda gave them to me for my sixtieth birthday," Mary had told them as she'd set the cups on the table and filled them with a fragrant jasmine tea. "She gave me the silver set last Christmas. We'd been using it for years, and she told me she wanted me to have it. I think she might have sensed that she wasn't going to be around much longer."

"Any particular reason?" Dirk asked, unimpressed with teacups or silver teapots.

Mary shrugged. "Not really. Just that she was getting up there and realized she wouldn't live forever."

Savannah studied the silver service set, admiring it. All three pieces—the teapot, the sugar bowl, and the cream jug—were heavy gauge silver, embellished with elegant rococo designs. Their interiors were gilt. "It's the most beautiful silver set I've ever seen," Savannah told her, resisting the urge to mention it must have been worth a fortune.

"It meant a lot to Lucinda," Mary said, running her fingertips along the top of the sugar bowl. "It was given to her when she was very young by a Russian ambassador. They were . . . friends. Very good friends," she added with a grin. "In her prime, Lucinda was quite friendly. With a lot of powerful, rich men."

"I'm sure she had a lot of stories to tell," Savannah said.

Mary nodded excitedly. "I told her that! I encouraged her to start a book years ago, all about her adventures, but she never got around to finishing it. I told her she should. Boy, she had some juicy stories. There were scandals back in the 'good ol' days' that would make today's gossip magazines look like church bulletins."

"I've heard Hollywood was pretty wild back then," Savannah said.

"Whatever you've heard, it was way worse. Lucinda told me things that would curl your ears."

"Do you have any idea where that book is now, the one she started?"

"I saw it a few days ago, there under her pillow where she was sleeping. But when I looked today, it wasn't there."

"Okay, enough about old stories. No recent juicy stuff?" Dirk said, getting back to business. "We need to find out what she'd been doing lately, what might have gotten her killed, not what happened sixty or seventy years ago."

"Nothing salacious lately, I'm afraid," Mary replied. "I

guess she was a bit past all of that at her age. Even a woman like Lucinda Faraday has to slow down sooner or later."

Savannah decided to take Dirk's lead and move the conversation back to the investigation. Surely, they had established a significant amount of rapport with her and could take a chance.

Jumping right in, Savannah leaned across the table in the housekeeper's direction and said, "Mary, if you don't mind me asking . . . What were you looking for so frantically there in Lucinda's sleeping area? Whatever it was, you seemed quite eager to find it. Some sort of paper?"

Mary looked as though Savannah had just delivered a karate chop to her solar plexus. For the longest time, she said nothing. Then she opened her mouth and—

There was a banging on the kitchen door so loud that all three of them jumped. Mary even knocked over the sugar bowl, spilling it all over the lace tablecloth she had spread in their honor.

"What the hell?" Dirk said, getting to his feet, as still another barrage of loud pounding began. He turned to Mary, who was pale from the double shock of Savannah's unsettling question and the angry attack on her back door. "Were you expecting somebody?"

"No! No one at all!" she replied.

He strode over to the door and jerked it open.

Savannah was on her feet at that point, too, and was standing beside her husband when they saw who was calling.

"Geoffrey!" they both exclaimed, surprised to see him and equally put off by his manner.

"What the hell are you two doing here?" the erstwhile great-grandson of Lucinda Faraday demanded.

"Investigating a murder. Why?" Dirk shot back. "Did you commit one?"

"I'm done talking to you. If you want to ask me something, speak to my lawyer."

Geoffrey tried to push past them, but if Savannah and Dirk were good at doing anything together, it was filling up a door-way. Nobody got around or through them uninvited.

"I'm here to talk to Mary, not you," Geoffrey complained. He stood on his tiptoes, trying to see over their shoulders. "Mary? Are you in there? Get out here. We have to talk!"

Mary tried to step up to the door, but Savannah placed her hand on her arm and gently pushed her back.

"You don't need to talk to him," Savannah told her. "At least, not while he's acting like a horse's rear end."

"She does too have to talk to me!" Geoffrey bellowed, his spray-on tan looking strange on top of his red, flushed cheeks. "Mary, I'm giving you notice to vacate this property immedi-ately! It's mine now, and you aren't welcome here, so get out! I'm giving you twenty-four hours before I send the sheriff out to evict you!"

"Wait a damned minute," Dirk said, holding one large hand in front of Geoffrey's face in his best Cop Directing Traffic style. "She doesn't have to go anywhere. She lives here and has for years. You can't throw someone out of their home with nothing but a twenty-four-hour notice."

"Not only that," Savannah joined in, "but who says this property is yours now?"

"Of course it's mine!" was the quick and angry response. "I'm Great-Grandma Lucinda's sole heir. Whose would it be? Everything that was hers is mine now. That's the law."

"Actually," Dirk replied, "a judge will probably be the one deciding who inherits your great-grandmother's estate. She may have left a will. She might've had other people she pre-ferred to leave it to. But either way, you can't come around here harassing this lady who took care of your great-grandmother while you ignored her."

"Ignored her? She's the one who abandoned me!" Geoffrey said, his face getting darker by the moment.

Mary managed to work her way around Savannah until she could see Geoffrey. The rage on her face matched his as she shouted back, "Miss Lucinda abandoned you? How dare you accuse her of that. She bailed you out of jail more times than you can count and paid your attorney fees, time and time again."

"She didn't that last time!" Geoffrey yelled. "She wouldn't raise a finger to help me when I needed it most!"

"It wasn't until you committed a crime so hideous that it made her sick to even hear about it that she cut you out of her life," Mary countered. "That wasn't abandonment. That was her coming to her senses and realizing what a monster you are!"

Geoffrey stuck his finger in Mary's face and shook it. Savannah got ready to grab the offending digit, give it a twist, and listen to it crack. But he lowered his hand and his voice when he said in an ominous, low tone, "*You* are the one who turned my great-grandmother against me, you bitch. You told her bad things about me and started the trouble between us. Don't think I've forgotten that. I haven't, and you're going to pay for it. Big time. Somehow. Someday, you're going to be very sorry for what you did to me. I promise you that!"

Dirk reached out and grabbed a fistful of Geoffrey's nicely pressed, expensive shirt. He jerked the smaller guy off his feet and pulled him against him, until they were almost literally nose to nose.

"What kind of idiot are you," Dirk shouted in his face, "to threaten a woman right in front of me like that? I'm the cop who's investigating you for murder, and you threaten someone in my presence? Are you completely stupid?"

154

Geoffrey went from enraged to terrified in an instant. He shook his head and muttered something that sounded like an apology under his breath.

Dirk pushed him, maintaining his grip on his shirt and backing him away from the house. "You leave this property right now, Faraday," he told him. "If this lady tells me that she even saw you looking in her direction from the other side of a street, we're going to have a long, serious talk, you and me. Do you understand?"

Geoffrey nodded feebly, and the instant that Dirk released his hold on him, he scrambled away, nearly tripping over his own feet as he stumbled to the black Porsche they had seen before behind his house.

As he drove away, Savannah heard Dirk mumble, "If there was any justice in this world, that man wouldn't be driving that car. He doesn't deserve it."

"Or the air he breathes," Savannah added, equally disgruntled.

They turned back to the kitchen and saw Mary collapsing onto one of the dining chairs, her face white, her breathing labored. A moment later, she began to cough again, those deep, wracking spasms that they had witnessed when they first met her, talking to Ethan on the front porch.

The attack went on for quite a while, alarming them both. Savannah stood behind her chair, her hands on the woman's shoulders, feeling helpless, unable to assist or even comfort her.

"Are you okay?" she asked, knowing how inane it sounded. Obviously, she was far from okay.

Savannah looked over at Dirk and realized from the alarmed expression on his face he was just as concerned as she was.

"Mary," he said, dropping to one knee beside her chair, "can we help you? You want us to call nine-one-one? Get you an ambulance?"

Mary continued to cough but shook her head emphatically.

"Okay, we won't then," Savannah assured her. "Just try to breathe, darlin'. In and out." Again, she felt stupid for even suggesting the obvious and momentarily worthless advice.

Finally, the spasms subsided. But they had taken their toll on Mary. She leaned forward, folded her arms on the table, and laid her head on them.

Savannah rubbed her back as Dirk tried to reassure her by saying, "Don't worry about that piece of crap, Ms. Mahoney. Really. I know his type. He's all mouth. He's not going to come around here bothering you anymore."

"But if he does," Savannah added for good measure, "don't you even open the door to him. You don't have to. You just call us, and Dirk'll deal with him. Believe me, Detective Coulter can get a lot rougher than that with him if he needs to."

Finally, Mary recovered herself well enough to speak, though in a shaky, weak voice. "I'm not scared of him," she said. "Not physically anyway. But I'm afraid he'll do exactly what he said, kick me out of my home."

"Try not to worry about that now, Mary," Savannah told her. "You can cross that bridge when and if you need to."

"I know I shouldn't get upset. It brings on those coughing fits. But I've lived here for so many years now. I can't imagine having to leave. Especially at a moment's notice, like he was saying."

"You won't have to," Savannah said, wishing she could believe her own words. She shot Dirk a questioning look, which he returned with a shrug of his shoulders.

Not reassuring.

Maybe she was advising the woman to be too complacent. Perhaps the threat was real.

"I think you should talk to a lawyer, Mary," Savannah said. "Just to set your mind at ease. An attorney who specializes in this sort of thing can tell you what to expect and how to protect yourself. Even one appointment could make a difference, give you some peace of mind."

Mary shook her head. "I don't think it would help. Like he said, he's her next of kin, her sole heir."

Dirk cleared his throat and said, "To your knowledge, did Ms. Faraday have a will?"

"Yes. She did."

"And . . . ?" Savannah asked.

"She left everything to him."

"Oh." Savannah glanced at Dirk, who was shaking his head and looking as disgusted as she felt.

Mary lifted her head and turned in her chair to face them. "But that was before he got arrested and convicted for holding those poor women who were being trafficked in the basement of that old house of his in Barstow."

Savannah perked up a bit. "Oh yeah?"

Mary looked up at her with frightened, sad eyes. "Yes. After that, she sat me down, here at this table, and told me that she didn't consider him family anymore."

"Understandable," Dirk muttered.

"She said I was the only person she trusted, the only one who had ever been kind to her, taken care of her. She told me I was her family. She said she had written a new will and left everything to me."

Suddenly, a light dawned in Savannah's head. "That's what you were looking for," she said.

Mary nodded. "That's what I was looking for. I've been looking for it since Ethan found her yesterday."

"A new will!" Dirk said, far too cheerfully. "Well, there ya go! You don't have anything to worry about."

Savannah rolled her eyes at him and gave Mary a comforting pat on the back.

Nothing to worry about?

Mary's future depended on a single document. A piece of paper hidden in a sixteen-thousand-square-feet mansion. Filled with countless cubic feet of garbage.

All Mary Mahoney had to do was find it.

No, she had no reason for concern, nothing to worry about. Not a blamed thing.

Chapter 16

As Savannah sat, parked in her Mustang, watching Brody run across the schoolyard toward her with a big grin on his face, she felt a rush of happiness. Other than little Vanna Rose squealing at the sight of her, having a child so thrilled to see her wasn't a joy Savannah had experienced much in her life.

Sometimes, Diamante and Cleopatra were especially excited when she came home, and they expressed their pleasure by making furry figure eights between her ankles as she walked from the front door, through the living room, to the kitchen. But she knew they were far happier that the Bestower of the Kitty Kibbles had arrived than that Beloved Mommy had made it home safe and sound.

They were gluttons. Pure and simple. She harbored no illusions about the fact that their love for her was based primarily on food. Petting, scratches behind the ears, and mumbled sweet nothings about how they were the world's smartest, sweetest, and most beautiful cats qualified as a distant second on their list of priorities.

Until that moment, sitting in the Mustang and watching Mr. Brody Greyson race across the grassy field toward her, Savannah had never fully experienced what Granny must have felt all those years ago when she had collected Savannah and her siblings from their school.

With her windows rolled down, Savannah could hear him yelling, "Hi! Hey, hey, Savannah!" from halfway across the field. She saw the light of happiness in his eyes and something even more important—peace. After less than twenty-four hours in her care, Brody looked like a different kid.

She couldn't recall ever feeling more deeply satisfied than she felt at that moment, as though she had accomplished something truly great.

" 'Hey' yourself, kiddo," she called out to him as he approached. "Get in this car right now and tell me all about your day!"

He jerked the door open, tossed his backpack onto the floorboard, and plopped himself on the passenger's seat.

The sneaky little smirk he gave her told her that he was deliberately trying to pull one over on her.

"You'll have to get up pretty early in the morning to put the shuck on me, boy," she told him.

His eyes widened with fake innocence. "Huh? Whaddaya mean?"

"Backseat," she told him.

"Huh?"

"Munchkins ride in the backseat. It's the law and a good one at that."

His face screwed into a scowl. "No way. My momma lets me ride in the front seat."

She turned toward him and laser-trained her intense blue eyes on his. "Don't even start with that 'But my momma lets me' junk. I'm not your momma, and it won't work. When you're with me, we do things my way. No arguments. Got it?"

He sighed and, acting as though his britches had a brick or two in each pocket, climbed out, pulled the seat forward, and slid into the rear.

He sat there, giving her the evil eye, as she glared back at him in the mirror.

"Don't look at me like that, boy," she told him. "You know darned well we wear our seat belts in this car. Buckle up."

"I don't know how."

"We both know that's a big ol' fib," she said. "You've done it several times since I met you. I saw you."

"I done forgot how."

"You'll remember. You're a fart smeller."

He giggled. "You said it wrong. You meant 'smart feller.'"

"Whatever. That's you. Get that seat belt on before you're a minute older. We've got a couple of cones waiting for us at the drugstore's ice-cream counter . . . if you were good at school, that is."

Two seconds later, she heard the metal snap of the seat belt.

"See there," she said, starting up the Mustang. "You're farter than you thought."

He giggled. "I was good at school, too. A perfect kid!"

"Glad to hear it. I was looking forward to a double scoop cone, fudge and butter pecan."

"I want chocolate chip mint and licorice," he said.

"Yuck. You lost me with the licorice there, puddin' head."

"Hey, it's what I like, and I was good! All day! It wasn't easy, neither. My teacher was cranky. I think she must've had her underdrawers on backwards or somethin'."

"Oo-kay. Whatever you say. Let's make tracks."

* * *

Half an hour later, they pulled into Savannah's driveway, both holding towering cones and wearing ice-cream mustaches. Hers chocolate. His licorice.

She saw two familiar vehicles—Gran's panel van and Ethan's GMC Sierra. She had company. Again. Granny hadn't yet left, and Ethan had dropped by.

Her house was full of love.

Long ago, she had decided that, if one wanted privacy and a personal life, it was best not to open a business in your house. Or have relatives who thoroughly believed the old saying, "My home is your home."

"Yay, Granny's here!" Brody shouted, nearly dropping his ice cream.

Savannah was more than pleased to see him so excited about seeing her grandmother again. Who said kids didn't appreciate the older generations?

But then he added, "If she's here, then the Colonel's prob'ly here, too! He's my favorite dog ever! He's a darned good wrestler!"

"What exactly constitutes a good dog wrestler?" Savannah asked as they got out of the car.

"He grabs hold of you with his big ol' mouth and throws you all around, but he doesn't hurt ya."

"I see."

"But he does slobber all over ya. If slobber was poison, you'd be dead as a three-day-old road-kill possum after a tussle with the Colonel."

"I can imagine." She shuddered. "Lord knows, I don't want to when I'm still eating my ice cream, but unfortunately, I can."

He continued to prattle on. About what, she wasn't sure, as she was wondering why Ethan had dropped by.

Probably not to wrestle with the Colonel.

If he was here for an update on the progress she had made so far, she didn't have a lot for him. Considering how generously he was paying her—at his insistence—she wished she could give him a great deal more.

Like the killer . . . tied up with a bright red bow.

Especially if it was rotten old Geoffrey, who was her favored suspect, as well as one of her least favorite people.

As soon as they stepped onto the front porch, a familiar and loud noise erupted from the backyard. A hound's plaintive, excited baying.

"The Colonel!" Brody shouted. "He heard us!"

"Smelled us is more like it," she replied, laughing. "He *is* a bloodhound, after all."

"He wants me to go back there and play with him."

"He does, and that's an excellent idea. But you go upstairs and change out of those new school clothes first. I don't want them ripped up the first day you wear them, by a champion wrestling hound dog."

"Okay!"

They entered the house, and the boy bounded up the staircase, looking as excited as the dog in the backyard sounded at the prospect of their next bout.

Savannah peeked into the living room and saw Granny sitting in her comfy chair, and Ethan on the sofa. Both were holding a coffee cup and balancing plates on their laps with generous slices of coconut cake.

Ethan saw her and jumped up to greet her, nearly dropping his refreshments in the process.

"Take it easy there," she told him. "That's some of the best cake on the planet. If it hits the floor, you'll cry, for sure."

"I would," he said, setting the plate and mug on the coffee table. "I've enjoyed a few bites already, and I'd agree with you. It *is* the best!"

He hurried over to hug her. She stood on tiptoe to kiss his cheek and thought of the teenage girls at the pier. She wondered how many women in the world would have been thrilled to see Ethan Malloy in the flesh twice in such a short period of time.

She certainly was.

Glancing over at Granny, she could see her grandmother was getting up, vacating the chair for Savannah.

While Savannah was touched and honored by the gesture, she wouldn't have it. Gran had raised her too well.

"Sit still," she told her grandmother, waving her down. "I'm going to snag a piece of that cake and some coffee and join you."

Granny eased herself back into the chair and said, "What's wrong with that hound dog out there? I haven't heard him bay like that since the cat next door at the trailer park got into his food dish and ate part of his supper."

"He wants Brody to come out and tussle with him again," Savannah told her. "The kid's as keen on it as the hound. I think you can safely say they've bonded."

"I had a redtick hound myself when I was about his age," Ethan said. "One of the best friends I ever had. He went everywhere with me. Slept with me. Even ate with me any time my mother wasn't looking."

"Boys and their dogs," Granny said, reaching down to pick Cleo up from the floor and set her on her lap. "They're best friends. Like a grandma and cats."

Savannah went into the kitchen and was in the middle of cutting herself some cake when Brody bounded through the kitchen, racing toward the back door. He was wearing his old shorts, which were now, at least, clean.

"Hey!" she called after him. "You want a piece of cake before you head out there? You might need some energy with all that tossing and tumbling you're about to do."

Brody hesitated, and she could see he was sorely tempted. But another bay from the Colonel sent him over the edge. "Naw. I'll have some when I come back inside," he said before he raced to the back door and disappeared.

Savannah headed back into the living room, her treats in hand. Sitting on the sofa, she turned to Ethan and said, "I was happy, as always, to see your car in the driveway when I came home. But I hope you didn't drop by for a 'murderer reveal' like on TV. We're good, but we take more than an hour to catch the culprits, I'm afraid."

He gave her a reassuring smile. "I'm sure you do. I have no expectations of a quick resolution here."

"Of course, we can always hope," she said. "But unless the killer's standing over the body with blood on his clothes and the murder weapon in his hand, it usually takes longer than sixty minutes."

Watching him take a sip of his coffee, then squeeze the mug tightly between his hands, Savannah could feel the stress radiating from him in waves.

"Truthfully," he said, "I'd be satisfied if I thought you'd be able to solve this case in two months. Even two years. Ever. I'm afraid you won't be able to, and Lucinda will never receive the justice she deserves."

"I understand. I won't lie to you, Ethan. That's always a possibility. Some murders are never solved."

Granny spoke up, adding, "Sometimes ever'body knows who done it, why, and with what. But for one reason or another, the police just can't nail the killer and put 'im away for good."

"That's true," Savannah said. "Knowing 'who done it' and proving it in a court of law are two very different things."

The look of sadness and anger on Ethan's face went straight to Savannah's heart as he sighed and said, "That's undoubtedly true. Bringing a killer to justice, I'm sure, is a lot harder in real life than it is on television or in the movies."

"It is," Savannah assured him. "Much harder. That's why detectives—private ones and cops alike—lose a lot of sleep during some cases. Believe me, we don't want to see a killer walk either. The thought that they're still out there and could do it again makes us crazy."

Ethan set his mug down, reached into his jeans pocket, and pulled out his wallet. "That's why I came over here this afternoon," he said. "After we talked there on the pier, I had a feeling this was going to be one of those cases that's really hard to solve."

"Okay," Savannah said. "You're probably right about that. But put your billfold away, boy. Your initial retainer was overly generous. We haven't come close to running through that and probably won't. I reckon I'll owe you money in the end."

"No. I won't be accepting any refunds from your agency, whether or not you catch the killer. Whatever happens, I know you and your team will be doing your best, and that's enough for me."

He reached into his wallet and pulled out a check. He placed it on the sofa cushion between them. "That," he said, "is a little extra effort on my part to catch this guy."

Savannah looked down, saw the amount, gulped, and said, "That's a mighty effort there, darlin'. What are you fixin' to do with that much moo-lah?"

"It's a reward," he explained, "for information leading to

the arrest and blah, blah, blah. If anybody tells you anything that takes this investigation forward, they get that. If a second, separate party comes forward with something else, I'll give them the same."

"Goodness!" Savannah nearly choked on her cake. "That's . . . wow! You really do want this guy caught."

"You have no idea. The more I think about it—the fact that Lucinda managed to live such a full, long, adventurous life, that she made it out of all sorts of dangerous situations and thrived, only to have her amazing life end in that pathetic, cruel way—I can hardly stand it."

"I hear ya, son," Granny said. "Not because I'm an old gal myself, but there is something particularly sad about an elderly person's life being taken that way. Like they lived all that time, maybe a good, peaceful life, and then, that's what their legacy is. What they'll be remembered for. It ain't right. Not a'tall."

"Exactly!" Ethan's face flushed dark with rage. "Lucinda should have been able to die naturally and peacefully with someone she loved holding her hand, not a murderer strangling her. She should have been allowed to keep her legacy, her reputation as a glamorous woman, a gifted actress, someone who inspired and helped a lot of people. But her killer robbed her of that, along with whatever years she had left. He stole her from us and the times we might have spent with her. I want him to pay for it."

Ethan paused, and Savannah could tell he was trying to get control of his anger.

She also knew he never would. Not about this.

"Murder is far more complex than the killing of a human being, as horrible as that is," she said softly. "There are always multiple victims. One person dies, but so many other lives are damaged, too. Some beyond repair."

"Catching the killer, convicting them, it's a good thing," he said. "I was so grateful to you and your team for bringing the murderer who ruined our family to justice. But it didn't bring back our dead, and we're still suffering the aftereffects of what happened. We always will."

Savannah studied the young man sitting next to her and thought of all he and his wife had endured. She grieved the loss of his marriage, his life as he had known it before they had been victimized.

"I'm going to do all I can for you," she told him, "and for Lucinda." She reached over and picked up the check. "This may help. There may be someone out there who knows something. The thought of a substantial deposit in their bank account might inspire them to share it."

Granny chuckled. "More than once, I've seen a person become inspired to do the righteous thing for a pile of filthy lucre."

Ethan looked confused. "Lucre?"

"That's Bible talk for money, son," Gran told him. "I'm just sayin', the Lord moves in mysterious ways."

Chapter 17

Once Ethan had left and Granny had settled down for a nap in the upstairs bedroom, Savannah decided to take a glass of lemonade out to Brody, who was still playing with the Colonel.

The boy had found a ball and was playing fetch with the hound. Although he was getting a bit frustrated. The Colonel was good at catching a thrown object, but he had never been inclined to bring it back to the human who had tossed it for him. He seemed to be of the opinion that, if he'd gone to the trouble of catching his prize, he should be able to keep it.

As a result, Brody was spending more time chasing the hound and prying the soggy ball out of his dripping jowls than throwing it.

The moment she stepped outside with his lemonade in one hand and a glass of tea for herself, she found the child standing, hands on his hips, glaring at the dog and giving him a piece of his mind.

"You ain't so good at this," he told the Colonel, who was prancing around the yard, his tail held high, the ball in his

mouth, and a self-satisfied look on his long face. "You're supposed to bring it back to me so's I can throw it again, you
knucklehead!"

Savannah laughed, took the glasses over to the wisteria-
draped arbor near the back of the property. "The Colonel
doesn't always play by the rules," she told Brody.

"No kidding. He seems to think it's a lot of fun for me,
watching him run around with the ball in his jaws. He ain't got
the hang of this a'tall."

"I hate to tell you this," Savannah said as she set the drinks
down on an accent table between the chairs, "but he's been
doing that since he was a pup and his father before him and
his granddaddy, too."

"You knew the Colonel's granddaddy?" Brody asked, amazed.

"I sure did. This is Colonel Beauregard the Third. His
grandfather was our first Colonel. Granny got him when I was
a kid."

"My age?"

"A mite older than you."

"Did you play ball with him, too?"

"I tried. He was as obstinate as his son, and his grandson
after them. Seems that particular brand of contrariness runs in
the Beauregard hound dog family."

Brody laughed. "I don't care. He's still fun. Watch this."

He scampered over to the dog and got down on his hands
and knees. Immediately, the hound dropped the ball, ran to
him, and with his nose, bowled the boy over onto his side.

Brody grabbed the dog around his saggy neck and dragged
him down on top of him.

That was when the battle began in earnest. Pseudo-fierce
growling on the Colonel's part, a lot of squealing from Brody,
as they rolled back and forth across the grass, neither willing
to let go of the other.

Savannah laughed, enjoying the moment of innocence and levity, having had little of either for the past twenty-four hours.

What is it about kids and dogs? she thought, watching them. *They bring out the best in one another.* Recalling all she had seen and heard at the Faraday mansion last evening and today, she added, *Too bad adult humans can't do the same.*

At that moment, she saw something that caused her to collapse in a fit of laughter. Colonel Beauregard III grabbed a mouthful of the seat of Brody's shorts, gave a mighty tug, and pulled them halfway down the boy's buttocks.

"Hey!" Brody yelled, trying to pull them up. "Knock it off, dog! Those are my britches! Let 'em go!"

But his struggles only added to the fun for the hound. He tugged at the cloth with typical canine enthusiasm, as though they were playing tug-of-war with a rope toy.

Savannah got up from her chair and sauntered over to give the boy a hand in retrieving his clothing and his dignity. "What's the matter, Mr. Greyson?" she teased. "Looks like he's getting the better of you. Or at least of your drawers."

She reached down to pry the dog's jaws apart, but before she could, she saw something that made her gasp and freeze, her hand on the animal's massive head.

"Stop! Colonel, drop it! Leave it!!" she commanded.

Normally the hound would have been reluctant to quit a game he was enjoying so much, but he seemed to sense the urgency in her voice. In an instant, he did as he was commanded, backed away from the boy, and sat down on his haunches, whining softly.

"What's the matter?" Brody said, sitting up and readjusting his clothing. "Why'd you make him quit? We was havin' fun!"

Savannah felt her knees go weak, so she sat down, abruptly, on the grass beside the boy.

Her mind raced, taking in what she had seen and frantically trying to think of the best way to discuss it with the child.

In the end, she decided to just be honest and forthright. But gentle.

"Brody, darlin'," she said, reaching over and smoothing his tousled hair. "Just now, when you and the Colonel were wrestling. I saw something."

He looked totally confused and only moderately concerned. "What are you talkin' 'bout? Did you bring me somethin' out here to drink?"

"Yes. I brought you lemonade, and you can have it in a minute. But I have to ask you about something I saw, there on your backside."

Instantly, the boy's smile disappeared, and his color deepened as he blushed. "Ain't nothin'," he said.

"I think it is, and I'm sorry, but we're going to have to talk about it." She stood and offered him her hand. "Would you prefer to go over there?" she asked, nodding toward the arbor, the chairs, and table with the drinks on it.

"No!" He refused her hand, sat up, and crossed his arms over his chest. "I don't want to go there. I want to go home. Call my momma and tell her to come get me right now!"

Savannah's heart sank. This was going to be even worse than she'd feared. "I can't, sweetie," she told him. "I can't call her where she is. Your mother couldn't come and get you right now, even if I did call her."

He started to cry. "But you tell her it's important. She said I should always call her and not say nothin' because—" He choked on the rest of the words, put his hands over his face, and sobbed.

Savannah felt a rage welling up inside her, stronger, darker, and uglier than she could recall in her entire life.

But she pushed it down, deep inside, so the child wouldn't hear it when she said, "Your mother told you that if anyone ever saw those marks, those sores on your bottom, you should call her?"

He nodded.

"And not tell anybody how they got there, right?"

"Yes," he whispered.

"Did she tell you that something awful would happen if you told anyone what happened to you?"

He looked up at her and seemed to be somewhat surprised that she knew.

"Yes," Savannah said. "I know about marks like those. The long ones are from a belt. From somebody giving you a whuppin' . . . a really hard one."

When he didn't reply, she continued, "Brody, I used to have bruises like that on me, too. On my bottom and on the backs of my legs. My momma made me wear long skirts, and long socks that came all the way up to my knees, even in the hot summertime, so the neighbors and the kids and teachers at school couldn't see them."

This time the boy was more than surprised. He was shocked. "You *did*?" he asked incredulously. "*You* did?"

"Yes. I sure did, and I remember to this day how bad those whuppin's hurt."

He nodded but offered nothing else.

"I saw something else on your bottom, too," she said softly. "You had something else done to you, too, besides the whuppin'. Something I didn't have done to me."

Staring down at the grass, he gave another little nod as teardrops rolled down his cheeks.

She took a deep breath and fought back her own as she said, "Those round, red sores, and the ones with black scabs on them . . . those are cigarette burns, aren't they?"

"I can't say anything," he protested. "My momma said, if I did . . ."

"I know. But you didn't tell me anything. You don't have to, darlin'. I was a police officer, and I know what causes marks like that. I also know who does it to kids. You didn't do anything wrong. You didn't tattle on anybody. I figured it out on my own. Okay?"

"Yeah. Okay. But she said if anybody saw them or if I tell anybody, something bad will happen. The cops will put me and her both in jail."

"That's not what's going to happen, honey. Nobody's going to put you in jail. I promise. Nothing bad is going to happen to you. Nothing like that is ever going to happen to you again."

She reached out her arms to him, and to her relief, he threw himself into her embrace, burying his face against her chest.

Even the bloodhound joined in by walking over to them and nuzzling the weeping child with his big nose and whining his sympathy.

"See there," she said, kissing the top of the boy's head. "The Colonel is letting you know that he's going to protect you, and I'm going to, and Detective Coulter, and even Granny, too. We're all plumb fierce about protecting kids and keeping them from being hurt. You don't have to worry anymore."

She felt him sag against her with relief, and that was what caused her to lose the fight with her own tears.

She held Brody Greyson, rocked him, and cried along with him. She wept for him and for the wounded child she had been so many years ago. She cried for all the children who bore the marks of adults' pain, frustration, and rage on their precious bodies.

* * *

Later, inside the house, Savannah left Brody snuggled up to Granny's side on the sofa as she read to him from one of Savannah's favorites, *The Blue Fairy Book*. She went upstairs to her bedroom, washed her face, and phoned Dirk.

She dreaded the call terribly. She knew he would be as upset as she was over this awful development. The last thing she wanted to do was tell him over the phone.

He sounded cranky when he answered with, "Yeah. Hi."

"Where are you?" she asked, anticipating his answer.

"This stinkin' place, sortin' through the stinkin' junk. That's what my life is now. Stinkin' garbage. Why?"

"I, um, I—" She swallowed, fighting back the tears that were threatening to resurface.

"What is it, babe? What's wrong?" he asked, all signs of grouchiness gone in his concern for her.

Don't tell him on the phone, her instincts warned her. *Life's best and worst words should be said face to face.*

"I know you're working, honey," she said. "I know you're busy. But could you . . . could you please come home?"

There was a long pause. "Now?" he asked.

"If you can, I'd appreciate it."

"Okay." Another lengthy silence. "Can you tell me what it is?"

Tell him, another voice in her head said. *You can't expect the poor guy to worry himself sick all the way home.*

In this case, the truth is worse than whatever he would worry about, argued another voice.

"Don't worry, darlin'," she told him. "It's not a life and death emergency. I just . . ." The tears started to fall. A knot rose in her throat, and it was hard for her to speak around it. Or even breathe. "I just need you."

"I'm on my way."

He hung up, and she clutched the phone to her chest, feeling his essence, his love and concern.

She knew her husband. She knew he was, as he said, on his way.

Bless his heart, she thought, *being Dirk, he's probably already halfway here.*

Chapter 18

When Savannah descended the staircase, she could hear Granny reading. Having practically memorized the book in her youth, Savannah could tell that Gran was near the end of the story.

She walked on into the kitchen, pulled a bag of dry dog food from the pantry, and took it back into the living room with her, arriving just in time to see Brody give Gran a hug around the neck and thank her for the story.

Not for the first time, Savannah marveled at the capacity children had for love. Even those who had dared to trust, only to have that trust violated, found the courage to reach out, again and again. Unlike most adults, who became bitter and withdrawn.

She walked over to Brody and placed the bag of dog food on his lap. "Would you do me a big favor?" she asked him.

He looked down at the sack, grinned, and said teasingly, "You want me to eat a bag of dog food?"

"Yes, absolutely," she replied. "If it's a bit dry for you to gag down, there's ketchup, mustard, and maple syrup in the fridge.

Put enough of that stuff on it and it'll slide down nice and easy-like."

"Oh, yum." He giggled. "Or I could go feed the Colonel for you."

"Yeah, there's that."

Granny gave her a questioning look. Usually Gran fed the Colonel, as she was more aware of his dining schedule. The bloodhound had always been inclined to overeat if left to his own devices.

Not unlike the rest of the Reid clan.

But Granny said nothing as Brody jumped up from the couch, tucked the bag under his arm, and headed toward the back door.

"Also, while you're at it," Savannah called after him, "would you give him some fresh water? You can fill the big stainless steel bowl there at the water faucet."

"Okay," he replied. "I don't mind earnin' my keep around here. Next thing, you'll be askin' me to chop firewood and plow the back field."

In spite of his pretended complaint, Savannah noticed that he had a certain swagger to his walk that she hadn't noticed before. She thought of what Granny had always told her grandkids: "Honest work don't hurt you. Tacklin' somethin' hard and doin' a good job of it—shows you how strong and smart you are."

What better work was there for a child than caring for an animal they loved?

"What's goin' on, Granddaughter?" Granny asked, reaching for her hand and pulling her down beside her on the sofa.

"I had to get him out of the house for a minute, so I could tell you."

"That's what I figured. Let's hear it."

Savannah paused, steeled herself, then let it out. "Dirk's on his way home right now. I called him and asked him to come."

"Okay. Why?"

"Because we have to take Brody to the hospital."

"Lord've mercy!" Granny's eyes, usually calm and gentle, searched Savannah's with obvious alarm and concern. "What on earth for? He seems fine to me."

"I know. He seemed okay to me, too. But when he was playing in the backyard earlier, the Colonel pulled his britches down, and I saw that he's been whipped. I don't mean a get-your-attention, run-of-the-mill spanking either. They're big, ugly bruises. He was beaten. Looks like a belt."

Granny closed her eyes and shuddered. "Oh, no. Poor child. I can't bear it!"

"I know. Me either, and there's more."

When Granny opened her eyes, Savannah could see tears in them. "What else?" she asked.

Gran's tears prompted Savannah's own. She wiped them away, glanced toward the back door, and said, "That bitch has burned him with cigarettes."

"No!"

Deep in the recesses of her mind, Savannah realized that she had just used a word that, out of respect and a healthy portion of fear, she had never spoken in her grandmother's presence. But Gran didn't seem offended, at least, not by the word.

She was too busy being outraged by the offense against a child who had already found his way into the centers of their hearts.

"Heaven forgive me," Gran said, shaking her head, "but hearing that makes me want to beat the tar outta that woman myself."

"I know. Don't worry. I'm sure Dirk will deal with it."

For a moment, Granny looked alarmed. Savannah quickly added, "Legally, of course."

"Of course." Gran mulled it over for a while, then said, "It'd be more satisfyin' to yank her bald, but I reckon that's against the law here in the fine state of California, where you can't even drink your soda pop with a plastic straw."

"They'd frown on yanking somebody bald, I'm pretty sure. You want to get away with that, you'd have to move back to Georgia."

Savannah glanced toward the door again. "I have to ask you something before Brody comes back in."

"What's that, darlin'?"

"Last night, when you bathed him, you didn't see those marks?"

Gran shook her head. "No. 'Course not, or I woulda told you for sure. When I offered to come into the bathroom with him, shampoo his hair and scrub his back for him, he let me know in no uncertain terms that he didn't want no female scrubbin' no part of him."

"Can't blame him for that, considering it was his own mother who hurt him."

"That's for sure. But I thought he was just bein' modest, and I aimed to respect that. He was old enough to be in a tub alone. I sat down the hall in the guest room with the door open and kept my ears out on stems, just in case he got in trouble."

"You did fine, Gran. I was just wondering if you'd noticed anything then. I didn't think you had, but I wanted to make certain."

"I understand, Savannah girl. You're doin' right by him, for sure. But why do you think he needs to go to the emergency room?"

"I don't think I could get an appointment this late in the

day with a pediatrician I've never used before. Some of those cigarette burns looked red, like they might be infected. Can't take a chance with things like that."

"True. Infection can spread fast, especially in a little fella like that, who's not been taken care of properly. He don't look as healthy as he should to me. Like he ain't thrived or somethin'."

"I think so, too. All of this has to be documented to bring legal proceedings against his mother, to make sure the boy doesn't wind up back in her care again."

"Heaven forbid."

At that moment, Savannah heard the front door open, then slam closed. She knew, within seconds, her husband would charge into the room.

Some knights arrived not on a white horse but driving an old, restored Buick. Sometimes, their armor was a faded Harley-Davidson T-shirt and a battered bomber jacket.

She was right.

In only a few heartbeats, he was in the room, and she was in his arms. He hugged her tight against his chest. Then he pulled back a bit, looked down into her eyes, and said, "Okay. I'm here. What the hell's goin' on?"

Convincing Brody that a trip to the hospital was both necessary and in his best interests proved more difficult than Savannah had anticipated.

When she first told him, he flatly refused. But, to her surprise and great relief, Dirk took over and, in his own gentle but firm manner, convinced the boy it was going to happen whether he wanted it to or not, but wouldn't be nearly as bad as he feared.

Dirk also assured him that they would both be with him every step of the way, to make sure he was well treated.

In the end, Dirk sealed the deal with a promise to take him to a Dodgers' game and buy him a cap and Dodger dog.

Savannah had often thought that bribing a kid was a lazy form of discipline. But after one thirty-minute battle with a child as determined as Brody Greyson, Savannah thought perhaps she should be less judgmental of parents who purchased their children's cooperation with cash and prizes.

Her new motto, concerning the raising of children, consisted of: "Whatever it takes."

Considering the fact that it was Dirk who had won him over in the end, she wasn't surprised when, upon arriving at the hospital, he had chosen Dirk to be his guardian and protector against probing doctors, nurses who insisted that he put on a paper gown, and anything even resembling a needle.

As Savannah waved good-bye to them and watched them disappear down the hallway, hand in hand, she decided she was happy to leave them both in the care of professionals.

The doctors were the ones with the fancy degrees and the paychecks to match. Let them find a way to haggle with the kid, now that Dirk had already played the Visit to Dodger Stadium bargaining chip.

She wished them luck, said a quick prayer, and headed for the one place in the hospital where she actually enjoyed spending time. The Serenity Garden.

When her brother, Waycross, had been in an accident, she had waited in that lovely, peaceful place for news of his condition.

The lush tropical paradise in the middle of the hospital complex had soothed her soul during that difficult time. Settled on a comfortable chair next to the koi pond, she watched the fountain send its glittering drops into the air and the lotus blossoms float on the swirling, crystalline water, along with tiny brass bells that chimed melodiously when they met.

Savannah found the place just as charming as it had been before. Possibly even more so, since the twilight version of the garden twinkled with tiny flickering fairy lights, adding to the magic of the place.

Sitting on the comfortable, cushioned chaise, Savannah realized how exhausted she was. Long ago, she had learned that there was no labor on earth as draining as dealing with human drama. She would have gladly picked cotton in the hot Georgia sun for a week rather than deal with something as upsetting as seeing the aftereffects of child abuse in her own home.

Her rage and sorrow wreaked havoc in her own body, leaving it aching from the stress.

Like Granny, the less evolved part of her brain desperately wanted to lay hands on Brody's mother and exact a generous measure of revenge on his behalf. Let her find out how it felt to be at the mercy of someone bigger than you, stronger than you, and definitely more outraged.

"She probably had it done to her, too," Savannah whispered to the enormous black and gold koi nearest her. "She can't help it. She just doesn't know any better."

Yeah, go on, make excuses for her, replied another less conciliatory voice in her head. *Of course she knows better. She knows full well what she's doing to her kid is wrong. Otherwise she wouldn't threaten him to keep his mouth shut about it. She's worried about getting busted by the cops for abusing him. But she's not worried about the pain she's causing him—and, by the way, if it was done to her, then she, of all people, should know how bad it hurts.*

Savannah's brain kept replaying the vision of those cigarette burns in her head. One particular detail screamed out to her that those wounds had been inflicted with cruel deliberation.

They weren't random.

They were carefully placed in precise, straight lines, equally spaced.

When Savannah thought of how much effort had been taken to do that, to methodically torture a precious, innocent, no doubt squirming child, her vengeful thoughts turned much darker than simple hair yanking.

She hated it, hated having such blackness in her own soul.

"Savannah, are you okay?" said a deep, kind male voice from the shadowed pathway nearby.

"Yes, love," said another, decidedly British, fellow in the darkness. "We called your house to speak to you, and your grandmother answered. She told us you were here and why. We came to see if we could help."

Savannah looked up and felt her heart rising from its black, angry abyss.

"Ryan!" she shouted, jumping up from the chair. "Oh, John!"

She rushed to greet two people she simply adored. Before she knew it, she was in the midst of a tight, loving three-way hug. "Thank goodness you're here," she said, melting against them. "You have no idea how relieved I am to see you guys!"

Chapter 19

Two and a half hours later, everyone, including Ryan and John, was back at Savannah's house, sitting at her kitchen table, happily making the rest of Granny's pot of beans disappear.

Although Ryan Stone and John Gibson were restaurateurs, who had traveled the world and enjoyed its best cuisine, they were chowing down on the southern countryfolk staple as though it were the finest French cassoulet.

"Have some more corn bread," Granny said, passing the basket to John.

The elegant, silver-haired, lushly mustachioed gentleman dug into the bounty with uncharacteristic enthusiasm. "I do believe I'll have another," he said in the posh, melodic tone that could only be achieved by British aristocracy.

Turning to his partner—in the restaurant business and in life—John said, "This corn bread is divine, so light that it will float out of your hand if you aren't cautious. Have another piece?"

"I most certainly will," Ryan replied. "This is the best corn bread I've ever had. The bits of onion and peppers really give it a nice kick, Granny. You've outdone yourself!"

As tall, dark, and utterly gorgeous Ryan helped himself to another piece, Granny blushed from all the praise the two were heaping on her. But then, Ryan and John caused a lot of females to blush . . . mostly because of the risqué thoughts they entertained about them. Fantasies that were mostly centered around the theme of reordering their sexual preferences.

At the other end of the table, Savannah grinned, watching her grandmother act the coquette as she exchanged flirtatious banter with them.

All seemed to be enjoying it, so there was no harm done.

Except, perhaps, to Dirk. Though he would never have admitted it, he resented the amount of attention the handsome twosome received from females.

"What a waste," he'd expounded on more than one occasion to Savannah during their private moments. "Gals throwing themselves at 'em, right and left, and them not even inclined to put on a catcher's mitt and nab one."

Savannah turned her attention to the little guy sitting next to her. Even Brody, after the tough day he'd had, was mowing through a bowl of beans as quickly as he could.

Ryan and John had attempted to engage him in conversation several times, but the boy seemed far more interested in filling his belly than making new friends.

Amazing, she thought, *what serving dinner a couple of hours late does for the appetite.* She had always considered "starvation" to be the best spice in her pantry.

When Granny offered the corn bread basket to Brody, she told him, "I'll be headin' on home tonight, so's you can sleep in the guest room in a proper bed, instead of all crunched up on the couch."

Instantly, Brody's face crinkled into a frown. "You ain't going home just so's I can have the bed, are you?"

Granny looked surprised. "Well, I—"

"Don't be goin' home on my account," he assured her. "I mean, if you need to, go on ahead. But if I had my druthers, I'd sleep on the couch and have you here."

Granny gave him a playful grin. "Don't go butterin' me up, boy. It's the Colonel you're frettin' 'bout. I know you and him's gotten to be fine friends."

She gave Savannah a helpless shrug and questioning look.

Savannah nodded.

Gran tousled the boy's hair. "I reckon, I could leave him here a couple days, and you two could—"

"No! It ain't just the hound dog," Brody protested. "He's a bunch o' fun, but I like you, too. Why don't you stay? Make yourself at home?"

Ryan and John burst out laughing, and so did Savannah. The boy's precociousness along with his ever-buoyant spirit were irresistible.

"Granny, if I may weigh in here," she said, "I think that, unless you've got a good reason for going home, like you miss your fine neighbors there at the trailer park . . ."

"The ones cooking meth or the hookers?" Dirk mumbled.

Savannah ignored him and continued, ". . . you should stay here with us as long as you, Brody, and the Colonel want to. With this case going on, we'll be out and about a lot anyway. It'd be nice if someone was here to keep an eye on the place."

Both Brody's and Granny's faces lit up.

"That sounds like a brilliant plan," John chimed in. "See what can be accomplished when great minds come together?"

Savannah was quite sure that, if the Colonel had been in the room, instead of snoring in his oversized doggy bed in her utility room, he would have been smiling, too.

* * *

An hour later, Brody was tucked into the upstairs bed, with the promise that Dirk would carry him downstairs and put him on the sofa once their company had all gone home and Granny was ready to retire.

"We don't want to keep you awake with all our chitter-chatting," was the explanation given to the boy.

It sounded so much better than, "We're going to have a meeting of the Moonlight Magnolia Detective Agency at the kitchen table, and we don't want to discuss the unsavory details of a murder a few yards from a kid on the couch who, instead of sleeping, would be lying awake in horror."

Savannah put a plate of cookies on the table, along with the obligatory coffee, and tea for John. Tammy and Waycross had been summoned, to complete the team. Savannah had mineral water for her, and a six-pack of root beer for him.

Baby Vanna Rose was snoozing, draped across Waycross's lap. Both the baby's and her daddy's fiery red hair glowed in the warm light of the stained-glass lamp. Unlike the overly streetwise Brody, the toddler wouldn't understand the morbid topics being discussed, even if she should wake.

"Let's start with you, Tamitha," Savannah said. "Did you dig up anything else on our principal players?"

Tammy grabbed her electronic tablet and referred to her notes. "Brooklynn Marsh is an interesting lady."

"Really?" Dirk said. "I didn't notice."

When Tammy gave him a long, confused look, Savannah said, "She's a pretty sad case."

"Plain. Mousy. Lackluster," Dirk interjected.

Savannah searched for kinder words but couldn't find any. "She struck me as a worn-out, dragged down, faded version of whoever she might have been if she hadn't hooked up with a jerk like Faraday."

"As unpleasant as that evaluation might sound," Tammy said, "I'll have to admit you may be right. She was a successful professional, the managing editor for a major magazine. Very fit and attractive, too, I'd say, judging from her earlier social media photos. She made a lot of money, owned a nice home. But then she met Geoffrey and her life took a major turn for the worse."

"In what way, love?" John asked as he added another bag of Earl Grey to his cup.

"Did he run them into debt?" Ryan asked.

Tammy nodded. "He certainly did. She spent all her money on his legal problems. Especially after his great-grandmother cut him off and refused to foot the bills for his shenanigans anymore. Brooklynn took out a second mortgage on her beautiful beachfront house to pay his attorney's fees."

"But he was convicted anyway," Savannah added.

"That's right. She even spent a couple of months in jail herself for 'obstruction of justice' when they figured out she'd lied and given him a false alibi. That led to her losing her job and therefore her home. Where they're living now is a cheap rental." Tammy laid her tablet down and took a sip of her water. "The poor woman's life has gone to the devil in a wicker basket since she hooked up with that guy."

"I don't doubt what you found there," Dirk said. "It may all be true, but he's driving a sports car now that cost more than a house."

"Let's just say"—Savannah turned to the always sharply dressed Ryan and John—"the two of you would covet his wardrobe. His suit, Ryan, is almost as nice as your bespoke Giorgio Armani."

Ryan gasped with pseudo-horror. "No! Tell me it isn't so!"

"But not as fine as my Brioni," John said.

"Oh, no. Of course not," Tammy assured him. "The suit has never been created that's as lovely as *your* Brioni."

John gave Ryan a nudge in the ribs and a good-natured laugh.

"If you guys don't mind," Dirk said, rolling his eyes, "we're supposed to be discussing murder, not fashion."

"We're determining the financial status of our major suspect," Savannah told him. "That's important."

"Yeah, yeah. Okay." Dirk threw up his hands. "The guy who couldn't pay for his own attorneys, whose fiancée is broke because she did, is now rolling in dough. That might be something we should check out."

"I'm on it," Tammy said.

"He's probably into something crooked," Waycross spoke up. "Sounds like he couldn't hold a job if it had a handle on it."

"Sounds like the only thing he's good at is livin' off womenfolk," Granny said.

Waycross nodded. "Yes, he does seem pretty good at that. But if he's got a lotta money and no job and his woman's flat broke, he's prob'ly come by it through skullduggery."

"Like he did before with the trafficking," Savannah said.

Ryan held up his hand. "We know a guy in the bureau who specializes in human trafficking. We can ask him to check around, see if maybe this guy's returned to his wicked ways."

"Thank you," Savannah said gratefully. As wonderful as it was to have successful restaurateurs for friends and part of her team, it was even nicer that they were former FBI agents.

"How 'bout that Mary Mahoney lady, the housekeeper?" Waycross asked. "She's got more access to the dead woman than anybody else. Also, not ever'body likes their boss. There mighta been some bad blood between them two."

"Oh, there was a bit," Savannah told him. "I think there was affection, too. She claims Lucinda made a second will, leaving the estate to her. But that doesn't always rule out murder."

"Could even be a motive," Gran said, "if she decided that the Good Lord was takin' too long to call Miss Lucinda home. She mighta got impatient to collect that inheritance and rushed things along."

"True," Savannah said. "A lot of killers have love-hate relationships with their victims. Those two emotions aren't mutually exclusive." She turned to her little brother. "You check her out, darlin'. See if anything pops up. Okay?"

Waycross blushed and said, "Sure. Glad to help."

It touched Savannah's heart that her brother was so grateful to have a place on the Moonlight Magnolia team. He was a valuable addition to their group. But since childhood, Waycross had never thought of himself as even worthwhile, let alone a precious commodity. His recent troubles with a prescription drug addiction had caused what little self-esteem he had to plummet.

But the entire family, even Dirk, had rallied around him. Especially his loving wife, Tammy. Little by little, he seemed to be coming around.

"Look, guys, we need to wrap this up," Dirk said, "or I'm gonna have to run out on you. I've gotta get back to work."

"You do?" Savannah asked, dismayed. Then it occurred to her that her earlier call had interrupted his workday. Instantly, she felt guilty. "I'm sorry, sugar. I'll go with you, help you shovel the garbage."

He gave her a sweet, understanding—if exhausted—smile. "You don't have to be sorry. Especially 'shovel garbage' sorry. You did the right thing calling me. I needed to come home for that business with the kiddo. I had to talk to him, question the doctors, take pictures, and all that."

"Are you gonna arrest that no-good momma of his for child abuse?" Granny asked, keeping her voice low.

"She's already under arrest," Dirk said, "behind bars even. Surprise, surprise, she couldn't make bail. But I'll be adding to her charges, big time. What she did to that kid—" His voice broke. He closed his eyes and shook his head. "I've seen way too much of that crap in my career, but this is one of the worst. He's such a sweet kid, too. It makes me crazy."

Granny reached across the table and placed her hand on Dirk's. "I know, son," she said. "It's a heartbreaker, for sure."

Tammy looked down at her baby, sleeping on her husband's lap. She said tearfully, "I'm quite sure I would kill somebody if I had to in order to keep them from doing something like that to my child. I can't imagine how a mother could . . ."

Waycross wrapped his arm around his wife's shoulders, leaned over, and kissed the top of her golden hair. "At least we don't have to worry about Brody's momma doin' nothin' like that to him ever again." He turned to Dirk. "Do we?"

"No. She'll be serving time for the drug charges, and now this? Any halfway sensible judge will make sure she's behind bars for most, if not all, of his childhood. She won't get her hands on him again. At least, not until after he's a grown man."

"And a lot bigger and stronger than she is!" Tammy added.

Dirk winced, reached up, and touched his badly bruised eye that Brody had pummeled. "Having wrestled with her and gotten punched by him, I'll tell you now, that family knows how to fight! I hope I don't have to tangle with either one of them again."

Dirk rose from the table, stretched, and popped a couple of cookies into his pocket. "Like I said before, I've gotta get back to the mansion, spend a few more hours rummaging around before I put this day outta its misery."

Savannah looked over at her grandmother and wondered if she dared impose on her again.

As always, Granny read her mind. "Go on along and help your husband. I can tell you're dyin' to. I'm stayin' the night anyway, since Mr. Brody invited me so sweet-like. Don't take more'n one of us to take care o' a sleepin' child."

Ryan gave John a questioning glance and John spoke up, as well. "We can come, too. Make a party of it. Four of us have twice as good a chance of finding something as two."

"Really?" Dirk looked like he couldn't believe his good luck. "Wow! Thanks!"

Tammy looked wistfully down at the baby sleeping on Waycross's lap. "Well, you guys have fun," she said, a plaintive tone in her voice. "You know we'd pitch in, too, but we're parents now, so—"

"So, nothin'," Granny said, reaching for the tiny redhead, who didn't stir at all as she transferred her from her grandson's lap to her own. "Get outta here and go catch a bad guy. The young'uns are gonna be asleep, safe and sound, the whole time. Remember, when it comes to takin' care o' kiddos, I'm a champion!"

Tammy didn't bother to hide her glee as she wriggled about, doing her "happy dance."

Dirk was astonished. "I never saw anybody so happy to wallow in trash as you are, Miss Fluff Head."

"Oh, shut up, Dirk-o," Tammy shot back. "You aren't the only one who takes their life's work seriously."

"Okay, okay." He held up both hands. "Since Gran's being so generous and willing to sit on the rug rats, I'll bring the kid downstairs and put him on the couch, then we can take off."

"I'll get the bedclothes for him," Savannah said. "Tammy, would you check under the kitchen sink and grab as many of those rubber cleaning gloves as you can find? Ryan, would you collect some trash bags? Lots of them. John, please run upstairs and get those bottles of hand sanitizer out of the bathroom cabinet. Waycross, in the utility room cupboard, in the earthquake emergency stash, there's a whole box of those little flashlights. Would you fetch 'em?"

They all stood, staring at her in amazement.

Finally, John said, "Is it truly that revolting, the Faraday mansion, the hoard inside it?"

"Oh," she said, "you have *no* idea. I'd suggest you all stop at home on your way there and change into work clothes. Clothes you won't mind burning later."

They stared at each other for the longest time, eyes wide, mouths open. Savannah thought she might have overdone it, lost Dirk the assistance he so needed.

Then Tammy said, "Wow! This sounds awesome!"

"Smashing!" John said. "I can't wait!"

A second later, they took off in all directions to collect the supplies.

Four minutes later, the four self-appointed crime scene assistants raced out the door.

Savannah watched as Dirk, black eye and all, gently laid the sleeping boy on the white sheet, made sure the pillow was fluffed under his head, and covered him with the blanket.

Reaching down, Dirk scooped up Cleo, his favorite feline sleeping partner, and tucked her securely under the child's arm.

"Good night, Brody," he whispered. "Tomorrow will be a better day."

Then he bent down and kissed the boy on the head.

As she watched, it occurred to Savannah that, in all the years she had known him and in all the situations she had watched him deal with people, she had never loved and respected her husband more than she did at that very moment.

Chapter 20

"There's an old sayin' we use down south." Waycross paused to wipe the sweat off his forehead with his shirtsleeve and catch his breath. "It goes, 'I'm up to my eyeballs' in whatever."

His fellow searchers welcomed the interruption, small though it might have been, to take a breather of their own. They laughed.

Not uproariously, by a long shot. Just dry chuckles.

Waycross and Tammy, Ryan and John, Savannah and Dirk, and even Mary Mahoney, had been searching the hoard for two hours.

The magic had worn off for all of them after the first twenty minutes. Since then, they had all been operating on pure work ethic and determination to find something, anything, to reward them for their efforts thus far.

Savannah looked across a pile of ancient magazines at her little brother, all grown up. His mop of red curls was the same as the little boy who used to tag along behind her, looking for opportunities to either amuse or annoy her.

The mischievous sparkle in his eyes had become more subdued with the years. Other than his beloved Tammy and their magical red-haired fairy fay, life had been more difficult than kind to Waycross, and it had taken its toll.

Savannah missed the jolly little guy who had frequently hidden frogs in his sisters' underwear drawers and who drew long, curly mustaches on every photo he could get his hands on—celebrities on yet-to-be-read neighbors' newspapers, wanted posters in the post office, Adam and Eve in Granny's family Bible.

But Waycross Reid was a good man. A devoted husband, father, grandson, brother, and brother-in-law. He was far more important than he realized.

He deserved a generous helping of self-confidence.

Savannah considered it part of her life work to help him attain it.

She laughed at his comment and said, "You never thought you'd literally be up to your eyeballs in garbage, huh?"

"None of us did," Tammy said, as she shined her small flashlight around the area at her feet. "I still haven't seen the floor yet!"

"I caught a glimpse of it about an hour ago," John piped up from his and Ryan's area, closest to where Lucinda's bed had been. "It's a beautiful hardwood parquet. Quite lovely, if I do say so."

"Along with the rest of the house." Ryan shifted an armful of clothing to one side, then had to grab a stack of books that threatened to collapse on him. "Obviously, this place is in need of some TLC, but—"

"No," Dirk said as he shoved a pile of papers into a brown evidence bag. "It's not in need of TLC. Our garage floor's got some grease on it and should be scrubbed. That's 'in need of some TLC.' This place doesn't need tender lovin' care. It needs somebody to set a match to it. Once we get our evidence outta here, that is."

John gave him a scandalized look. "Torch it? This magnificent, historical work of art? I hope you're in jest, lad."

"I agree," Ryan said. "If you can look past the mess, this home is an art deco masterpiece! Not to mention the treasures that are scattered among the junk at our feet."

They all looked down. Other than John, everyone wore a doubtful frown.

"I hate to contradict you, Ryan, but I don't know about that," Tammy said, "unless there's a market for used toothpaste tubes, empty cold cream bottles, and naked paper towel rolls."

Ryan held up a book as Exhibit 1 of his argument. "This, for instance, is a 1902 copy of *The Hound of the Baskervilles*, by Sir Arthur Conan Doyle. It's easily worth between five and ten thousand dollars."

Dirk gasped and so did the rest.

"Seriously?" Waycross asked. "I'm up to my eyeballs in junk worth thousands of dollars?"

"You're practically swimming in dough, mate," John told him. "Makes you see things a bit differently, no?"

"Yes!" Waycross returned to his task with renewed vigor.

"Good," Dirk said. "Maybe you'll find that will Mary was talking about, or a threatening letter, or a scandalous diary."

"To heck with that," Waycross said, digging in up to his elbows. "I'm fixin' to find another book like that 'un!"

* * *

Half an hour later, the search team heard someone coming through the tunnel in their direction and glass clinking, along with what Savannah thought sounded like the tinkling of ice.

Refreshments? she thought. *Somebody's brought us energy-restoring, soul-refreshing goodies? What a delightful idea.*

"Do I hear food?" Dirk said, turning to face their new arrival.

"Just beverages," said Mary Mahoney as she appeared around the curve in the path. She had a tray in her hands, loaded down with what Savannah hoped with all her heart was lemonade.

It was. Fresh squeezed and well sugared. Savannah's all-time favorite.

Other southerners could extoll the virtues of sweet tea, and of course, she loved it, as well. But there was nothing like real lemonade to quench the thirst and recharge a dehydrated, calorie-deficient body.

"You've been working a long time," Mary said as she found a reasonably clean spot atop an old overturned laundry basket to place the tray. "I thought you might need something to wet your whistles, as Lucinda used to say."

"Lucinda drank a lot of lemonade, did she?" Dirk asked, a sarcastic tone in his voice.

Savannah suggested his skepticism might have something to do with the enormous amount of empty Irish and Scottish whiskey bottles they had uncovered in the hoard.

"Not really," Mary said. "My lady preferred beverages with a little more kick, to be honest. But back in the old days, when we entertained frequently, she would ask me to make lemonade for our guests."

"I can't imagine how beautiful this place must've been back then," John said as he hurried over to help her pour and serve the lemonade. "It's such an elegant estate, and those were such glamorous times."

Mary's eyes sparkled as she handed Ryan his glass. Like most females, she looked him over thoroughly from head to toe, taking in his dark hair, pale green eyes, and his body, which many hours on the tennis court had honed to perfection.

"Oh," Mary said, "you wouldn't believe the people she entertained here. Everybody who was anybody came to Qamar Damun in its heyday. Everybody wanted an invitation to this place. Some arrived even without an invitation. If we invited fifty people to a party, a hundred would show up. They weren't all well behaved either, if you know what I mean."

"We've heard tales," Savannah said, accepting the tall, frosty glass that John was handing her. "I understand some not-so-nice things happened here, too?"

Mary nodded solemnly. "It's true. I won't deny it. Let's just say, the police became very well acquainted with Miss Lucinda and her guests."

Dirk took a long drink from his glass and wiped his mouth with his sleeve. "Something tells me she might have crossed quite a few cops' palms with silver on a regular basis back then."

"Silver, gold, Rolex watches," Mary replied with a grin. "Not to mention, regular invitations to the best parties. But those were usually reserved for high-level law enforcement officials. State prosecutors, county judges, important people like that."

Tammy gently refused when offered the glass full of sugar and said, "Tell us, Mary, of all these people who came and went in this house over the years, did Ms. Faraday have any disagreements with any of them, arguments, hurt feelings, stuff like that?"

"Of course she did," Mary admitted. "Ms. Faraday was a spirited, opinionated, feisty woman who said exactly what she thought at all times. That's not always the best way to make and keep friends."

"Did she have any friends, serious friends?" Savannah asked.

Suddenly, Mary looked sad, as if remembering something unpleasant. After refilling Dirk's glass, she cleared some clothing off an old chair and sat down on it, groaning slightly as she did. Apparently, her arthritis was acting up.

"Miss Lucinda did have a friend, a best friend, for a long time. Delores Dinapoli."

"I guess she's dead now," Dirk said with his usual tactful, delicate manner.

"No, Miss Delores is still around. She's over twenty years younger than Ms. Faraday. They got along well for a long time. I'd even say they loved each other like a mother and daughter. Better than some mothers and daughters."

Considering how sad Mary looked to be discussing this topic, Savannah thought it might be important.

She probed a bit deeper. "May I ask what happened between them? Did their friendship end at some point?"

"It did. With a bang, so to speak."

Now she had everyone's attention.

"What happened?" Tammy asked.

"The same sort of thing that happens in too many friendships. Betrayal. Of the worst kind."

"Who betrayed whom?" Ryan asked.

"I'm ashamed to say it, but my lady was the one who destroyed that relationship, as she ruined others. She was a flawed person in many ways, but the best I ever knew."

"You're a loyal person, I can tell," Savannah said softly, taking a step closer to Mary. "I know it must be uncomfortable to say unflattering things about your former employer and friend. But right now, we need to know all we can about her and her relationships."

"I understand."

"Good, because unfortunately, when a murder occurs, luxuries like privacy go out the window. Sometimes, having one seemingly small secret revealed can solve a case."

Mary looked up at Savannah and nodded thoughtfully. "I'm sure it does happen that way sometimes."

"Then, if you can bring yourself to do it, would you tell us what happened between Delores and Ms. Faraday?"

Savannah could tell that Mary was struggling with her conscience, but in the end, practicality appeared to win the battle.

"Miss Delores was married to Dino Dinapoli, a very wealthy man, a good-looking man. He was an extremely sexy man, if you want me to be honest."

"We do," Dirk assured her. "That's exactly what we want. Go on."

"That was how Ms. Faraday liked her men—good-looking, sexy, and wealthy."

"Lemme guess," Waycross said, "Ms. Faraday took a serious likin' to Miss Delores's husband."

"She did," Mary admitted, "and she made sure he felt the same."

Savannah did a bit of quick math in her head. "Was Dino closer to Lucinda's age than Delores's?"

Mary shook her head. "No. He and Miss Delores were

about the same age, which, yes, means that he was around twenty years younger than Ms. Faraday."

"Wow," Tammy said. "That Ms. Faraday must've really had a way with men, to be able to seduce somebody twenty years her junior."

"Oh," Mary said, "she had a way with men, all right. She had *her* way with them. I never saw her go after a man she wanted and not get him. She just had a way of pulling them in, like a fish on a line. She'd bait them with that whole glamorous silver-screen star facade, slather them with all that buttery flattery, and the next thing you knew, they were her next tasty dish. Of course, once she had eaten what she wanted, she threw the leftovers into the garbage, wiped her mouth, and pretended nothing had happened."

"Unless a wife found out," Dirk said. "Then the meal might end badly."

"It did. Frequently. Ms. Faraday wasn't nearly as discreet as she thought she was. Pretty much everyone around her knew exactly what was going on at any given time. I'm sorry to say she ruined quite a few marriages."

"Are any of those wounded parties still alive, other than Delores, that is?" Savannah wanted to know.

"No. Just Miss Delores."

Mary paused to take a sip of her own lemonade, and Savannah noticed that her hands were trembling. She used both to hold the glass, and even then, she nearly spilled it.

"A few years back," Mary continued, "I remember Miss Lucinda telling me, 'All of my enemies are dead now.' I thought how strange it would be to say that. Even to think that."

It would be strange, Savannah thought. To have lived so

long that almost everyone you knew, all of your contemporaries, at least, had passed on.

She imagined it must be a lonely feeling. Though, apparently, a relief, if most of the people you knew had been enemies rather than friends.

"I don't doubt she said that," Dirk added. "But I wouldn't have to be a detective to tell you, I saw her body, and Lucinda Faraday was wrong. She still had at least one enemy left, for sure."

Chapter 21

The next morning, when Savannah returned from dropping Brody off at school, she pulled together a small breakfast of cinnamon rolls, miscellaneous fruit, freshly squeezed orange juice, and percolator brewed coffee.

Just as the cinnamon rolls were coming out of the oven, the members of the Moonlight Magnolia Detective Agency—plus Ethan Malloy and his three-year-old son, Freddy—began to arrive.

Since the weather was crisp and cool, and because she thought Freddy and Vanna Rose might enjoy playing on the grass in the backyard, Savannah ushered everyone out the back door and over to the picnic table beneath the wisteria arbor.

Granny and Tammy helped her put the goodies on the table, while Waycross and Ethan introduced the children to each other and the joys of rolling about on Savannah's lush lawn.

"You're still using only natural fertilizers on your grass, right?" Tammy asked, checking out the nearly perfect and weed-free green expanse.

Savannah couldn't help herself. Tammy brought out the worst in her. She gave her a wicked smile and said, "I've used only organic fertilizers since that long conversation we had last spring. Except for the dandelions, of course," she added. "A good squirt of arsenic is the only thing that gets rid of those stubborn, nasty things."

Tammy gasped and nearly dropped the cinnamon rolls. "Arsenic? You're kidding, right? But you shouldn't be, because nobody should joke about arsenic. Do you know what that stuff does to the human body?"

"As a matter of fact, she does," Granny said, rescuing the rolls and conveying them safely to the table. "My granddaughter knows more about poisons and ugly stuff that kills people than 'most anybody I've ever known. 'Cept me, of course. Being part of a private detective agency, I have to keep up on that sorta thing."

"Of course," Tammy said, simmering down almost immediately.

That was something else that Granny knew more about than Savannah did, and Savannah was the first to admit it. Granny could calm a mad hornet who'd just been stepped on and turn him into a honeybee in three seconds flat.

It was a gift that Savannah wished she had inherited, knew she had not, and had surrendered any hope of developing herself.

She looked over at her brother and Ethan and saw, to her delight, that the two men were rolling around on the grass with the kids. Even the Colonel had joined in the fun. She noticed that the hound was being far gentler with little Vanna than he had been with Brody. Like most good dogs, he sensed that she was smaller and more delicate, a puppy to be coddled and not wrestled.

He was nudging her with his soft nose, his long velvety ears brushing her pink cheeks, causing her to squeal with delight.

Ethan reached out and grabbed his three-year-old son, who was trying to climb on top of the dog's back. "Watch it there, Freddy boy," Ethan said. "That's a hound dog, not one of your granddaddy's packhorses. You might hurt him."

Freddy threw a tantrum, kicking his legs and screaming as though he were in agony, rather than being cradled in his father's arms.

"I know, I know," Ethan told him. "I'm a cruel father, not letting you ride every dog you get your hands on."

Ethan looked up and saw that Savannah was watching. He said, "I took him to my dad's ranch for Christmas and made the mistake of going riding with him. He loved it."

"There aren't a lot of horses to ride here 'bouts," she said.

"Tell me about it. That's why I have to watch out for any dogs that cross his path."

Granny walked over to Ethan and Waycross, holding a plate that she had filled with strawberries, orange slices, banana slices, and grapes cut in half. She sat down on the grass beside the children and told their fathers, "You fellas get over there to the table and have some breakfast before you start discussin' business. I'll watch out for these young'uns. I'll even keep that cowboy there off the hound dog."

"You don't mind, Granny?" Waycross asked his grandmother. "Seems like you've been doin' nothin' but babysittin' lately. We don't wanna wear you out."

Granny laughed and offered a bit of strawberry to Vanna. "Don't be silly. At my age, I'm plumb thrilled to death to be of some use to somebody."

She looked down at the children with a light of joy and purpose in her eyes. "Just a few years back, I was askin' the Good

Lord why He was keepin' me here, walkin' above grass instead of layin' under it. I wasn't sure what I was supposed to do with my life. Then, one day your little Vanna Rose showed up, and now some others, too, and all of a sudden, I know exactly what I'm here for."

She pointed over to the table, where Savannah, Dirk, Ryan, John, and Tammy were sitting down and helping themselves to the refreshments. "Y'all got an important job to do, a holy mission, looking for justice. If I can help you in any way to get 'er done, I'm grateful for the chance."

Ethan stared at her for a long moment, then said, "I think I'm in love with you, Ms. Reid."

She blushed and tittered like an eighth-grade girl who'd been asked to her first prom. "Why, Mr. Malloy. You say things like that, you'll turn my head."

"How's about I adopt you? Is that a possibility?"

She gave him a flirtatious grin that surprised everyone who saw it. "Oh, I reckon somethin' could be arranged, sir. We'll work on it."

Savannah chuckled and shook her head as she listened to the exchange. *You can take the belle outta the South*, she thought, *but you can never take the South outta the belle.*

"Good thing," she whispered, "'cause what a loss that would be."

Before long, the last cinnamon roll had been sent to Pastry Heaven, the coffee and tea were mostly gone, and thanks to the children and Tammy, the fruit had disappeared.

With the important tasks finished, it was time to get down to business.

"Okay," Dirk said, leaning back in his chair, his hands behind his head. "We all know what we didn't find last night."

"The will," Tammy replied. "I must say I felt bad for Mary.

It's so important to her. I really wish we had been able to locate it for her."

"We haven't abandoned the task yet," John added. "I, for one, would be glad to go back there today and look again."

Ryan nudged him. "Yeah, we know what you want to go back and look for. The possibility of finding more first editions, not to mention that amazing coin collection and the Ming vase you uncovered last night."

"That was brilliant!" John exclaimed. "I'll remember that moment for the rest of my life. If it's authentic, and we can find the will that leaves the mansion and its contents to Mary, she could be a wealthy woman just from that one vase alone."

"I so wish we'd found that document," Tammy said. "Mary seems like a good person. She took care of Lucinda, and we all have a feeling that wasn't an easy job, for all those years. It's only fair that she would be the heir, not that worthless great-grandson who never even visited Lucinda."

"Unless he wanted her to bail him out or pay his attorneys," Dirk added. "What a dirtbag. You guys are hoping to find the will. I'm hoping I can lock that guy away again. Maybe this time, he'll stay behind bars, where he belongs."

"Hear, hear," John exclaimed. Lifting his teacup, he said, "A toast to better days for Mary and far worse ones for our friend, Geoffrey Faraday."

Everyone toasted with whatever beverage they had in hand. But a moment later the enthusiasm, the levity died down, and reality set in.

"Okay," Dirk said, "it's not like we came up empty handed last night. Waycross kept us from getting totally skunked with his find of the evening."

Savannah lifted her coffee cup again and said, "To Waycross and the discovery of the night. The diary!"

"To Waycross!" everyone exclaimed. "To the diary!"

Everybody at the table went wild with applause and cheers, except for Dirk, who simply smiled and nodded. He was somewhat phobic when it came to overt expressions of approval. Unless, of course, he was watching a boxing match and his favorite fighter knocked his opponent to the mat.

In that case, all hell broke loose, and the otherwise reserved Dirk could be heard baying more lustily than the Colonel in the act of treeing a giant raccoon.

Savannah looked across the table at her ginger-haired brother, who was blushing almost as red as his curls. She wasn't sure if he was wallowing in the joy of his team's recognition or if he was embarrassed half to death. She decided it was probably a bit of both.

"Actually, Sis," he said, "it was *you* who found it, not me."

Savannah shook her head. "You pointed to the box that was under my feet and told me you had a hunch it was in there. I opened it, and there it was. But believe me, I wouldn't have if you hadn't suggested it."

Ducking his head, he said, "Aw, shucks. Quit it."

John reached over and gave the young man a shove that nearly knocked him off his chair. "Learn to take a compliment when it's given to you, lad," the older man told him. "Not that many sincere ones come a man's way in a lifetime. Embrace them whenever possible."

"Okay. Thanks." Waycross lifted his head, straightened his back, and said, "It was my pleasure to help out. I'm just glad we've got it. I remembered Miss Mary sayin' that whiskey was one of Miss Lucinda's favorite things in the whole wide world. With the diary bein' so personal and all, I just figured the two might go together."

"You figured right, little brother," Savannah said. She felt the urge to glance around her backyard, just to make sure no one was eavesdropping. But, as always, her property was private, thanks to the high fence she had installed and the thick shrubs she'd planted. Privacy, and the resulting ability to walk outside on one's own property in your underdrawers at any time, day or night, was important to Savannah.

But the topic she was about to broach wasn't one they wanted to share with the public at large—or anyone outside the Moonlight Magnolia team. Except in this case their client, Ethan Malloy.

She lowered her voice and said to Tammy and Waycross, "Did you guys get a chance to read it last night? Did you find anything good?"

Tammy also gave a conspiratorial glance around herself before whispering, "We read it and found good stuff!"

Waycross turned to Dirk and quickly added, "We did exactly what you said though. We wore those stupid, hot, sweaty as all git-out surgical gloves the whole time."

"I didn't even let him eat potato chips over it while we were reading," Tammy added proudly. "Didn't want to get any crumbs between the pages."

Dirk groaned under his breath and mumbled, "Good. I can just imagine what cranky Eileen there at the lab would say when she found those. She'd be all over me, griping about 'chain of custody' and all that junk."

Savannah raised one eyebrow. "All that junk? It's kind of important, keeping evidence from getting contaminated."

"Yeah, yeah. But how many times have you seen Eileen chowing down on some of those cookies you take there to bribe her and get on her good side, while she's checking out the interior of a suspect's vehicle, or looking at some bloody gunk under the microscope?"

Savannah nodded. "True." She turned back to Tammy and

Waycross. "We've established that you didn't get potato chip crumbs inside the diary or your fingerprints on the cover. That's important. But what did you actually find inside?"

Tammy and Waycross looked at each other, and Savannah could have sworn they both blushed. She also thought how charming it was that there were two people left in the world who actually blushed anymore, and that they happened to be married to each other. What a sweet couple. She glanced over at the baby on the lawn, who was lying beside the big sleeping hound, her head on his neck.

Savannah thought of Brody and wished she could somehow infuse a bit of that sweetness and innocence into his life, poor kid.

"Tell us what you found," Savannah told her brother and his wife, "and don't hold back any of the salacious details out of modesty or courtesy or anything like that."

"Yeah," Dirk said. "None of that courtesy or modesty stuff allowed around here." When Savannah gave him a funny look, he added quickly, "Not in the middle of a murder investigation anyway. Spill whatcha got."

Tammy and Waycross stared at each other, as if waiting for the other one to begin. Finally, Tammy sighed, crossed her arms over her chest, and said, "We read all night and got through most of it. I can tell you now, Lucinda Faraday was a very unhappy lady."

She glanced over at Ethan, saw a sadness on his face, and added, "I'm sorry, Ethan. I know she was your friend, and you had a lot of affection for her. I'm not saying she was a bad person. From a lot of the things she said in the diary, I can tell that she cared about other people and tried to help them as much as she could. There were certain things that really hurt her in her life. Some she never really got over."

"Like what?" he asked.

Tammy gulped and looked down at the table. "The one thing that seemed to bother her the most was an abortion she had years ago, when she was only sixteen. She wrote about it, there in her diary, off and on for the rest of her life. She never got over the hurt of it, her pain of losing that child."

"What made it way worse," Waycross added, "was the abortion wuddin' her choice."

"What?" Savannah was horrified. "They did it against her will?"

"Absolutely," Tammy assured her. "Her manager insisted, said an unwanted pregnancy would end her career. He wasn't going to let one night of her being stupid ruin all he'd done for her."

"What he'd done for himself is more like it," Ryan said.

"He set it up and forced her to go and even helped to hold her down when they did it."

Ethan put his hands over his eyes, as though trying to unsee what he had just heard.

Savannah reached over and placed her hand on his shoulder. "I'm sorry, sugar," she said. "This must be hard for you. It's hard for the rest of us, and we didn't even know her."

He rubbed his eyes with his fingers, then turned to her and said, "It's just that I remembered something she said one time when she'd had a bit too much to drink."

"About this?"

"Maybe. I asked her if she had children. She said two, a boy and a girl. When I asked them their names, she said the boy's name was Martin, but she wouldn't tell me the girl's name. She just said, 'She died.' I felt so bad for her. I could tell she was in a lot of pain when she said it. I just figured it was an older child. Not something like this."

"Forgive my ignorance," John said, "but could she have even known the gender of the fetus?"

"It would depend on how far along she was," Savannah told him.

"She was only a little over two months pregnant," Tammy said. "Savannah's right. She couldn't have known at that point. Certainly, not back then. In those days, nobody knew the child's gender until it was actually born."

"Then how did she . . . ?" Dirk asked.

Tammy shrugged. "From what I could tell, reading what she wrote, she just had a sense it was a girl. A very strong sense. Years later, she even described the child in the diary as having long, curly blond hair, pale skin, and light blue eyes. She wrote that her little girl loved strawberry jam, white kittens, and ballet. She said her daughter was funny and sweet and could dance and sing beautifully."

"How sad," Savannah said. "It sounds like Lucinda's lost pregnancy was a lost child to her in every sense of the word. She believed she knew her daughter intimately, as she would have known her had she been born."

"She was so young," Ryan said. "It would have been very difficult for her to raise her child on her own."

"She knew that," Tammy told him. "She says so in her diary. She was fully prepared to carry and deliver the baby, then give it up to a good family to raise. But she said her agent wouldn't let her do that either. He said the baby's father wouldn't allow it. Apparently, he was a celebrity of some sort, too, and had a reputation to protect. She mentions the father was there the night the procedure was done but was no comfort at all to her. Quite the contrary, in fact."

Savannah imagined Lucinda grieving for the child she had never known, then she thought of Geoffrey. "But she had a child at some point," she said, "and a grandchild. Or she wouldn't have a great-grandson."

"She did," Tammy said. "I checked some family tree records and found them. She had a son named Martin. Must have been the one she told you about, Ethan. Martin died in his forties of alcoholism. Martin's only child was Jeffrey. He was killed in an automobile accident, driving drunk. Also in his forties. Geoffrey was a teenager at the time."

"Those must be some of the losses that Mary referred to, that Lucinda had suffered," Savannah observed. "Losing a son and a grandson, both in their primes, and to alcohol."

"Apparently, it runs in the family," Ethan said. "Though we never discussed it plainly, I have no doubt that Lucinda was an alcoholic. I believe a lot of her depression was rooted in that. Or vice versa. It's always hard to know which comes first with that disease."

They all sat in silence for a moment, letting the information sink in. Finally, Savannah said, "As tragic as all these things were, I'm not sure how losing her sons to alcoholism or an unwanted pregnancy and horrible termination about seventy-five years ago would have anything to do with her being murdered today. Her sons are gone. The participants in the abortion—her manager, the baby's father, whoever performed the procedure—are probably long dead by now."

"True," Dirk said. "Let's move along. What else was in the diary?"

Waycross looked down at his notes. "The other thing that seemed to upset Miss Lucinda somethin' awful was what happened between her an' her good friend, Miss Delores. She never did get over that neither. Was writin' about it up to the very last."

"What did she write?" Savannah asked.

"Mostly that she felt she'd done a terrible injustice to her friend." Waycross shrugged. "I wuddin' argue with the lady 'bout it. You could tell by what she wrote 'bout ol' Dino, he wuddin' worth warm spit."

"Then they weren't in love?"

"Not a bit. She just thought he had a wicked eye, and she was gettin' old and didn't get looked at that much anymore, so she crooked her finger, and he was on 'er like a duck on a June bug."

Dirk mulled that over for a moment. "A duck enjoying a bit of hanky-panky with a June bug, whatever the hell that is."

Savannah turned again to Ethan. "I hate to ask this, but was that sort of thing routine behavior for Lucinda?"

"What? Sleeping with men much younger than she was?"

"Something like that."

He thought it over for a minute. "I guess so. She didn't worry much about age. It wasn't an issue for her either direction, older or younger. I never saw anybody turn her down because she was older than they were. Men were pretty happy to be invited into Lucinda's boudoir." He winced and added, "Back when she had a proper bedroom, that is."

When a silence settled over the table, Ethan looked around, lifted his chin, and said, "Since nobody's going to ask, but apparently everyone wants to know—the answer is no. I guess she drew the line at a guy young enough to be her great-grandson. Either that or she just didn't take a shine to me."

Savannah looked him over and grinned. "The former, darlin'. I assure you."

"Yes!" Tammy said, far too enthusiastically.

"Absolutely. Without a doubt," Ryan and John agreed in unison.

Dirk rolled his eyes, "Oh, good grief. You people are shameless."

Savannah turned to Tammy and Waycross. "Was there anything else we need to know about in the diary? Like, did she mention if Delores Dinapoli threatened her?"

Tammy nodded. "If you call it a threat to tell somebody, if

they don't stop what they're doing, you're going to rip off their arm and beat them to death with it."

Savannah thought it over for a moment. "Naw, parents down south use that threat on their kids all the time. It's just an affectionate, colorful . . . promise, of sorts."

"I read some of that stuff she wrote during that time, too," Waycross said. "I figure Miss Lucinda was a mite scared of her friend. I don't think Delores meant it the same way Granny did when she used to threaten us."

"Okay. I think I should go pay a visit to Delores Dinapoli," Savannah said. "I'll shake her tree and see if any ripe fruit falls."

"Sounds good," Dirk said. "Thanks."

Ryan raised a hand. "We just want you to know that we followed up this morning with our friend in the bureau. The trafficking guy. He said he was well aware of Geoffrey Faraday and the circles he used to travel in. He swears everybody but Geoffrey's still behind bars. Neither he nor anybody he spoke with on our behalf has gotten so much as a whiff of Geoffrey since he's been out."

"Darn," Savannah said.

"Yeah," Dirk added. "I was really hopin' to go after him."

"You can," Tammy told him. "In fact, you should."

"Oh yeah? Why?"

"Because I checked him out this morning, too, after I uncrossed my eyes from reading that diary most of the night. I was able to go even deeper than before."

"You hacked into his bank accounts," Savannah said. She knew Tammy. Fortunately, she fought on the side of the angels. If she ever turned to the dark side, heaven help humanity.

Tammy giggled. "Let's just say I know more about him than I'll bet his fiancée does—or she'd probably leave him."

"Did you find anything good?" Savannah asked.

"Something intriguing and inexplicable."

"Let's hear it."

Tammy looked down at her electric tablet. "All of a sudden he's turning up with all sorts of expensive stuff. That suit, the watch, the cuff links, and of course, the Porsche. Not bad for a guy who, a month ago, didn't have two nickels to rub together. Meanwhile, his fiancée, who spent all her money on him, is now flat broke. I find that curious."

"Me too," Dirk said. "I'm going to put Jake on him, have him tail him for a few days, see who he's meeting where and when. Maybe we can at least find out what sort of nastiness he's up to this time."

"With any luck, it'll be something really bad," Savannah said. "It'd be so much fun to watch you arrest him."

"Ah-h-h . . . the stuff fantasies are made of."

Chapter 22

As Savannah drove to Delores Dinapoli's home in Malibu, she decided that being a private detective had to be the best job in the world. At that moment, the primary reason she thought so was the Southern California coastline.

Miles of beach that varied between smooth, golden, and sandy to rocky and strewn with tide pools, home to all sorts of exotic sea life. Then there were the palm trees that lined those beaches. The oleander bushes that lent a feminine softness to the borders of the otherwise soulless freeways. The crimson bougainvillea that draped itself over a multitude of manmade structures, lending those concrete and steel buildings their gentle beauty. Then there were Savannah's favorites, the wildflowers that grew in profusion on the hillsides, due to the extra heavy spring rains.

She especially loved the poppies. She couldn't think of another place in nature that particularly vivid shade of orange existed.

Yes, if being a PI meant she "had" to drive along the Pacific Coast Highway, smell the salt sea, admire the flowers and palms, all while passing the homes of the world's most beloved movie stars . . . oh, well, she'd find a way to suffer through somehow.

With clear skies and the sun shining brightly, the ocean sparkled as though it had been sprinkled with a million tiny crystals. The "diamonds" seemed to dance on the water as the tide brought them to the shore, where they appeared to melt into the sand.

If I were back in Georgia, she thought, *I'd be waiting tables at the Burger Igloo or doing the books at Butch's garage. There's nothing wrong with waitressing or working in a garage if that's what you want to do. But for me, this is better. Way, way better.*

She thought of how she'd told Brody that he would be rewarded for his courage with a better life.

Oh, how she hoped she could help him receive that reward. She wasn't sure she had ever met anyone, man, woman, or child, who was braver than that little boy.

He was just a kid and yet, she admired and respected him more than most adults she knew.

She was looking forward to going back home to him, once her business was completed.

Delores Dinapoli's home wasn't hard to find, like some of the estates tucked away in the hills to the east of the highway. Nor was it difficult to access, like the mansions with high, impenetrable fences and 24/7 manned security gates.

Her house was a simple gray Cape Cod affair situated right on the edge of PCH. It looked like it would feel more comfortable on a beach in Maine than in an area where the majority of the homes were stucco with red tile roofs, like in San Carmelita and, farther up the coast, Santa Barbara.

As she pulled onto the gravel driveway, Savannah looked eagerly for any indication that someone was home. She hadn't called first. Years ago, she'd discovered that it was easier to tell a person, "No, I don't want to talk to you," on the phone than in person.

With that in mind, she had come to visit Delores Dinapoli unannounced, hoping she would be home and willing to be coerced into a conversation that she probably wouldn't want.

The first sign that she might be in luck was the late model SUV parked in front of the house. Its back door was open, and a woman was unloading tennis rackets and an oversized ball bag.

She recognized the woman as Delores Dinapoli from several pictures that Tammy had found on social media and sent to her.

She was tall, lean, and deeply tanned. Her blond hair was cropped short and she moved with a powerful, no-nonsense strength that might have made her appear less than feminine. But her grace more than made up for it.

She spotted Savannah right away, tossed the equipment back into the SUV, and waited for Savannah to park the Mustang.

Then she walked over to the car, peered at her with strange golden eyes, and said, "Hello. May I help you?"

"I certainly hope so, Mrs. Dinapoli. In fact, I'd say you might just be my last hope."

That was enough. She was invited inside.

Although Delores wasn't the warmest woman Savannah had ever met, she was friendly enough to invite her to sit down when she told her she was a private investigator.

Savannah suspected her hospitality was born of curiosity, if nothing else. Few people had a PI call on them, and they found it intriguing. Thankfully. Otherwise Savannah's job would have been much harder.

Delores offered her a seat on the sofa and a cold drink. Even though Savannah was about to float away from all the coffee and tea she'd already had that day, she accepted a soda. Experience had also taught her that some people were too polite to throw someone out of their house who was holding a beverage they had just given them.

Accepting a drink usually bought her the amount of time that it took her to consume it.

Savannah could sip a standard twelve-ounce can of soda for a minimum of fifty-seven minutes. She could also find out most of what she wanted to know in that time.

But once she had the security of the frosty drink in her hand, she stopped beating around the oleander bush and admitted to Delores Dinapoli the true reason for her visit.

She had a feeling the proverbial manure would hit the fan blades and become airborne.

She was right.

One mention of Lucinda's name and, as her southern, non-cussin' lady granny would say oh-so-delicately, "The pooh done flew."

"You've got a lot of nerve coming to my home to discuss something like that with me!" Delores shouted at her as she jumped to her feet and charged toward her, stopping only a few feet away from the sofa. "You get your rotten, stinkin' ass outta my house! Now!"

Apparently, Savannah thought, *Delores Dinapoli ain't a southern lady*.

But she *was* clearly enraged, and Savannah was surprised to realize how unsettling it was to be the subject of that rage.

Savannah even took a second to remind herself that her Beretta was in its holster, should she need it.

If she had been honest, she would have admitted that, even

though she was twenty years younger and quite a few pounds heavier than the other woman, and trained in karate and standard police defense and offense tactics, she was a wee bit scared of Delores Dinapoli.

Go figure.

"It's truly not my intention to offend you, ma'am," she said, holding the soda in front of her and hoping the outraged woman was persnickety enough about her housekeeping to not attack her and risk having soda splash all over her furniture, rugs, floor, and silk accent pillows. "I just thought you might prefer to speak to me before you have to talk to the police. Maybe I can get you up to speed, before they come knocking on your door."

"I have no idea why you or they would knock on my door about anything having to do with Lucinda Faraday. She's been out of my life for years now. Good riddance too. The last thing in the world I want to do is talk to you, the cops, or anybody about *her*."

"Do you know that she's dead?"

Delores stood still, completely void of expression, displaying one of the best poker faces Savannah had ever seen. Either she hadn't heard and wanted to hide her surprise, or she did know and wanted to conceal her feelings on the topic.

Finally, she whispered, "Yes."

"How did you find out . . . if you don't mind me asking, of course."

"I saw it on the news. Like almost everyone else, I suppose. Lucinda didn't have contact with many people. She'd lost almost everyone who ever meant anything to her."

"Including you, and I don't blame you," Savannah said softly.

She could tell Delores was taken aback by the gentle reply,

but she quickly recovered herself and charged ahead. "If you can say that, then you must know the circumstances under which our friendship ended. Therefore, I'll tell you again. You have a lot of audacity coming here to talk to me about something as personal and painful as that."

"Actually, you said 'nerve' the first time, not 'audacity,' but you're absolutely right. I have a lot of both. As, I suspect, do you. I think a woman has to have more than her share to get by in this world, don't you?"

Again, Delores seemed shaken. Savannah could tell. Under different circumstances, Savannah believed Delores might have actually liked her. Kindred spirits, and all that.

As Savannah was waiting for Delores to decide whether to slug her or have a conversation with her, the cell phone in Savannah's jacket pocket began to play the frantic, annoying little tune she had chosen for Dirk.

"Don't worry. I won't answer it," she told Delores, who was still standing less than a yard away from her, glowering down at her. "This is too important for us to be interrupted."

The cell phone finally quit, but the two women still stared at each other, waiting.

Only a few seconds later, the phone began again. Two calls in a row, one right after the other. That was her and Dirk's code for: This is serious! Pick up!

"I'm sorry, Delores," she said, reaching inside her pocket. "Apparently, it's important. I'll only be a minute."

Before the other woman could reply, Savannah answered with, "Yes, Detective Sergeant Coulter. How can I help you?"

"Are you still intending to drop in on that Dinapoli gal?" he asked.

"No, sir, I'm in Malibu with a Mrs. Delores Dinapoli. How can I help you?"

"Oh, gotcha," he replied. "Well, watch yourself with her. She could be dangerous."

"Just a pleasant conversation about the case you and I are both working on. She's most cooperative."

"Yeah, I'll bet she is. I wanted you to know that Ryan and John just called me from the mansion. They found two boxes of letters in the heap. One's full of love letters from that gal's husband to Lucinda. Over-the-top gushy stuff. The second's stuffed with some of the nastiest threatening letters you'll ever read, and they're from that gal there."

"Yes, I told her you'll be wanting to question her. She'll be happy to speak with you, sir, I'm sure."

"Watch her close, Van. Anybody who'd even write the sick crap that's in those letters is nuts."

"I'm sorry, but I won't be able to do that, Detective. Anything Ms. Dinapoli tells me is confidential. If you want to know anything about her and Ms. Faraday, you'll have to question her yourself."

"Yeah, yeah, yeah. Get outta there as quick as you can and call me the minute you're on the road."

"I'm sorry, Detective Coulter, but that's my position. Good-bye."

As soon as she replaced the phone in her pocket, Delores walked over to a chair and sat down. "Okay, what do you want to know?" she asked.

"Please tell me when you last communicated in any way with Ms. Faraday."

"It will be fifteen years ago on the tenth of June. That's when I told the woman I loved like a mother that she had broken my heart and shattered my life. That was the day when I lost the two most important people in my life—my husband and my best friend. I'm not likely to ever forget that day."

225

"No, I'm sure you won't. There is no pain quite like betrayal, and that has to be one of the worst kinds."

Delores studied her for a long time, then asked, "Has it happened to you?"

"Yes."

"A husband?"

"A fiancé."

"Did he do it with your best friend?"

"Three of them."

"Ouch."

"Yeah. He was stupid. Couldn't figure out how to close a zipper."

They both laughed. A little.

Delores picked up a pack of cigarettes from a nearby table. She removed one and offered it to Savannah. When Savannah shook her head, Delores lit up, her fingers fumbling with the lighter.

Once she'd drawn several long drags, she asked, "Did you leave him?"

"Moved to the other side of the country. If I'd gone any farther, I'd have fallen into the ocean."

"I hear you."

"I gather you divorced yours."

"Naw." She released the smoke slowly from her nose.

"Oh?" Savannah couldn't hide her surprise. Delores didn't seem like a woman who would continue to cohabitate with an adulterous husband.

"He fell down a staircase. Broke his neck." She grinned. "Oh, darn."

Their eyes met, and a shiver ran through Savannah, colder than she could recall feeling in a long time.

"Oh. Wow," was all she could manage.

Delores's weird smile was as chilling as her strange gold eyes. "You asked when I last communicated with Lucinda, and I told you. Now, ask me when I last communicated with that worthless jackass of a great-grandson of hers."

Savannah felt her pulse rate jump. "Oo-kay. When did you last communicate with dear, darlin' Geoffrey?"

Again, the cold, creepy smirk. More smoke pouring out of her nostrils. "Yesterday."

Chapter 23

The instant Savannah pulled onto the Pacific Coast Highway, she used her hands-free car phone to call Dirk.

He answered with a breathless, "Are you outta there?"

"Yeah, safe and sound. But that woman is one creepy freak-o and a half. She's got me thinking she might've even murdered her own husband."

"We can check into that later. Did she kill Lucinda?"

"I'm honestly not sure. But she told me something you've just got to hear."

"Okay, lay it on me."

Savannah was so excited that she had to concentrate and remind herself that she was driving. The Pacific Coast Highway was beautiful, but it was dangerous, too. The sharp curves were fairly unforgiving, especially to someone who didn't travel it every day and hadn't memorized every twist and turn.

She drew a deep breath, held it, and slowly released it. Then she said, "Geoffrey Faraday is blackmailing Delores Dinapoli."

"Get outta here!"

"I'm not messing with you. That's what she told me. Showed me the e-mails and everything."

"What's he got on her?"

"What he's got is his great-grandmother's tell-all manuscript, the book that Mary told us about. The one she said Lucinda was working on for years. Her autobiography, including all the craziness back in the good old days."

"Let me guess," Dirk said. "There's a chapter in there on the Lucinda-Dino affair?"

She laughed. "Did I ever tell you that I married you because you're smart?"

She could hear the smile in his voice when he said, "You never mentioned it before. But I'm glad you finally came to that conclusion."

"Oh, that's not why I married you, darlin'. I just wondered if I ever told you that."

"Smart-ass. I want to hear more about this blackmail scheme of Geoffrey's. How did he contact her? How much did he ask for?"

"Like I said, with an e-mail. She showed it to me. He even scanned the pages of the chapter that talked about them. She let me read them. They weren't very complimentary to either Delores or Dino."

"In what ways?"

"Lucinda called Delores a frigid witch who neglected her husband, physically and emotionally, and she wrote something about Dino's dicky-doo being 'dinky' and 'stinky.'"

"O-o-o-o, brutal!"

"He wants half a million for the manuscript."

"Does she have any intention of paying him for it?"

"No way. I got the idea she's been called a frigid witch and worse a few times already and doesn't mind that much. I also have a feeling she pushed ol' Dino down a staircase and broke

229

his neck, so I doubt that she cares if someone says she neglected him or if they denigrate his wiener."

She could almost hear the wheels in his head spinning, as hers had been for the last half hour.

"Okay," he said. "Here's the plan. I'm going over to Geoffrey's house—or should I say his mousy little fiancée's rental—and ask him what the hell he thinks he's doing."

"He'll deny it."

"Of course he will. But I can get a read on him, and I can shake him up, letting him know that I'm onto him."

"Sounds doable. Want company?"

"I want *you*. Always. Even if you don't think I'm smart."

"Oh, you misunderstood me. I think you're *brilliant*. But that's not why I married you."

She heard him chuckle and the deep sound went right through her. "Tell me why," he said, "my good looks, my charm, my impeccable table manners."

"Certainly not the latter."

"Then what?"

"Many reasons. Lawn maintenance. Cleo likes you. Granny adores you. You set the garbage cans out on the curb every Thursday."

"Gee, I can feel my head swelling by the minute."

"But mostly, I married you for your not-at-all-dinky, never-the-least-bit-stinky dicky-doo."

"Yay! I knew it!"

She ended the call and continued to maneuver the treacherous curves of the Pacific Coast Highway, still enjoying the beautiful view, still proud of herself for taking a chance and moving to California.

But mostly she was glad she had married Dirk—a guy who was so easy that one silly little joke could set his world right.

"Easy" was good. Almost as good as "peace."

* * *

Savannah and Dirk rendezvoused at a corner, a block away from Geoffrey and Brooklynn's house, then drove the rest of the way in the Buick.

When they got out and walked up the sidewalk, both were too excited to even speak.

At the door, he gave his customary Papa Bear knock.

Savannah could feel her heart pounding as they waited. As usual, under stressful circumstances, she found herself thinking the silliest things. Like: *Will Geoffrey be wearing a different amazing suit, or does he wear the other one all the time? Even to bed? Will Brooklynn have washed her hair yet? For cryin' out loud, stop it! What are you, the Queen of Stupid Questions?*

The moment the door opened, one of those questions was answered instantly.

No, poor Brooklynn hadn't washed her hair or changed out of her pink teddy bear pajamas.

Savannah couldn't help feeling sorry for her. Depression was a hideous disease, as evidenced by the woman standing in the doorway.

"Hello again," Dirk said with more congeniality than Savannah had expected. "Is Geoffrey at home?"

"No."

"Where is he?"

"At work."

Dirk gave Savannah a quick sideways look. "Where's *work*?" he asked.

"He has a job now. An important job, and he makes a lot of money."

Seeing that Dirk wasn't getting anywhere fast, Savannah decided to give it a try. "Have you ever been to this place where he works, Brooklynn?" she asked with as much patience as she could muster.

"We drove by it once. I didn't go in, but I saw it."

"Was there a sign on the building?"

"Yes."

"What did it say?"

"City Hall."

Again, Savannah and Dirk exchanged looks. Sure. Geoffrey Faraday, ex-con, was now working at San Carmelita's City Hall, performing some important job that paid megabucks. Enough to buy diamond-encrusted watches and top-of-the-line Porsches.

And if frogs had wings, Savannah thought, *they wouldn't bump their little butts when they hop.*

"May we come inside, Brooklynn?" Savannah asked. "We'd just like to talk to you for a minute. No big deal."

Brooklynn looked back over her shoulder at the living room behind her. "The place is kinda messy. The girl who comes in to clean forgot to come this week."

"Don't you just hate it when that happens?" Dirk said as he opened the screen door.

His body language said he was coming through, so she stepped back and allowed them to enter.

Once inside, Savannah could tell that Dirk was anxious to get down to serious business before Geoffrey appeared. Finding him gone was a stroke of luck that just might pay off handsomely.

Brooklynn started to clear the debris off the sofa, when Dirk said, "Oh, don't bother with that, ma'am. We're not gonna stay long if Geoffrey's not here. It's just that we need a certain item, and we think Geoffrey might have it. I was going to ask if I could borrow it from him."

"Oh, right. Hm-m-m." She glanced around and said, "If you tell me what it is, and I know where it is, maybe I could get it for you."

"Sure." Dirk brightened considerably. "It's a stack of papers. A manuscript. Does that ring a bell?"

She thought it over but looked confused. "Not really."

"It might be in a box," Savannah offered. "Or some kind of manila folder, or . . ."

"No. I haven't noticed anything like that lying around."

Dirk pasted on his sweetest, most benign smile. "Would you mind if I just looked around a bit? I wouldn't ask, but like I said, it's really important, and I'm super busy today. It'd be great if we don't have to wait until Geoffrey comes home."

Again, she glanced around at the clutter and looked embarrassed. "I don't mind if you look around," she said. "As long as you don't yell at me about the mess. Geoffrey always yells at me about the mess, but he never picks up anything himself. Just drops stuff wherever he wants and leaves it."

"Men!" Savannah said with a laugh that sounded fake even to her. "They'll leave their sunglasses in the toaster oven and their socks in the freezer if you don't watch them every second."

She shot a Get-on-With-It look at Dirk.

The legal renter, whose name was on the lease, had just given him permission to search the place.

This is no time to let moss grow on your backside, she thought, giving him a knowing nod toward the bedroom.

"If you can just find that manuscript," she told him, "we can get out of here and leave this poor woman alone. I'm sure she has other things to do than chat with us."

Brooklynn shrugged. "Not really. My show's coming on in half an hour, but until then, you're welcome to hang out and do whatever you need to do."

"Oh, then maybe I'll help Detective Coulter search, if that's okay with you," Savannah said.

"Sure. Whatever. Do what you gotta do."

Savannah turned to Dirk. "What the heck, Sarge. Let's do what we gotta do."

They both headed into the bedroom. No time to waste. The master of the house might come home at any moment, and for all they knew, the lady of the house might come to her senses.

Heaven forbid.

When Savannah and Dirk emerged from the bedroom Savannah was carrying a small silver laptop, and Dirk had a bright red leather satchel under his arm.

Brooklynn was lying on the laundry on the sofa, her feet up on its arm, watching a soap opera. She smiled when she saw them. "Oh, you found something! Is it what you were looking for? The manuscript?"

"Yes. It's here in this." Dirk held up the satchel.

"Oh, right! *That* thing! I didn't know what was in that, but Geoffrey brought it home the other day. I think it's new. He's been buying so much stuff lately. He likes nice things."

Instantly alert, Dirk said, "He brought this home the other day? Which other day, exactly?"

"Um . . ." She squinted her eyes, thinking. "It was the same day you came by here to tell us about poor Great-Grandma Lucinda's passing. He was gone for a while. When he got back home he had that with him. He took it into the bedroom. I didn't know there was a manuscript in it, or I would have told you about it. Where did you find it?"

"Between the headboard and the wall," Savannah told her.

"Really? What a weird place to put it. That Geoffrey!"

"Yes. That Geoffrey." Savannah tried to laugh with her, but it was all just too strange.

"We're leaving now," Dirk said, heading for the door, his prize under his arm.

"Tell him we said hi. That we're so proud he landed that important job at City Hall," Savannah added. "Maybe you can put some of that money he's making toward the wedding or a nice honeymoon."

Brooklynn smiled broadly and pranced across the room toward them, her hand held out. "That's done taken care of," she said. "The deed is done!"

It took Savannah a while to notice that there was a tiny, modest band next to the equally nondescript engagement ring. Not that there was anything wrong with inexpensive wedding sets, but a guy who wore a diamond-studded platinum watch and gold designer cuff links should have done better, in her humble opinion.

However, the bride seemed thrilled, so who was she to judge?

For some reason, Savannah recalled how many abused women had told her that the real mistreatment had begun right after they'd said, "I do." Sometimes, the first blows were struck on the actual honeymoon.

She looked down at the PC she was holding and was pretty sure it was Geoffrey's. It was a high-ticket model. Brooklynn wouldn't have owned anything so expensive.

She thought about how Geoffrey was going to react when he came home and realized they had come and taken his property without a warrant. If he found out Brooklynn had given Dirk permission to search . . .

Savannah handed the laptop to Dirk, reached into her purse, and pulled out one of her cards. When she handed it to the woman, she said, "Brooklynn, I hope you never need this. But if you ever find yourself in any trouble. Any kind of trouble. With anybody. Like maybe even Geoffrey. Promise me you'll call me. I can help you. Detective Coulter can help you, too, and we will. Okay?"

Brooklynn looked puzzled as she stared down at the card. Finally, she said, "Yeah. Okay. I don't think I'll need it."

"Just hide it away someplace where nobody but you will see it. Remember it's there, and don't be afraid to use it, any time, day or night. Got that?"

"Yeah, okay. Thanks."

"No, thank *you*. You have no idea how much help you've been," Dirk said. He looked like he was about to break into song and dance at any moment.

Savannah decided to get him out of the house before he did.

Considering the hell the woman was going to catch for what she had done, it just didn't seem appropriate.

Chapter 24

"Lord have mercy! As a fan of romance novels, I've read a lot of steamy stuff in my day, but this here plumb takes the cake!" Savannah looked up from the pile of papers on her lap and over at her grandmother, who was sitting on the sofa, the other half of the manuscript on hers. Both wore surgical gloves.

From the expression on Granny's face, Savannah could only imagine what Gran's half of Lucinda Faraday's tell-all book contained.

Granny glanced up from her reading, held up a traffic-cop hand, and said, "Sh-h-h. Don't interrupt me. I just got to the good part. I mean, the bad part." She reconsidered for a moment. "No, the good part. Oh, mercy, I'm all twitterpated."

"I know! Here I thought y'all used to behave yourselves back in the old days. This stuff is worse than we ever—"

"Hush!"

Savannah giggled. "Okay. Sorry."

If the manuscript had been a published, bound hardcover, she couldn't have convinced her grandmother to read a sentence of "such filth." But along with being a modest woman who guarded the sanctity of her eyes, mind, and soul, Granny Reid was a true detective, a card-carrying member of the Moonlight Magnolia Detective Agency.

When Dirk had left an hour before, his instructions were, "Get that thing read as quick as you can. I gotta know what's in it and who else Geoffrey Numb-Nuts might be blackmailing."

Savannah had made a huge pitcher of sweet tea, piled some cookies on a platter—Reid women needed fuel for their tasks—and she and Gran had settled down, each with a cat cuddled next to them, and applied themselves with a fervor.

Tammy sat at the rolltop desk in the corner, her daughter asleep in her lap, the computer on and ready to go. Every few minutes, Granny or Savannah would bark out a person, place, or thing for her to research. So far, she had studied the life histories of at least thirteen of Lucinda's lovers, with whom she had shared from one night up to a year.

All were well dead and unlikely to care, let alone kill her.

"Okay, Tams, how about this fella?" Savannah said a few minutes later, having found a story that was darker and more disturbing than the others. "A guy by the name of Jacob Stillman. I gather he was in his early forties in 1948."

Tammy turned eagerly to the desk computer. "Then his birth date would have been, let's say, 1900 to 1910. Got a location? Anywhere he might have lived?"

"Los Angeles."

"I'm on it."

Granny looked up from her pages. "That rings a bell."

"It does," Savannah said. "It sounds familiar to me, too. But I can't quite place it."

"What'd he do?"

"He and Lucinda spent some, um, quality time together when she was fifteen and he was forty-two."

"Jerk. Oughta had his tallywhacker tied in a knot."

Tammy added, "Around his neck."

They all had an instant mental vision of Lucinda's body and made a face. "Sorry," Tammy said. "My anti-child-molester zeal got the best of me there. Since I've become a mother, my live-and-let-live attitudes have flown out the window. I'm starting to sound more like you Georgia gals."

Savannah smiled and nodded, but she was barely listening, as her eyes skimmed the pages. "She was in love with him," she added. "Very much in love."

"Of course she was," Gran said with a sniff. "She was fifteen. You don't fall a smidgeon bit in love at that age. It's head over hiney or nothin'."

"What else?" Tammy asked, typing away at the keyboard and staring at the various Web pages popping up on the screen in rapid succession.

"He was the father of the baby that was aborted."

"Apparently, he didn't mind having sex with a minor," Tammy said, "but he wasn't ready to marry and raise a child with a teenager. Nice guy."

"He wasn't a nice guy, and not just for what he did to Lucinda," Savannah said, studying the papers in her hand. "He worked for Lucinda's manager, who was a gangster himself. Definite ties with organized crime."

"Back in those days," Granny added, "gangsters were the roughest ruffians around. They were shootin' the puddin' outta each other on a daily basis. They had the police and politicians and judges in their hip pockets. Them that weren't cops and governors and judges theirselves, that is."

"Lucinda writes that Stillman didn't want her to have the baby and give it up for adoption because he intended to be a judge when he grew up someday. Figured he could help out his mob buddies if he was in position to rule on cases against them."

"Of course he could," Tammy said. "That'd make him an extremely popular, and no doubt wealthy, fellow in that time and place."

"Nothin' like havin' a squad o' rich mobsters on your side back then," Gran agreed. "He'd have been set for life. Did he ever get to be a judge, heaven forbid?"

Tammy nodded. "He did. In 1949. Served for the next twenty-two years."

"That was twenty-two years of corruption and judicial misconduct, I'm sure," Savannah said.

"Oh, that's not all," Tammy said, sounding most excited. "That was the turning point for his particular branch of the Stillman family. They did quite well for themselves after that."

"In what way?" Savannah asked.

"Every way! He married into a wealthy family and had two sons. One also served as a judge, the other built an extremely successful shipping company."

"Wait a minute! I got it!" Granny exclaimed, startling the sleeping Cleo curled beside her. "That nice-looking young man who wants to run for governor, Mr. Clifton J. Stillman. Wasn't his daddy a super-rich guy who made his money in shipping?"

Tammy gasped. "That's right! Clifton's on fire! They say he's the rising star of his party here in California. Some are saying he could be president someday! I've watched him debate a couple times, and he's brilliant. I think I heard him say his grandfather was a judge. That his family is all about public service and justice."

"Not to mention a bazillion bucks from shippin' and who knows what other skullduggery," Granny added.

Savannah listened with one ear, but she had reached a part of the manuscript that was so horrifying, she could hardly breathe. She read it as quickly as she could to the end.

Laying the pages down on her lap, she reached for her tea, her hand shaking. As she was taking a long drink, to wet her dry mouth, she heard Granny say, "Savannah girl? You okay, sugar?"

"Not really," she replied, "and when you hear this, you won't be either. I've gotta call Dirk."

Savannah, Dirk, and Granny sat at the kitchen table, while Tammy sat on the sofa, close enough to join in the conversation, as she nursed her daughter.

"Are you absolutely sure about all of this?" Dirk asked. "'Cause if I move on it with a guy like Stillman . . ."

"If Lucinda's manuscript is true, and it sure has the ring of authenticity to me, then it's true," Savannah told him. "That's the best guarantee I can give you."

"Run it past me one more time before I leave. If I'm gonna go rattle the cage of a guy who might be president someday, I gotta be well informed."

"Okay." Savannah drew a deep breath and began. "Lucinda got pregnant by this older guy, Jacob Stillman, who was in cahoots with the mob and wasn't the least bit interested in raising a baby with a kid."

"I got that much. Go on."

"Her manager and Stillman were mob buddies. The manager arranged to take Lucinda and Stillman out on a high-level mobster's yacht. They also invited a girlfriend of Lucinda's, named Belinda, along. Belinda was sixteen and she was also pregnant. The father of her baby was the mobster who owned the yacht."

"We didn't hear about Belinda in the diary," Tammy spoke up from the living room.

"No," Savannah said. "The tell-all is a lot more forthcoming than even her personal diary. Anyway, they told the girls that it was going to be a party, and they didn't bother to mention that they had also invited an abortionist. Not a real doctor, of course."

Dirk shook his head with disgust. "Of course not. A coat hanger, back alley kinda guy."

"Tragically, yes." Savannah took a long drink of her tea and realized that her thirst was from her nerves, not dehydration. No amount of liquid was going to wash away the terrible taste left behind by what she had read. "If you want all the gory details," she told Dirk, "you can read the manuscript. It's quite graphic. Very sad. But the upshot is: Both girls received abortions that neither of them wanted. Lucinda survived hers, obviously. Belinda did not. She was, I guess you would say, 'buried at sea.' Lucinda witnessed everything that happened to her friend, as well as suffered her own loss."

"Damn," Dirk said.

"Yes," Granny agreed. "That poor little Belinda, and no wonder Miss Lucinda was haunted by that night for the rest o' her days. Somethin' like that'd scar the mightiest of souls, to be sure."

Dirk sat back in his chair and crossed his arms over his chest. Savannah recognized the gesture all too well. He was guarding his heart.

Unfortunately, in a cop's world, if you had a heart at all, protecting it from the tragedies you witnessed every day was impossible.

"Okay," he said, "what else?"

"I don't know how true it is," Savannah continued, "but Lucinda wrote that some months later, Jacob Stillman had the nerve to actually blackmail the mobster who owned the yacht. He threatened to go to the cops about the murder if the mobster didn't use his influence to help Stillman get the judicial appointment he was after. I guess the mobster decided it would be handy to have a guy like that in his pocket. They formed a sort of sick, symbiotic, parasitic relationship, each feeding off the other. The mobster even invested in Stillman's son's shipping company, guaranteeing its success."

Dirk nodded thoughtfully. "So, we have this guy now, Clifton Jacob Stillman, the grandson, with his family's wealth and judicial experience—not to mention who knows how many unsavory connections—getting ready to run for governor of California. Nice."

"He might be," Tammy piped up from the living room. "I like him. He seems to be a real man of the people with a lot of compassion."

"That's a rare commodity in the world of politics," Savannah said. "But maybe he doesn't know his family's history. Maybe he doesn't realize that their wealth and influence began that night on a yacht where a couple of girls had their babies stolen from them, and one lost her life."

Dirk stood, picked up his phone from the table, and shoved it into his pocket. Turning to Savannah, he said, "I'm off to Los Angeles to find out how much he knows and doesn't know. You want to come with me?"

She glanced at the clock. It was twelve-thirty. The drive to Los Angeles could easily take an hour, maybe more. Plus, who knew how much rigmarole they would have to go through to see a man as important and busy as Clifton J. Stillman?

"I don't think we could make it there and back before

Brody gets out of school," she said. "I'd better stick around here."

She saw the disappointment in her husband's face. The same disappointment she felt at having to turn him down. There was nothing she wanted more than to be there and watch this interview. She owed it to Ethan if nothing else.

"Oh, for heaven's sake," Granny said. "Have y'all forgotten already that you have a built-in babysitter here, one that's more than willin' and eager to take that little guy off your hands?"

"But you'll have to pick him up from school and everything," Savannah replied.

Granny put the back of her hand to her forehead and feigned a dramatic faint. "Oh dear, oh dear, whatever shall I do? I've never picked up a child from school before, and it's a whole, what, two blocks away? I might get lost or plum wore out before I get there and back."

Savannah laughed. "Okay, okay. That's enough. I'll leave him in your extraordinarily competent hands, Gran."

"I'll probably just walk over with the Colonel and get him. Somethin' tells me Brody'll score points there at his new school by showin' off his four-footed friend."

"I think that's the best idea ever. Thank you, Granny."

"My pleasure, darlin'." Gran turned to Dirk. "Go to Los Angeles and talk to that Stillman man. I'll bet you dollars to doughnuts that weasel, Geoffrey, already has."

"We can hope," Dirk said. "Never hurts to hope."

As they headed for the door, Dirk stopped and looked back at the brown paper evidence bag on the kitchen table that held the manuscript. "You're absolutely sure," he asked Savannah, "that you and Granny are the only ones who touched that thing."

"Yes, and before you ask, we were wearing gloves the entire time."

"Good." He rushed over to the table and scooped up the bag. "After we get back from LA, I'll drop this over to the lab and make Eileen dust every single page for fingerprints."

Savannah gave him a *tsk-tsk*. "And you wonder why that gal's not a fan of yours?"

Chapter 25

Traffic was light on the way to Los Angeles, and Savannah and Dirk had no trouble at all finding Clifton J. Stillman's campaign headquarters. His operation was not being run from a shabby first-floor converted bodega in a tough part of town, like some politicians who claimed to be "for the people."

No, Clifton Stillman didn't bother to hide his wealth. His headquarters covered the entire fifty-third floor of one of the tallest buildings in downtown Los Angeles. Glass and steel, and an atrium four stories high with full-sized palm trees and a waterfall announced his wealth to anyone visiting the heart of his operation.

"I hear they have a penthouse suite in this place that would knock your socks off," Savannah told Dirk as they walked to the elevator bay and watched as herds of rich Californians, dressed in their ultra-expensive pseudo-casual attire poured out of the various doors.

Savannah felt a little underdressed in her simple white cotton shirt and her linen slacks and jacket. She decided she should have at least worn heels instead of her trusty loafers.

As they stepped into an elevator, she looked Dirk over, taking in his standard uniform: faded jeans, Harley-Davidson T-shirt, bomber jacket, and scuffed running shoes.

He must really be embarrassed, she thought. But only briefly before remembering—he was Dirk.

He did fill out those jeans quite nicely, though she doubted that would impress Clifton Stillman as much as it did her.

She had always enjoyed walking behind Dirk, and since he walked twice as fast as she did, she frequently got the opportunity to savor the view.

It took a while for the elevator, fast and modern as it was, to get to the fifty-third floor. It wasn't a particularly pleasant trip, as neither she nor Dirk enjoyed elevators. Usually, they were alone when riding one, and they passed the time and reduced the tension by making out.

She supposed they could have followed their routine. Californians weren't known for being overly judgmental about those things. But with a dozen other people inside the tiny enclosure, riders constantly getting in and out and jostling for positions, she decided it would hardly be worth it.

She looked over at Dirk and saw he was grinning down at her. The twinkle in his eyes told her he was thinking the same thing.

He bent his head down to hers and whispered, "Thanks for the thought anyway."

She chuckled. "You too." Then she added for good measure, "Don't worry. This'll go okay."

"I know," he said with typical Dirk nonchalance.

Not for the first time, Savannah wished she could feel as confident about anything, even once in her life, as her husband did about almost everything.

How nice it would be not to have inherited the Reid

Worry-All-The-Time and the Second-Guess-Yourself-Every-Dang-Chance-You-Get genes.

She would never know. She suspected those two anomalies made up 90 percent of her DNA.

Finally, they arrived at the appropriate floor and exited the elevator to find themselves in an expensive, elegant office foyer.

The design and furnishings were ultra-contemporary. A lot of industrial style cement, black leather sofas and chairs, a gas fireplace, and one of the biggest widescreen televisions she had ever seen. It was showing, predictably, Clifton J. Stillman giving a speech and looking quite gubernatorial, even presidential, doing so.

To their far right, behind a black and chrome desk, sat a beautiful young woman, impeccably dressed in a designer suit that even Geoffrey Faraday would probably approve.

They walked over to the desk, and Dirk took his badge from his jacket pocket.

Holding it out for her inspection, he said, "Good afternoon. I'm Detective Sergeant Dirk Coulter. I need to speak with Mr. Stillman."

Savannah couldn't help noticing that he had neglected to mention the fact that he was with the San Carmelita Police Department. She didn't blame him. Nothing could be gained by drawing attention to the fact that you were from another jurisdiction.

The young woman smiled, showing a full set of perfect teeth. "Is Mr. Stillman expecting you? Do you have an appointment?" she asked.

"No, I don't," he admitted, "but—"

"Oh, what a shame," she said with a sympathetic shake of

her perfectly coiffed head. "Mr. Stillman is extremely busy today and won't be able to see anyone without an appointment."

"I understand," Dirk said in a tone that suggested he was anything but understanding. "Ma'am, this is concerning a very serious matter, and I assure you that Mr. Stillman would want to know that I'm here."

The young woman looked both irritated and curious when she said, "May I ask what this is regarding?"

Dirk gave her a chilly smile and said, "Just tell him that it's about Lucinda."

"Lucinda?"

Savannah watched her closely to see if she appeared to recognize the name. If she did, she gave no sign of it.

"Yes," Dirk assured her. "Tell him it's critically important, and it's about Lucinda."

The receptionist picked up the phone, punched in a few numbers, and after a brief pause said, "I'm so sorry to bother you, Mr. Stillman, but there is a gentleman at the front desk, a Detective Coulter. He doesn't have an appointment, but he says he has a matter of critical importance to discuss with you. He says it has to do with Lucinda."

She listened briefly, and Savannah watched as the semi-smirk slid off her face, to be replaced by incredulity. "Yes, sir," she said. "I'll send him back right away." Again, she listened for a few seconds, then replied, "Of course, Mr. Stillman. I'd be happy to escort the detective and his companion directly to your office."

She ended the call and walked around from behind the desk. Savannah could tell that it irked her a bit, but she pasted a smile on her face, gave a gracious wave of her hand, and said, "Follow me, please."

As Savannah and Dirk fell into step behind her, he turned to Savannah, gave her a wink, and whispered, "He knows."

She nodded vigorously, resisting the urge to giggle. "I know . . . that he knows. Cool."

The receptionist led them into the center of the action, and unlike the quiet reception area, this part of the campaign headquarters was abuzz with activity.

The enormous room was filled with busy, bustling people and the cacophony of phones ringing constantly with myriad ringtones. On the wall to the right were several televisions, most of which were tuned to news stations. One was showing the same speech as in the reception area.

Another wall was decorated with a large American flag, as well as a California flag and a gigantic calendar. All sorts of Post-its and notecards were stuck to its various squares. Some areas had lines drawn through them. *Perhaps when Mr. Stillman is out of town?* Savannah wondered.

On the third wall was the largest map she had ever seen. It was the state of California, showing all of the voting precincts. They were color coded in a way that made no sense to Savannah, but she assumed they were crucial to the campaign.

No one even looked their way as they followed the receptionist to the far end of the room. Savannah couldn't remember ever seeing so many people so busy.

She reminded herself to never work on a political campaign. It appeared to be the exact opposite of peace.

Finally, after what seemed like a major hike, they arrived at a glass-enclosed office in the very back of the room.

In an instant, Savannah recognized the man inside, sitting behind the desk. It was the handsome, dynamic, up-and-coming Clifton J. Stillman himself, in all his glory.

Although he didn't look particularly glorious when he glanced up and saw them walking toward him. In fact, he looked quite worried.

She took that as a good sign.

Anything but have this long trip turn out to be a fool's errand with her playing the major nitwit.

The fact that Stillman appeared bothered, rather than simply curious, told her that he knew exactly who Lucinda was.

At least, she could hope.

The receptionist started to knock on the door, but Stillman waved them inside.

The three of them entered. She announced Dirk, who then introduced Savannah, and Stillman gave the receptionist a dismissive nod.

At first, Savannah thought he wasn't even going to invite them to sit. Then, he seemed to decide a cooperative approach might be best.

"Would you like a cup of coffee, Ms. Reid, Detective?"

"I'll pass," Dirk said, plopping himself on a chair without waiting to be asked.

Savannah sat a bit more gracefully and said, "No, thank you."

Dirk pulled his badge from his pocket and quickly showed it to him. Again, he wanted to show his authority but not necessarily his jurisdiction.

But this time, he was dealing with a candidate with his sights on the White House, not a receptionist.

Clifton J. Stillman was a sharp cookie.

"You're with the San Carmelita Police Department?" he said, his intense gray eyes taking in every detail of their attire, sizing them up in an instant.

It made Savannah uncomfortable and reminded her that she and Dirk did the same to people every workday.

"Yes," Dirk replied. "How did you know that, sir?"

Savannah was sure Dirk hadn't given Stillman time to read any of the fine print on his shield. It was a good question. She could see the man struggle for a moment to come up with an answer. Her only question was: would he be honest?

Something about the way he sighed and dropped his shoulders, as though in defeat, suggested to Savannah that he had chosen to be truthful.

"A couple of days ago," he began, "I saw on the news that Lucinda Faraday had been found dead in her mansion, Qamar Damun, in Twin Oaks, which I believe is still part of San Carmelita. I assumed you're with the SCPD."

"You're right. I am," Dirk admitted. "I appreciate you taking time to talk to us."

Stillman turned his intense gaze on Savannah. "May I ask what your involvement in this case might be?"

She decided to be completely honest with him, too. It would only make things simpler for everyone.

"I'm a private detective, also from San Carmelita . . . and Detective Coulter's wife."

"You're helping your husband solve his case?"

"I'm trying, sir. I formerly served with the SCPD. We were partners, in fact. However, I'm investigating this murder on behalf of a client."

"Who?"

"I'm not at liberty to say, Mr. Stillman. Someone who was very fond of Ms. Faraday and wants to see her murderer brought to justice."

"Okay."

His brow furrowed with concentration, and she could tell he was evaluating everything they'd said, as well as their demeanor.

She could also tell he had a lot at stake. For all of his cool alpha male demeanor, she sensed he was highly stressed.

"Mr. Stillman," Dirk said, leaning forward in his chair, "could you tell me what personal knowledge you might have of Lucinda Faraday?"

Stillman sat back in his chair. Way back. He laced his fingers together over his belt buckle and said, "Before I heard about her murder, I knew very little. That she was a pretty lady, an old-time movie star, who did some sort of racy calendar shot back when she was still underage. Maybe in the forties?"

Savannah nodded. "Yes. When she was fifteen."

"That's disgusting," Stillman said.

"You don't know the half of it," Dirk added. "Or maybe you do."

Stillman just gave him a deadpan stare that said nothing.

Dirk returned the stare with his own, and as Savannah watched, she was glad she had never been on the receiving end of that.

Dirk was very good at glowering. He watched a lot of Clint Eastwood movies and practiced in front of the mirror.

He denied it, of course—all that rehearsing. But finally, his efforts paid off; Stillman caved first. "If you have questions for me, Detective," he said, "please ask them. I have a very tight schedule."

"Okay. We'll get right to it then," Dirk told him. "Do you know a guy named Geoffrey Faraday?"

Savannah saw and heard Stillman's sharp intake of breath.

The question seemed to both surprise and maybe even frighten him.

It took too long for him to answer with, "I don't know him personally."

"Have you communicated with him in any way lately?"

Again, she watched Stillman wrestle with the decision: lie or tell the truth?

He held his hands up, almost as though he were surrendering, and said, "I have."

"Thank you. I appreciate you telling me the truth. We'll get along a lot better that way. Would you please tell me about that communication? I need details."

Stillman looked past them, through the glass at the people working in his giant war room. Several of them were staring at the office, as though trying to discern what was happening.

The floor-to-ceiling glass hid little.

Transparency may not always be the best policy, Savannah thought.

Stillman stood and walked around his desk. For a moment, she thought he was walking out on them. The expression on Dirk's face told her that he thought so, too.

But when Stillman got to the door, he turned his back to the glass.

At least his employees and volunteers couldn't see the distress on his face when he said, "Detective, I'm being blackmailed."

"By Geoffrey Faraday?" Dirk asked.

"Yes."

"With a tell-all manuscript?" Savannah asked.

"Yes. Apparently, Lucinda Faraday wrote one of those kiss-and-tell books before she died, and it included some stories about my grandfather that were . . . unflattering, at best."

"I know," Savannah said. "I've read them."

"Then perhaps you can understand why I'm upset. With me running for office, this is the last sort of publicity I need."

"I'm sure it is," Dirk said dryly.

"But the worst part, the most painful aspect of the whole sordid thing is that I loved and respected my grandfather. He was an old fellow and died when I was a kid, but I remember him as a loving, funny grandpa. He was a good man, who left the world a better place than he found it. He instilled that same conviction in my dad and in me. I'm devastated to hear about this other side of him."

Savannah couldn't help pitying the man. The pain in his eyes convinced her that he was telling the truth. Whatever he might be lying about or faking, the hurt was all too real.

"When did Geoffrey Faraday contact you?" Dirk asked him.

"The same day that they found her body. Late that evening, actually." He sagged against the glass behind him, as though too exhausted to stand. "To be honest, if you hadn't come here, I think I would have contacted you anyway. I almost did this morning. It occurred to me that he might have actually been her killer. I know he's her great-grandson and all, but he wouldn't be the first sonuvabitch to murder someone in their own family."

"How did he communicate with you?" Savannah asked.

"An e-mail."

"Can we see it?" Dirk asked.

"Yes." Stillman took his phone from his pocket, found what he was looking for, and turned it around so they could see the screen. "That's the e-mail," he said, "and those are the pictures he attached. They're the pages of the manuscript that pertain to my granddad."

Savannah looked them over and told Dirk, "These are the same as the others. The threats are almost word for word. Just different pages, of course."

"Others?" Stillman asked, intensely curious. "What others?"

"Let's just say you aren't Geoffrey's only target," Dirk told him. "That tell-all book is bad news for more than just you and your family."

"The guy needs to be stopped," Stillman said.

Dirk handed his phone back to him. "I absolutely agree." He pulled a card from his pocket and handed it to Stillman. "My e-mail is on there. Would you please forward those to me?"

"Sure. Anything else?"

Dirk stood, and Savannah did likewise.

"Yes. If you hear anything from him or anyone, or if you re-member anything we haven't discussed here already, call me right away."

"Okay, I will. Thank you."

As they headed for the door, Stillman offered his hand. When they shook it, he said, "Detective, Ms. Reid, I'm torn. Do I pay him? I can't stand the idea of having this campaign destroyed before it's even begun. Too many people have worked too hard. So many will be hurt. My whole family dev-astated."

Savannah watched Dirk struggle with the answer for a long time and appear to come up with nothing.

She decided to step in and rescue him, even if she couldn't rescue Clifton J. Stillman. "No one can tell you what you should or shouldn't do, Mr. Stillman. You're the one whose fu-ture is on the line. If you decide to pay, be sure to let us know exactly what's going on and when. Maybe we can nab him in the process."

"Yeah," Dirk said. "Meanwhile, we'll keep workin' day and night to put the guy away. Then you won't have to worry about it at all."

Stillman looked sick—to his stomach and in his soul. "I hope you do, Detective, put him away, that is. But something like this—it's out there now or will be very soon. There's really no stopping it."

Chapter 26

As Dirk drove them home from Los Angeles, Savannah decided it was less stressful to call the office than concentrate on his city driving and flinch, gasp, and grab the arm rest every fifteen seconds.

Peaceful, it was not.

"Tell me something good," she told Tammy, when she got her on the phone.

"I thought *you'd* be the one with good news," Tammy replied. "You both seemed so hopeful when you left. Downright cheerful, and we both know a Cheerful Dirk sighting is a rare occurrence, indeed."

"We do have good news, actually. Stillman was pretty open with us, told us that Geoffrey's blackmailing him, the same way he did Delores Dinapoli. Showed us the e-mail and everything."

"Great, and by the way, I found a dozen or so versions, like practice runs, of those blackmail letters and the pictures he took of the pages on the laptop that Dirk left here. I hope that'll be enough for Dirk to arrest him for blackmail while he's building the murder case."

"Good work, Tams. I'll tell him what you found. But he'll probably want to tie up a few loose ends, just to make the case as tight as he can. He'll drop me off at the house in a few minutes and then he's going to take Lucinda's manuscript to the lab for fingerprinting. Geoffrey's prints should be all over it, and that'll be another nail in his coffin."

"Good deal! This case is turning out to be fun!" Tammy sounded so positive, so bouncy, that Savannah could hardly stand it.

As always, Savannah had to balance her joy for her friend that she was so darned healthy with wanting to tie her down and take a transfusion of all that energy for herself.

"How's Mr. Brody?" Savannah asked. "Did Gran have any problem picking him up?"

"No. She took the Colonel with her when she picked him up, like she said. He was thrilled to death."

"I'll bet. What are they doing now?"

"I just took a peek out the utility room window. The three of them and Vanna, too, are in the backyard. Brody and the Colonel are running around on the grass while Granny squirts them with the water hose. Vanna's crawling, watching the circus and laughing. They're all in heaven."

"I'm sure they are. I'm sorry you have to work."

"I *love* to work. Tell Dirk-o that I checked out City Hall, and there's no way anybody there hired a dirtbag like Geoffrey Faraday. That can't be where he's making the money to buy all that expensive stuff, like he told his girlfriend. Like we ever thought it was, duh."

"He's not making it from his blackmailing career either," Savannah said. "Stillman hasn't paid him anything yet, and

Delores told him to take a hike. I guess he'll have to find another line of work."

"Or keep doing whatever he's doing that's paying for those clothes and that car."

"Stay on that, would you, sugar? See what you can dredge up."

"Sure! I love it when you keep me busy."

"Thanks for everything, puddin' cat. We just passed the pier. See ya soon."

"Toodles."

As Dirk pulled up to the house to drop Savannah off, she felt a twinge of regret to be sending him off on his own.

"This isn't the way we usually do it," she said with the door half open and one foot on the ground.

He looked a little sad, too, as he leaned over to give her a second good-bye kiss. "I know. But as long as the kiddo's staying with us, we'll both have to put some time aside for him. You go play with him now, and I'll take him off your hands when I get home."

"Okay. Sounds like a plan."

"One more thing," he said, grabbing her arm. "Did you call the CPS gal today to see if they've found a foster home for him yet?"

"Um, no."

Savannah searched his face to see if he was angry. He looked more relieved.

"Good," he said. "Why don't we just leave her alone. Wait for her to call us. They get really busy there and—"

"Wouldn't want to bother them, make a nuisance of ourselves. They'll call us when they're ready. Until then . . ."

"Yeah, till then. Go have fun. You deserve it."

Savannah could hear Brody's squeals of delight and the

Colonel's unearthly baying coming from the backyard, along with Granny's and Vanna's laughter. "Okay," she told Dirk, "I will. Thank you."

"Thank *you*, babe."

As she walked up the sidewalk to the front door, she turned to watch him drive away. She waved. He beeped the horn a couple of times. She smiled.

Marriage was turning out to be nicer than she'd thought it would be.

Once inside the house, Savannah headed straight for the desk in the corner of the living room, where Tammy was slaving away at the computer.

Savannah placed her hands on her friend's shoulders and gave her a quick rub. "Can I ask you for a favor, darlin'?" she asked, knowing the answer. Even without a massage, Tammy was always eager and ready to please.

Savannah was convinced that if the Chinese had a Tammy to help them build their Great Wall, it would have sprung up overnight.

"Could you get Mary Mahoney's phone number for me? I've misplaced it, and I'd like to make a quick call to her."

"Sure! No problem."

Savannah was sure it wouldn't be. Tammy Hart-Reid could tap into bank accounts and most government service records in less than ten minutes. A phone number, no challenge at all. Savannah would have bet she'd have the number before she got back from the utility room.

She passed the washer, dryer, and noticed the cats' filled water and food bowls. *Brody's doing*, she thought. At the window, she stopped and looked outside.

The scene was every bit as charming as Tammy had described. Only now, Granny was holding Vanna Rose in front of her and Vanna was doing the squirting with the hose gun. She had a pretty good aim for a toddler, and both boy and dog were completely drenched and utterly joyful.

"One phone call and I'll be joining you," Savannah whispered.

Then she heard Tammy shout from the other room, "I've got it, your phone number, that is!"

"Of course you do," she replied. "What would I do without you? What would I do without any of you?"

Savannah settled into her rose-print chintz chair to make the call to Mary. She knew she wouldn't be enjoying it long, but lately, she'd had to snatch "comfy chair" moments as often as she could. They were few and far between.

Mary answered after one ring. "Savannah! How's it going?"

"We're cautiously hopeful, ma'am. So far, so good. I called because I have a few quick questions for you."

"Okay. Let's hear them."

"First, I want to double check on something you told me earlier. Where did you say you last saw that tell-all manuscript that Lucinda was writing?"

"It was under her pillow, there where she was sleeping."

"Is that where she usually kept it?"

"For as long as I can remember, even when it was only a few pages, she'd tuck it under her pillow. I think she wanted to make sure no one saw it until she was ready to show it to the world."

"Okay. Can you remember exactly what day it disappeared?"

"No, I'm sorry. I know it wasn't long ago. Days ago, not weeks."

"Did you see it at any time after she died?"

"No. Definitely not."

"Okay, thank you. My next question is very important. To your knowledge, when was the last time Geoffrey was in the house? For any reason. Even for a moment."

"It's been a long, long time. Before he went away to prison. He and that fiancée of his—"

"His *wife* now, actually. They tied the knot."

"Foolish girl."

"I know."

"They came by here to try to talk Lucinda into paying for his bail and his attorney. She wouldn't. They stormed out in a huff. Well, the girl wasn't the sort to storm or huff anywhere. But he was furious."

"Was the house"—Savannah struggled to find the words—"in the condition it's in now?"

"Upstairs, but not downstairs. Lucinda entertained them in the parlor, and it was clean and neat at the time."

"Did they see the rest of the house, any of the messy part?"

"No. I'm sure they didn't. I was with them the whole time. They were only here about ten minutes."

"Okay, and now, one last question: Is there any chance Geoffrey has a key to the mansion or knows a way in?"

"A key? No. A way in? Sure. The place is falling apart. Right now, you could find at least a dozen places where you could walk or crawl in, if you wanted to. That's part of why I refuse to live inside the big house itself. That and the filth. At least, my apartment door has a sturdy lock on it and windows that lock. I wouldn't feel safe in there."

Savannah thought of Lucinda, strangled in that house only a few days ago, and stated the obvious. "You're absolutely right to be concerned. As it turns out, Qamar Damun isn't safe at all."

263

* * *

When Savannah had finished her call with Mary, she debated whether or not to phone Ethan, as well. She knew he was eager for any tidbit of information she could give him.

However, there were a little boy and a baby girl in the backyard who she knew would be delighted to have her join them, even for a few minutes. Not to mention a grandmother whose face always lit up at the sight of her.

A strange feeling was creeping over Savannah, trickling through her veins. Born of a dilemma she'd never faced before.

She felt torn. Guilty.

She hated it.

She took pride in the fact that she followed her grandmother's teaching: "Whatever your hand finds to do, do it with your might." She had lived by that and found satisfaction in doing so.

But now she didn't know what to do. How could she give all of her might to being both a private investigator and a guardian for a child who needed her? There was only one of her, and when she had to juggle those two responsibilities, both would surely suffer.

She glanced over and saw that Tammy was watching her from the desk in the corner. "It's tough deciding between working or doing the 'mommy thing,' huh?" her friend said, with eyes that were kind and wise for her age.

Savannah nodded. "It sure is. How do you working mothers do this, handle both roles?"

"We don't. Nobody can," Tammy replied. "We do one at a time, back and forth. We try to find a balance."

"Every day?"

"Every hour. Sometimes every minute. It's really hard."

"How do you ever feel good about yourself? How do you take pride in having done a great job?"

"Do a *good* job. *Great* is overrated. Good is fine. You can take pride in the fact that you did your best. Be proud that you tried."

"Does it ever balance out?"

"Sometimes you can have all the balls in the air, going around and around and not dropping. But most of the time, like I said, you just try. That's enough."

Savannah thought again of her career, her number one reason for living most of the years of her life. She thought of Dirk, of how little he asked of her and how grateful he was for whatever she gave him. She thought of little Brody out there, having fun. But not as much as he'd be having if she would join him.

"I gave enough to my career for one day," she said. "I'm going outside to play."

"Good for you," Tammy said. "I'm proud of you."

"Balance, you say. Just try."

"You got it!"

Savannah disappeared upstairs and returned two minutes later, wearing her swimsuit top, a pair of shorts, and flip-flops. Her hair was pulled back and fastened with a barrette.

As she sailed through the living room, past the desk, Tammy yelled, "Whoopee! Look at 'er go! Teach those kids how to properly use a garden hose sprayer!"

"Let's just say, you won't need to give Vanna a bath tonight, not when Auntie Savannah's done with her!"

Savannah bounded out the back door, and, if she had entertained doubts before about how she should spend the next hour—work or play?—those concerns evaporated the instant she saw the love lights in those three precious people's eyes. Even the Colonel bayed joyously, ran to her, jumped up and put his big, muddy feet on her shoulders. The next second, she received the wettest kiss ever given to her by a male.

"Ew-w-w!" she yelled. "Dog slobber! Quick, gimme that hose! Quick!"

Considering the attitude of the crowd gathered in her back-yard, she realized that was a poor choice of words as a jet of ice-cold water filled her left ear, then hit her full in the face.

"No! No! Oh! Dadgum!" she spewed and sputtered, trying to shield herself from what felt like a fireman's hose blasting away her eyebrows, nose, and ears. "That's *not* what I meant! Turn it off! Oh-h-h, when I get my hands on that hose, you are so-o-o gonna regret—There! Yeah! How do you like *that*!? Yeah, you'd better run. Run, you turkey butts! Run! Run! Run! A-ha-ha-ha!"

Chapter 27

Tammy had just set the table, and Savannah and Granny were dishing up the fried chicken, gravy, and potatoes, when Dirk walked through the back door.

"What happened out there?" he asked, pausing in the utility room to remove his muddy sneakers. "That backyard looks like somebody tried to fill the swimming pool and then realized we don't have one."

Savannah paused halfway to the table with the platter of chicken to give him a kiss. He looked at her stringy, damp hair and flushed cheeks. Then he glanced around the room and saw that everyone else, except Tammy, had the same wet, flushed appearance. Granny, Brody, and Vanna all looked like someone had dunked them in the ocean, then left them on the beach to dry in the noon sun.

"We had fun," Savannah said simply.

"Obviously," he said. Then he noticed the chicken and thoughts of anything else fled. "Oh, wow, does that ever look and smell good. I thought I was starving before, but now . . ."

He headed straight for the table, pulled out his chair, and

plopped down on it. Picking up his knife and fork in his fists and pounding on the table, prison dining hall style, he said, "I want some grub! I want some grub!"

Brody scrambled onto his seat, grabbed his own flatware, and joined in the chant.

Savannah just gave her husband a sad look and shook her head.

"What?" he said. "I'm setting a bad example for the kid? You don't approve, and I don't get dessert?"

Brody giggled, but Savannah still wore the same grim expression.

"You're not sending me to bed without my supper, woman. I'm not kidding. It's been so long since I've eaten that I'm fartin' cobwebs."

"Dirk!" Granny shouted. But when she clamped her hand over her own mouth everyone could hear her giggling.

Brody nearly fell off his chair, helpless with laughter.

Savannah was still unmoved. She walked over to the kitchen counter, picked up a paper lunch sack, and handed it to him. "I knew you'd be starving," she said, "so I made this up for you."

"What is it?"

"Same as this," she said, waving her hand to indicate the table and its bounty.

"But why would you make me a sack lunch? I hadn't even come home and misbehaved yet."

Savannah turned to Tammy and said, "Go on. Tell him."

Tammy ran over to him and parked herself on a chair beside him. She produced her tablet and began to scroll down its screen. "Savannah told me to try to find out how Geoffrey's making all that money. He doesn't have a job and is failing miserably at blackmail."

"Okay. And I'm still hungry."

She shoved the tablet under his nose. "See this charcoal suit? Does that look like the one he was wearing?"

Dirk looked. "Yeah. I guess so."

She searched, then showed him the screen again. "Is that the diamond-encrusted platinum watch he had on?"

"Looks like it," he replied, moderately interested.

She displayed Exhibit C. "His gold cuff links, also with diamonds?"

Dirk sat up straight in his chair. "Yeah, I believe it is."

"And the coup de grace." She showed him a picture of the Porsche.

"Where did you get these pictures?" he demanded. "Come on! Stop playin' with me here. What's up?"

Tammy laughed. "You're about to apologize to me that you ever called me a bimbo, an airhead, a dumb blonde, a—"

"Hey, hold on! I never called you a dumb blonde. Savannah'd smack the crap outta me if I did. Now what have you got?"

"A luxury menswear shop was burglarized a week ago. A trio of three guys broke in and stole numerous high-end suits, including that charcoal one, jewelry, including that watch and those cuff links, the owner's laptop, which is sitting in there on the office desk. Yes, I'm sure. I checked the serial number against the one that was stolen. Then, the frosting on the cake . . . they took his Porsche. I have the VIN number if you'd like to make a comparison."

"Wow! Thank you! I will never call you a fluff head again."

She gave him a "yeah, right" look. "I've heard that before."

He sniffed. "Then you should probably take it with a grain of salt."

Savannah leaned over the table and patted Tammy's hand. "Go on, kiddo. Tell him the very best part."

"This cake has *two* frostings?" Dirk asked.

"The other two guys were caught."

"Did they rat him out?"

"Not yet. But they all three shared a cell together in prison."

Dirk leaped out of his chair and, without a word, raced out the back door.

A few seconds later, he ran back inside, his stocking feet soggy with mud. He grabbed his shoes off the floor, snatched the lunch bag out of Savannah's hand, and took off. Again.

Other than a ten-minute period, when Savannah snuck away to her bedroom to call Ethan and give him a quick catch-up, she had the privilege of enjoying what she found out later was commonly called a Family Movie Night.

She was astonished that it could be so much fun for the three of them—Granny, Brody, and herself—to lounge around in the living room, devour bowls full of homemade savory popcorn, washed down with root beer floats, and watch an old Disney classic together.

They allowed Brody to choose, since he was the most recently added guest, and he picked *Aladdin*, because as he put it, "That blue genie dude just cracks me up!" Though he did put one of Savannah's best accent pillows over his face and make mooing sounds during the romantic scenes, smearing popcorn oil on the pillow's silk cover in the process.

When the evening was finished, and both Granny and Brody were in bed, Savannah retreated to her upstairs sanctuary, the bathroom, and pampered herself with a luxury she hadn't enjoyed for days. Her ritual bubble bath.

Dressed in her fluffy white bathrobe, she took her latest romance novel, her phone, and clean undies and went into the room that she had decided long ago was the most peaceful place in the world.

Her world, anyway.

Running steaming hot water into the tub, she added a generous squirt of bubble bath scented with star jasmine.

Having pulled down the blinds, she lit several pink votive candles and set them, here and there, around the room. Then she flipped off the light.

Standing in the middle of the room, she took a moment to look around, as she had hundreds of times, and enjoy what she had done. Because she, alone, had created this lovely space.

It was as feminine and soft and dreamy as her life was hard and harsh and all too real at times. She felt like a woman within these walls, even after a day when she had wrestled a bad guy to the ground, blending her sweat and sometimes her blood with his.

The wallpaper with its tiny red and pink rosebuds, the mahogany wainscoting beneath it, the black and white ceramic tiles on the floor, the Victorian pedestal sink, and her favorite, the claw-foot tub, all drew her into a magic world that soothed all of her senses.

Even her taste buds were to be pampered. On a tiny china saucer sat two dark chocolate, raspberry-cream-centered truffles.

"Ah-h-h," she said. "You did good today, Savannah. Well, you tried. You did the best you could, and Tammy says we all get credit for that. So, enjoy."

She dropped the robe and lacy knickers on the floor and slipped slowly into the sparkling pile of bubbles. The water was hot, almost too hot, but that was exactly how she liked it.

She lay back in the suds and wondered why she didn't just insist on living here, 24/7. Never, never, ever to step out of that tub again.

She closed her eyes, drew a deep breath . . . and the phone rang.

"Damn it!"

She cursed herself for not turning off the phone, although she knew she never had and never would. She had too many people who loved her and might call her, desperately needing her help. She'd been a cop. She knew what could happen to perfectly innocent people out there. She could never allow herself to be truly "off duty."

She leaned as far as she could, trying to reach the phone, which she had left on top of the wicker hamper.

It was too far. She'd have to get out.

If that loved one in desperate need on the other end wasn't already dead, she was going to kill them.

Finally, she retrieved the cell phone and instantly melted when she saw the caller ID.

Alma Reid.

Savannah didn't want to admit that she played favorites with her siblings, but she did. Absolutely. Hands down. Waycross was her favorite between her two brothers, and sweet, gentle, smart, and funny little Alma was the only sister she liked.

She loved them all, of course. There was some rule book somewhere that said you had to. That you were a rotten person if you didn't.

But she actually *liked* Alma, too. She enjoyed her. She missed her.

"Hello, darlin'," she said into the phone as she settled back into the bubbles that were about half gone. "I'm so glad it's you. I've been missing you lately somethin' fierce. Even more than usual, that is."

"I've been missin' you a bunch, too," said the soft, gentle, southern voice, so like her own . . . when she was in a good mood and not irked at anyone.

"When are you going to come out for a nice California vacation? I'm working on a case now, and I've got some extra money. I'll pay your way."

"Actually, I was thinking of doing that. But you wouldn't need to pay my way. I've got some saved back."

"That's wonderful! Tell me when you're coming, and I'll bake a cake!"

"One of your German chocolate ones with the pecan and coconut frosting?"

"Any kind your little heart desires."

"Okay. How does next week sound?"

"Oh, don't toy with me, girl! Don't get my hopes up and—"

"I mean it. I'm so tired of living here in McGill. I miss you and Granny so much it hurts. You're my people. Well, you're the ones I like."

They shared a hearty laugh at their siblings' expense.

"You know I feel the same way," Savannah told her. "Why don't you pack several suitcases and a few boxes, too, and spend a long, long time?"

"Do you mean, like, move there?"

"It's been done."

"You and Granny and Waycross are braver than I am."

"Hey, it's only change, and change won't kill you."

There was such a long silence on the other end that Savannah thought they might have been disconnected.

"You there, kiddo?" she asked.

"Yes. That's the problem. I'm here, and I'd much rather be there. With y'all, and the sunshine, and the beaches, and Disneyland."

Savannah felt as if her heart was overflowing. "Oh, honey," she said. "Do it! I'll help you any way I can."

"I know you would. I think about it all the time. But it's hard to leave everything you know. I've spent my whole life here."

"All the more reason to try something else for a change. If for any reason you find you don't like it, McGill ain't going anywhere. You can always go back. You've got nothing to lose and maybe a whole new life to gain."

"I'm going to!" she said. Savannah could tell by the joy and excitement in her voice that her sister had made her decision.

"Oh, darlin', that is wonderful! Wonderful! You have no idea how glad I am that you're doing this! Thank you!"

Suddenly, the bubbles in Savannah's tub sparkled more brightly and their jasmine scent was sweeter. She was pretty sure that if she bit into one of those truffles it would taste better than anything she had ever put in her mouth.

Happiness just did that to you.

Chapter 28

Savannah was never more contented with her lot in life than when she was in her kitchen, cooking good food for her loved ones. The only thing she enjoyed more was when she was in the backyard barbecuing for them.

So, that was exactly what she did the following evening.

All of her California family was present: Granny, Tammy, Waycross, and Vanna Rose. Ryan and John were there, as well as Ethan and little Freddy.

Savannah and Dirk had billed the occasion as an opportunity for everyone to get to know Brody better.

While that was true, the grown-ups were in a particularly festive mood for a reason they weren't sharing with the children.

Geoffrey Faraday was in jail! Not for murder, as they were still building that case. But Dirk had him dead to rights for blackmail, burglary, and grand theft auto. Considering his previous record, there was no doubt that Geoffrey Faraday would be incarcerated for a very long time. Unless, of course, they could nail him for first-degree murder, and then he would be going away forever.

Ryan and John had brought a set of horseshoes and were showing Brody how to play the game. Unfortunately, more than once, the Colonel had mistaken their intentions when throwing the horseshoes and had scampered after them, trying to pluck the heavy metal objects from the air.

"Don't do that, you fool hound dog," Brody yelled at him. "If you catch one of those things, you're going to knock your teeth out. You'll be the only bloodhound in town sportin' dentures."

Savannah had solved the problem by luring the dog over to the barbecue grill with tiny bits of the tri-tip she was cooking. After one bite, he had no interest in sinking his teeth into a horseshoe.

Dirk was tending the barbecue. Outdoor grilling was his only foray into the world of cooking, but he was getting better at it all the time. Although lately, he had decided it kept the meat moist if he poured some of the beer he was drinking over it from time to time.

Savannah decided to call it "basting" and hope her guests wouldn't object to eating food that had been splashed with one of Dirk's half-consumed beers.

When she saw Tammy staring at him as he performed the ritual, Savannah whispered, "The heat burns off any germs that might be on the meat. Don't you think?"

"Sure," said the ever cooperative and nonjudgmental Tammy. "You bet. But I'm a vegetarian. I wasn't going to eat it anyway, and I'm certainly not going to with Dirk-o spit on it."

Ethan was talking to Waycross, while Vanna and Freddy played on the grass nearby. Freddy found a dandelion that had escaped Savannah's scrutiny. He picked it and attempted to stick it in Vanna's bright red curls. Unfortunately, his little friend would have no part of it. She reached up, pulled the flower out, and promptly stuck it in her mouth.

Savannah saw Tammy give her a dirty look.

Shrugging, Savannah said, "What? I only put arsenic on the ones in the front yard, so what's your problem?"

"Very funny," Tammy said, reaching around Dirk to put one of her vegetarian burgers on the grill beside the tri-tip.

"Hey," he complained, "get that wanna-be burger off my grill. Only manly man stuff gets cooked here."

Tammy crinkled her nose at him. "Your manly man tri-tip *and* my veggie burger. That's what's going to be on your grill, and don't spill any of that spit-polluted beer on my burger."

"I don't spit in my beer! Who the hell do you think I am? I'll have you know I have perfect control over my saliva. It goes where I tell it to and when."

"He does," Savannah assured her. "I know. I've seen him spit on bugs in my garden before. He's surprisingly good at it."

Tammy rolled her eyes and walked away to join Waycross, Ethan, and the babies.

Dirk motioned for Savannah to come closer. He whispered in her ear, "Is it really a bad thing for me to pour my beer on the tri-tip? Or is that just her being persnickety?"

"She might have a point," Savannah said. "Why don't you open a new beer and just use it exclusively for the meat."

He thought about it for a minute, then said, "If there's anything left in that meat-only bottle, can I drink it when I'm done?"

"Of course, darlin'. When I bake a cake, I get to lick the beaters and the bowl. We cooks need a few perks for slaving over hot stoves."

As she walked away she saw him head for the cooler and another beer, grinning all the way.

He was so easy.

But just as he was lifting the bottle out of the crushed ice, she heard his phone ring, and she knew who it was by the Alfred Hitchcock theme song ringtone.

She hurried over to him to see what Dr. Liu would have to say. This was the phone call they had been waiting for. The final nails in Geoffrey Faraday's coffin. He was a murderer, and they wanted to make sure he didn't just pay the price for burglary, blackmail, and car theft. That particular conviction was the only thing that would have satisfied Lucinda Faraday—murder in the first degree.

"Yes, Doctor," Savannah heard him say. "Whatcha got for me?"

He put the phone on speaker, so Savannah could hear the conversation, too.

"I have lab reports on Faraday. They show there was a drug in her system. Quite a lot of it."

Savannah said, "I'm here, too. What kind?"

"Hi, Savannah. It's a prescription strength sleeping pill, called dimazepin. It's one of the strongest ones, a controlled substance."

"How much had she taken?" Dirk asked.

"Ten times the amount it would have taken to kill her."

"Wow, then there's no way that was an accident," Savannah said.

"Absolutely not."

Savannah wondered about the strangling, which seemed like overkill if you had already given a woman ten lethal doses of medication.

"Why didn't he just let her die from the pills?" Dirk asked. "Why the strangling? Why the posing?"

"He was cruel," Savannah said. "He didn't want her to die peacefully or easily."

"I agree with Savannah," Liu said. "The pills were just so he could kill her more easily."

Savannah glanced around the yard and realized almost all of the adults were watching them, Ethan in particular. They had known that calls from Dr. Liu and the lab were imminent. She could tell they were waiting to hear, and at this point, she didn't know if this was good news or bad.

"I have another piece of information for you," the doctor continued.

"What's that?" Dirk asked.

"I heard from Eileen at the lab. She asked me to call you."

"Why didn't she call herself?"

"She isn't speaking to you. She's furious with you for sending over so many items for them to process. She says it'll take six months, and frankly, I don't know if she'll do ten percent of it."

Dirk mumbled something that sounded moderately obscene under his breath.

Savannah stepped in. "Did she at least take time to search the manuscript for fingerprints?"

"Yes. Apparently, that's what she's maddest about. Said it was a waste of time."

Savannah didn't want to hear that! "How?" she asked. "A nuisance I can understand, but a waste? Really?"

"She didn't find one print on it that belonged to your suspect, Geoffrey Faraday," Liu told him. "It was covered with prints. The victim's."

"Obviously," Dirk said. "She wrote it, so she would have handled every page."

"And one other person, which we thought is a bit strange."

"Who?" Savannah asked.

She waited for what felt like an eternity for Liu to say the words. Finally, she did. "The prints that were all over it, other than the victim's, belong to Brooklynn Marsh. Geoffrey's new wife."

The backyard barbecue had turned into an emergency meeting of the Moonlight Magnolia Detective Agency.

Savannah and Dirk quickly filled everyone in on the latest developments, especially the one about them having a brand-new number one suspect.

"Who woulda thought Miss Mousy had it in her?" Dirk said, shaking his head as they gathered around the picnic table beneath the arbor.

"I agree," Savannah said. "She didn't look like she'd be able to say 'Boo' to a goose."

"I always wondered about that southern phrase," Tammy observed. "Do you people down there go around scaring geese a lot?"

"You mean more than here or in Maine or North Dakota?" Savannah asked.

"Do you mind?" Dirk barked.

"Sorry." Savannah cleared her throat. "Hearing this new thing about the fingerprints on the manuscript, it makes sense. If I was engaged to a horse's rear end like Geoffrey, I'd be looking to get rid of him, too."

"Yes, and the woman invested years of her life with him," said John. "She'd be looking for some sort of payoff."

Ryan added, "She bankrupted herself for him. Lost a career. She'd want major financial compensation of some sort, if she could manage it. Probably emotional payback, too."

Savannah glanced over at Brody and saw that he was trying to teach the two toddlers how to throw the horseshoes. They seemed oblivious to the adult conversation taking place on the other side of the yard.

She was glad for that, at least.

Turning her attention back to the group, she said, "If it was a woman who killed Lucinda, it would make even more sense that she would drug her first. No struggle, less work that way."

"Is Brooklynn large and strong enough to carry Lucinda from the bed area to the place where I found her?" Ethan asked.

"Hm. I'm not sure about that." Savannah tried to recall the woman's basic build. It had been hard to tell under the baggy pajamas. "We'll have to think about that one."

"I'm still not sure why she got moved from her bed to there anyway," Dirk replied. "Doesn't make sense."

"Maybe I was wrong and the whole thing went down right there where the body was found." Savannah turned to Ethan. "You said that Lucinda liked her Irish whiskey."

He nodded. "A lot."

"Did she have a nightcap?"

"Every night without fail. Told me she'd never get to sleep without it."

"Tell me about that. If it was a nightly pleasure for her, she probably had some sort of ritual."

He nodded. "Yes. She did. She had a special cut-crystal glass. Short, wide, with red flashing around the top and a gold edge. Beautiful. She told me a lover gave it to her. She didn't say which one. I had the feeling it might have been her son's father. Anyway, it meant a lot to her. She always drank her nightly whiskey from that."

Savannah turned to Dirk. "Did the team find a glass like that at either the bed location or where her body was found?"

"No."

"Are you sure?"

"Yeah. A fancy glass like that would've stood out in all the ugly garbage. I'll check with the CSU team, but they were all showing me anything they thought was different or special. There was nothing like that found in either place."

Waycross had been sitting quietly, adding nothing to the conversation, stroking Colonel's glossy copper ears and keeping an eye on the children. But he turned to them and added, "If I wanted to put somebody to sleep, big time, and I knew they downed a glass of whiskey ever' night before they called it a day, I'd spike that whiskey. Then after I'd done the stranglin' thing, I'd been sure to get rid of that bottle and glass, 'cause they'd have a bit o' that poison in or on 'em. That's prob'ly why we didn't find 'em there. If that Brooklynn gal was the killer, she'd a took 'em with her."

Savannah mulled that over and thought it made perfect sense. She said to Ethan, "If that glass is half as pretty as you say it is, I don't think she'd throw it away, either."

"If she pulled this off," Tammy said, "on some level, I think she'd be feeling proud of herself. She'd want to keep it as a little souvenir, don't you think?"

One by one, the team members thought about it, then nodded.

"I'd keep it," John said.

"Me too," Waycross added.

"Even I probably would," Dirk admitted, "though it'd be stupid. You'd just kinda have to, to remind yourself of what you'd got away with."

A cold determination started to build in Savannah. She thought of the old woman whose life had been difficult already, taken from her by a young one whose only motive would have been greed, pure and simple.

She stood and turned to Dirk. "I don't like the fact that, if she did it, she's feeling proud of herself. I want to upset her apple cart, right and proper. Would you mind if I go have a little talk with Miss Brooklynn?"

"Not as long as you're wearin' a wire, and we're in the van right outside."

"Overly protective, are we?"

"We are that," Ryan said. "Especially where you're concerned."

"We're fond of you, love," John added. "In case you hadn't noticed."

"I've noticed," she said, feeling a blush coming on. "I appreciate it, too. Apparently, our Miss Mousy ain't as timid as we thought."

Chapter 29

When Dirk dropped Savannah off, a block from Brooklynn's modest Spanish home, he said, "One more time."

She sighed, knowing the microphone John had hooked inside her collar was working fine. But Dirk was a worrywart. At least where she was concerned.

That was endearing and occasionally annoying.

"Testing, testing. One, two, three, four, five, gonna skin that man alive . . . if he doesn't let me get out of this here vehicle and go do my job."

In her earpiece, she heard Ryan say, "Loud and clear, Dixie Darlin'. Go get her."

"They've got it," she told Dirk.

"Yeah, me too," he said, adjusting his own earpiece.

She leaned over, gave him a kiss for luck, and left him to listen and worry.

She knew, between the two of them, she had the easy part.

Crossing her fingers and saying a little prayer that their gal would be home, she hurried up the sidewalk and onto the little house's porch.

One more time, she ran the details of her plan through her mind. What she would say and when.

Yeah, like it matters, she thought. *No matter how prepared you think you are, the plan always flies out the window in the first ninety seconds.*

Savannah knocked on the door, and it took quite a while for it to open. When it did, she could hardly believe what she was seeing.

Standing there was Brooklynn Marsh-Faraday, but she was a totally different woman. Savannah was shocked by the transformation that a stylish outfit, makeup, and hairdo could make.

Brooklynn was wearing a figure-hugging dress, tights, and booties that showed she did, indeed, have a body and was quite physically fit. Her makeup was impeccable, accenting her slightly slanted eyes, and giving them a beautiful, exotic quality. Her hair was not only washed, but styled, full and glistening as it flowed over her shoulders to her waist.

Brooklynn was a knockout! Go figure!

"Wow," Savannah said. She almost added, "You clean up good," but changed it to, "You look very nice. Going somewhere?"

"Just hanging out," was the casual reply.

Savannah thought she smelled alcohol on her breath, but she couldn't be sure. If it was booze, the gal had started a bit early in the day.

Celebrating, perhaps?

"May I come in?" Savannah asked.

"Oh, yeah, sure."

Brooklynn opened the door and stepped back so she could enter.

The house had gone through a transformation, too, though

not as drastic as the lady herself. Some of the clutter had been put away and the smell of urine was less. Apparently, some kitty had a newly cleaned litter box.

"What's up?" Brooklynn asked, motioning for Savannah to sit and doing the same herself.

"I've been thinking about you. Wondering if you're doing okay."

"Really?"

Savannah noticed that the look on her face wasn't one of appreciation, but suspicion.

Brooklynn gave her a not-so-pleasant smile and added, "How nice of you."

Savannah couldn't recall hearing the word "nice" spoken with such sarcastic coldness.

Yes, this was definitely not a mousy miss sitting in front of her. This gal was hard, cold, and for some reason, no longer trying to hide it.

Savannah took a deep breath and got a nearly dizzying, strong smell of alcohol.

Whiskey.

No doubt about it. A lot of it.

"I've been thinking it must be hard for you," Savannah continued, "what with Geoffrey being arrested. Again. You all alone here. Again. With you just a newlywed. I'm sure you were hoping for more."

"Much more," was the simple, blunt answer.

"Are you going to be okay?" Savannah asked. "Do you have anyone to support you during this—"

"I don't need support. I'm fine. But thank you for caring."

Again, with the sarcastic tone.

This Brooklynn was the exact opposite of the one who was

sitting on the floor, weeping about never being able to repair their relationship with Great-Grandma.

Was the change in her personality due to drinking? Savannah wondered. Some people turned into someone else as soon as they downed alcohol.

But Savannah didn't think the strong stench was coming from Brooklynn. She only had a bit on her breath. This smell was so powerful, Savannah would have been reluctant to strike a match.

"I suppose you're wondering about the estate," Savannah said, venturing into dangerous territory.

"What's to wonder about?" Brooklynn said. "She died, he's going to jail, we're married, I don't have to worry about paying the bills anymore. Or his ridiculously high attorney bills."

"I see."

For just a second, the harsh exterior seemed to slip, and Savannah thought she saw a bit of fear flit across her face.

"You do?" she asked in a voice more like Timid Brooklynn.

"I think so. You put so much into this relationship. Years, money, time, effort. I can't imagine Geoffrey was easy to live with. If you wind up benefiting from his great-grandmother's passing, and he doesn't . . . oh, well."

A broad smile lit up Brooklynn's face. Apparently, it felt great to be so "understood."

"That's exactly what I was thinking," she said. "I'm sorry she died, but still, some good should come from it."

A slight breeze came through a nearby window and Savannah got another strong smell of whiskey.

Wow, that girl must've bathed in it this morning, she thought.

Then the breeze shifted slightly, and she realized the smell was coming from behind the sofa.

She flashed back on their first visit, when there had been a flurry of activity tossing things into the corner behind the furniture.

Slowly, Savannah stood, knelt on the couch, and looked behind it. "I'm sorry, darlin'," she said, "but I think you might've spilled something back here. Smells like vanilla flavoring or—"

That was when she saw it. An empty bottle of whiskey, a large, fresh puddle of the stuff on the floor, clothes, and other items that had been thrown there. But more importantly, there was a beautiful small crystal glass with ruby flashing along the top, finished off with a stripe of gold.

Savannah reached into her pocket, pulled out a surgical glove, and slipped it on. "Oh, lookie! What have we here?" she said, reaching down and retrieving the glass.

She held it up for Brooklynn to see. For the sake of the men waiting outside and listening, she said, "A lovely glass with a red top and gold trim. How nice! Where did you find something like this, Brooklynn?"

For a long time, the women stared at each other. Brooklynn wavered between a "mouse in a trap" look and her cold, nasty persona. In the end, the icy gal won.

"I think you know where I found it," she replied. "I think we both know what it means."

"We do." Savannah took a small brown paper bag from inside her purse and slipped the glass inside it. "It means Geoffrey's done a lot of bad stuff. But it was you who drugged and strangled his granny and left her in that awful pose. You wrote those blackmail e-mails. All the while, you were framing Geoffrey for it, bringing that manuscript over here and giving us permission to search. Very smart, lady."

Brooklynn gave a slight nod. "That's an interesting theory you have there. Do go on."

"I can understand what you've got against Geoffrey. But how about Lucinda? You acted as if you liked her the other day."

"She was horrible to me. Treated me like dirt the first I met her. She looked me up and down, and she decided right then I wasn't good enough to be in her family. Knowing what a pig Geoffrey is, you can imagine how offended I was."

"Of course. He didn't deserve you."

"So true! Then after I found out what a mess she was living in over there, I knew she was crazy to pass judgment on me."

"That must have been when you went back to scope out the place and plan the murder."

"What?"

"The last time you were there as Lucinda's guest, you only went into the parlor, and it was still clean. If you saw the mess firsthand, it must've been when you went there uninvited. When you broke in, looked around, memorized those stupid tunnels, and planned how you were going to do it."

Brooklynn said nothing, but gave her a funny little smile, as though she was enjoying herself.

Savannah could tell she was aching to talk about it. Killing another human being is the biggest event in most murderers' lives. They always want to share it. With somebody. Anybody. Especially someone who understands.

"I understand, you know," Savannah assured her. "I probably would have done the same thing."

"No, you wouldn't. You're a *nice* person."

Again, "nice" was spoken as though it was the most horrible word in the English language.

"I'm nice to people who deserve it. Not to people who don't. Geoffrey didn't deserve good things. His great-grandmother had a ton of nice things, but see what she did with them? You worked

289

hard your whole life, and thanks to him getting in trouble and her not helping him, you lost it all. You deserved reimbursement, one way or another."

"Yes! That's exactly what I thought!"

"She wasn't going to live that much longer anyway."

"Exactly!"

"What good was her money doing her . . . her living there in a landfill."

"I know!"

"By knocking her out with the drugs first, she wouldn't even feel it."

"Well, that was the plan." Brooklynn slumped back in her chair, less jubilant than before. "It didn't work out the way I'd hoped."

"I hate it when that happens. You think you've got it all worked out and then . . ."

"One little thing."

"What went wrong? Looks to me like you covered your bases just fine."

"She passed out before she could show me where the . . . where something was that I wanted. That was actually the reason for drugging her. I thought if she was woozy enough, I could tell her to give it to me or else, and she would. Plus, she wouldn't fight me so much. She took me to the area she said it was in, but then she passed out and wouldn't wake up."

"Oh, man! That must have been frustrating!"

"It was! But nobody's gonna find it . . . that thing . . . anyway in all that mess, so it all worked out okay."

"The will, you mean. The new one that leaves everything to Mary Mahoney."

Brooklynn looked dumbstruck. "You know about that, too?"

"Let's just say there are two very smart women in this room right now. One of whom is going to be very, very rich."

They shared a laugh, then Savannah said, "How did you get Geoffrey to marry you so fast? I mean, you needed to be married so you'd have the money once he went off to prison."

"That was the easy part. He heard those guys he'd done that burglary with had been arrested. He figured they'd be giving him up any minute. I told him if we were married, they couldn't make me testify against him. Now that was a stroke of luck. I think it was the Man Upstairs looking out for me, don't you?"

"Oh, I'm sure He's watching . . . and listening, too."

A small voice in her earpiece said, "Every word. We got it all."

"There's just one thing I can't figure out," Savannah continued.

"What's that?"

"If you gave Lucinda a fatal dose, and she'd already passed out, she was dying anyway. Why the strangulation? Why the posing?"

"That nasty old bitch made me feel really bad when she put me down like she did. Even after I left her that day, I kept seeing the disgust in her eyes. I saw it constantly, from the time I woke up in the morning until I went to sleep. I saw her eyes, and I thought how I was going to get even with her. When I'd start feeling bad, I'd imagine what I was going to do to her someday and feel so much better."

"So, when the time came . . . ?"

"I couldn't just let her go to sleep. Nice people die that way. No, it had to be *my* way, exactly the way *I* imagined with the world seeing her for what she was—a dead, old, ugly slut."

"Okay. That's it."

Those were the code words for Dirk to come in and take over.

In seconds he'd come charging through the door, and that was a good thing. Because Savannah desperately needed to go outside and get some fresh air. She thought there was an excellent chance that she was going to be sick.

Chapter 30

Since their previous backyard celebration had been interrupted, the Moonlight Magnolia gang, friends and family, decided to throw another party a week later. Life was good. They had so many wonderful things to celebrate.

It was a group affair with everyone contributing in their own way. Dirk was manning the barbecue by popular demand. Several bottles of meat-dedicated, room temperature beer had been placed tactfully within his reach by the grill. Loathing a warm brew as he did, there was no chance he would be stealing sips from it.

Tammy brought trays of fresh fruit and vases of wildflowers, picked in the hills that morning. After Freddy stuck several of the blossoms in Vanna's curls, she decided to decorate the Colonel by putting daisies in his collar. Brody quickly intervened on behalf of his buddy, telling her, "I know you mean well, Miss Vanna, but no self-respectin' hound dog wears flowers. Not a *boy* hound, anyway."

The moment she turned away, Brody removed them and

set them aside. He promised to help her decorate Cleo's and Diamante's collars later.

Waycross supplied the music. He rigged up a set of powerful car speakers to a battery, and as self-appointed DJ was playing tunes chosen for everyone present: Johnny Cash, classical, rock, and the staple—good ol' California beach songs from back in the day.

Ethan provided a tent, for those who might prefer to be out of the sun. Inside he had set up a high-tech audiovisual presentation that was a memorial to Lucinda, showing the highlights of her life. The positive ones. The sunshine and none of the darkness.

Mary Mahoney sat in the tent, watching, weeping, and laughing with the others who ventured inside to view. She had helped Ethan assemble the photos and videos into a loving remembrance of a colorful life, flawed as it was, lived with gusto and courage.

Savannah had prepared a dozen side dishes the night before. Everything from her signature potato salad to a few southern favorites, salads that contained nary a vegetable, but plenty of fruit-flavored gelatin, whipped topping, and marshmallows. She set them out on the table, knowing that Tammy would soon be pointing out the folly of calling something a "salad" that contained nothing but man-made chemicals.

Granny had insisted on doing the baking. Savannah suspected it was so she could enjoy the company of her favorite kitchen assistant, Alma. The younger Reid sister had arrived the day before, and Savannah felt her home was now complete, just having the dark-haired, blue-eyed, gentle beauty under her roof.

So much to celebrate!

As John passed around the trays of exquisite gourmet hors

d'oeuvres from ReJuvene, Ryan offered some to the group standing around the grill. When he got to Savannah, he said, "I'm so happy to know your sister. She's absolutely delightful. Sort of a mini Savannah."

"No, she's her own person," Savannah said, though pleased with the compliment. "Younger."

"Well . . ." Ryan shrugged.

"She's a lot nicer, too," Savannah added.

"That's for sure," Dirk said, earning him a swat with a dish towel.

John walked up to them and said, "Is it me, or does there seem to be something going on between your little sister and our Ethan?"

He nodded toward the makeshift dance area where Way-cross was playing a sweet love ballad. The only couple on the "floor" was Alma in her brightly flowered sundress, her hair in a graceful updo, slowly swaying to the music in the arms of Hollywood's leading man.

They were chatting away, giggling, lost in their own world.

Savannah could hardly believe her eyes when she saw Ethan rest his cheek on the top of Alma's head and close his eyes, a look of pure bliss on his face. To watch them, she could imagine they had been dancing together for years.

Could it be? Her little sister and Ethan Malloy?

"Holy cow!" she said. "Can you imagine? What if they . . . ?"

"Don't look now, but I think they already have," John said. "What a fine thing. She's just what he needs."

"She is?" Savannah thought of her sister, the darkness of their childhood, the poverty, her total lack of what the world would consider "sophistication."

"It would be wonderful, but they're so different," Savannah told him. "She's just a simple country girl, and he's a man of the world. She's a one-eighty-degree turn from Hollywood."

"That's exactly why he'd want her. Why he needs someone like her. She's real."

They watched as little Freddy walked up to the dancers, reached up, and tugged on the leg of his father's slacks.

Startled out of their reveries, Ethan and Alma looked down, saw the child, and laughed.

"Hey, are you cutting in on me, young man?" they heard Ethan say to his son as he picked him up in his arms. "You want to dance with my girl?"

As though understanding exactly what his father meant, Freddy held his arms out wide to Alma.

She laughed and eagerly took him, placed their arms and hands in the appropriate dancing positions, and waltzed him across the lawn.

As everyone cheered, Ethan threw his hands up in surrender and walked over to join them by the grill. "Did you see that?! I change that kid's dirty diapers, and he goes and steals my girl!"

Something about the way he'd said "my girl" caused Savannah's heart to soar. John was right. She had introduced Ethan to her sister three hours ago, and he was already calling her his girl.

She glanced over to the dessert table to see if Granny was watching and saw that she was taking it all in and grinning broadly. When the two women's eyes met, Gran laughed, put her hands together as though in supplicating prayer, then raised them, palms up, to the heavens, as if giving praise.

Savannah laughed. For years, Gran had been praying for a good man for her little Alma. If there was one thing Savannah knew, it was that sooner or later, the good Lord always answered Granny's prayers. Savannah suspected it was because she wouldn't quit until she plumb wore Him down.

Ethan reached over and took hold of Savannah's elbow.

"Excuse me," he said. "I don't want to take you away from your hostess duties, but could I have a word with you?"

"Sure."

She led him over to a bench behind the vegetable garden, farther away from Waycross's speakers and all the gabbing going on around the food area.

As they sat down on the bench, she saw him cast a couple of looks at Alma and Freddy, who were still enjoying their waltz. They had been joined by Brody and Vanna and, considering that the toddler had just learned to walk, Brody was doing a pretty good job of showing her how to sway back and forth, standing on one chubby baby foot, then the other.

"I hope somebody's getting that on video," she said. "It's about the sweetest thing I've seen in a long time."

"It certainly is," he said. But Ethan wasn't watching Brody and Vanna. He was enjoying the sight of his son and the pretty girl who was twirling him around and around, making him squeal with joy.

Ethan seemed to make an effort to pull himself back to the business at hand. He shook his head, reached into his pocket, and pulled out a check. He took Savannah's hand, opened it, and placed it in her palm.

"This is for you," he said. "Don't even start to make a fuss because—"

She glanced down at the sum and gasped. "No way! You already paid me! I got the bank transfer three days ago!"

"This is a bonus, and that is the fuss I just warned you not to make."

"But it's too much, really," she said, trying to shove it into his tightly closed fist. "I can't possibly take it."

"Well, I'm not taking it back, so you're stuck with it." He gave her a warm, brotherly look and said, "Savannah, please let me do this for you. For your family. You do so much for others. It would make me so happy if you'd take this money and spend it on something special. Maybe something you've wanted for a long time but couldn't . . . you know."

"Afford?"

"Yeah. That. Isn't there something you'd really like to have for yourself, or someone else you love?"

Savannah looked across the yard at the people who mattered most to her in her life. Such good people. So deserving. So content with so little.

"There is one," she whispered.

"Good." He smiled his big famous breathtaking smile. "I'm so glad. Thank you!"

"No, thank you!" She leaned over and kissed his cheek.

She saw him cast yet another lovesick look over at Alma and Freddy, who had ended their dance and were clapping along with everyone who was watching them. "Wait a minute," she said. "This isn't a bribe . . . so that I'll put in a good word for you with my sister, is it?"

His eyes followed Alma as she led Freddy over to Tammy's fruit table and gave him a chocolate-dipped strawberry. "No," he said softly and quite seriously. "That's a situation I hope I can handle all by myself."

"I think you can, too, big boy."

"Yeah?" He looked so hopeful, like a little kid on Christmas Eve.

"Oh yeah. I know her. I know you. Go for it!"

The next thing she knew, she was sitting alone on the bench, and he was headed for the fruit table.

"Hm," she said to herself. "Reckon he's got a powerful hankering for a chocolate strawberry!"

Savannah lingered on the bench long enough to make a telephone call, collect some information, and solidify her plans.

Then she strolled over to the magnolia tree, where Granny was sitting in a chaise, enjoying the shade and a glass of lemonade. The Colonel lay beside her chair, snoring as she stroked his back.

She raised her legs, vacating a seat for Savannah on the foot end of the chaise.

Savannah sat down and pointed to the hound. "He's worn to a frazzle from all this socializing with energetic kiddos."

"It's good for 'im. It's good for all of us. Kids keep ya young."

"Looking at you, I believe that. We were your fountain of youth."

"You and Alma and Waycross were. The rest . . ."

They laughed.

Savannah reached over, took her grandmother's hand, and folded it into hers. "I've got some good news to tell you," she said.

"Oh, I done heard about how Mary found that will, right where you told her, where that lady's body was."

"Yes, that's good news, but—"

"I know she might sell the mansion to Ryan and John, too. They asked her, and she said she'd think about it. That she prob'ly would, 'cause it wouldn't be the same for her if Miss Lucinda ain't there. Plus, she don't think it's good for her health, bein' there."

"I hadn't heard! How wonderful! Can you imagine what Ryan and John could do with that place, with all their good taste and sophistication! It would be glorious!"

"Once they got all the junk out."

"Well, yes. There's that. But neither of those things are my good news."

"Oh, I know. Waycross and Tammy done invited Alma to stay at their house till she finds a place of her own. Your house's about full to the brim."

"I don't mind one bit and neither does Dirk. But that's not my news."

"I'm plumb outta ideas. What is it?"

Savannah looked down at the hand in hers and remembered when it had far fewer lines. When its veins had not been purple but had been smooth. When there were no age spots or misshapen knuckles.

She thought of all that hand had accomplished in its eighty-plus years. All the diapers it had changed, noses it had wiped, wounds it had tended, backs it had patted, troubled heads it had soothed, meals it had cooked, and broken things it had mended. Including hearts.

She wouldn't have changed one thing about that hand, lines, veins, or spots. Or the woman who owned it.

"I was just given a gift," Savannah began. "A very special gift that I didn't particularly deserve and certainly wasn't expecting."

"That's wonderful, child! I'm happy for you!"

"The person who gave it to me told me to use it to do something good for my family. Something I've wanted to do for a long time."

"Really! Bless their hearts! Although I'm sure you deserved it. You're my Savannah girl, and you deserve more than this whole world could give you."

"So do you, Granny. That's why I'm so happy to give you my good news."

"What's that, child?"

"I just made a phone call to that beautiful mobile home park down on the beach."

"The one that's right on the water?"

"Yes. The one that I know you've had your eye on ever since you moved here."

"Oh, sugar." She chuckled and squeezed Savannah's hand.

"That's just a daydream for me. One o' them fantasies you play around with in your head that you know ain't never really gonna happen. It's just nice to think about. Livin' right there by the water, where all you gotta do is walk out your door and there's the Pacific Ocean! Feelin' them fresh breezes all day and all night. It's just a dream."

"But we Reid girls believe that dreams can come true."

"Sure, we do. Just look at us, livin' here in California and—"

"In a rusty trailer that's parked among a bunch of yahoos making meth and turning tricks and who knows what else."

"I'm contented. Nobody's gonna bother me. I got the good Lord watchin' out for me, and if He ever dozes off on the job I got the Colonel and a twelve-gauge shotgun full o' rock salt."

"That's all well and good. I'm glad you're contented with what you have. But I want you to have more than living in Dirk's old rusty trailer. I want you to live in a nice mobile home in that wonderful park. I want you to walk barefoot on the beach every day, just like you've dreamed, for the rest of your life and watch every sunset and soak up as much of that sunlight and enjoy as many of those breezes as you can."

Tears filled Gran's eyes as she clung to Savannah's hand. "Granddaughter," she said. "I know you mean well, and I love you for it. But I won't go into debt at my age, and I refuse to let you either. There's no way we could—"

"We can. We will. Pay cash, that is."

Granny gasped. "That was the gift you got? Enough money to buy a mobile home and a space in a place like that?"

"Yes, and we'll furnish it any way you like. I called the park, and they have three units for sale. Would you like to go with me tomorrow and pick one out?"

Granny didn't answer. She couldn't. She was blubbering far too hard to speak as she grabbed her granddaughter and folded her into a breath-robbing hug.

301

Savannah happened to glance across the lawn, and who did she see watching their exchange but Ethan. Of course, he couldn't know what his gift had bought, but he knew who had received it, and he obviously approved.

He smiled, nodded, and threw her a kiss.

She reached up in the air, "caught" it, and held it to her heart. Where it would remain. Forever.

Chapter 31

As Savannah stood at the picnic table, scooping leftovers into plastic containers and sealing others in zip bags, she remembered one of the reasons why she loved her younger sister so much.

Alma helped with after-dinner cleanup.

"If you'll toss me one of those bigger bags, I'll stick the leftover corn on the cobs in it," Alma said from the other end of the table.

Savannah slid the box of bags down to her and said, "This brings back memories, doesn't it? All those dishes I washed. All those pans you dried?"

"It sure does." Alma smiled across the table at Savannah with eyes the same cobalt blue as her own. "I can't say I enjoyed it all that much at the time. Mostly because I was frettin' about the fact that the others weren't lending a hand. But now that I look back on those evenings, I wouldn't give them up for anything."

"Me either. But only because of you. You actually managed to make kitchen cleanup fun."

"You too. When we were little, we blew bubbles at each other. Then when we got older, we talked about boys. Told each other our secrets. That was always fun."

Savannah glanced around to make sure no one was listening. "Speaking of boys, I couldn't help noticing that you and Ethan seem to be getting along well."

Instantly, Alma's eyes twinkled even brighter. "Oh, we are, Savannah. I knew he was handsome, of course, and a great actor, but I had no idea he was so nice."

"I'd say he's even nicer than he is handsome, and that's saying something. It looked like you were enjoying each other's company."

"We were! The dancing was just . . . Oh, wow, Savannah. His little boy is a sweetie, too. We took to each other right away."

"I could see that. I'm excited for you, Alma. You've barely arrived in California, and you're already fitting right in."

"Thank you for telling me to come. I don't think I would've had the courage otherwise."

"*You?* Lacking in courage?" Savannah shook her head. "Oh, Alma. Do you remember that time when I had gone out with Granny, and you younger kids were home all alone, and Cordele set the house on fire?"

"I'm not likely to forget that. Ever." She shuddered. "It was the scariest thing I ever went through."

"I'm sure it was. But you got all the rest of the young'uns outside and put them under the old tree in the front yard, like Granny told you to do if there was an emergency like that."

"The worst part was when I couldn't find Jesup. Momma hadn't put her to bed before she left for the tavern. I finally found her laying on some dirty laundry in the bathtub."

"Yeah, Shirley wasn't much of a tuckin' in kinda mom."

"I didn't think I was going to get us out of there alive. I kept thinking Jesup's gonna die, and she's only six years old! It's gonna be all over for her before she even gets started!"

Savannah pictured the sweet little girl with the bright blue eyes and dark hair, who had dragged her sister to safety that night with no concern for her own. "Yes, Jesup was only six, just starting out. But do you know how old *you* were at the time, darlin'?"

She could tell by the way Alma stopped and considered it that she'd never given it any thought. "I'm two years older than Jes, so I must have been eight."

"You were just starting out yourself."

"When you put it like that, I reckon I was."

"But you got her out. The firemen were so impressed that you were able to carry her like you did through all that smoke and heat."

Savannah stepped closer to her sister, wrapped her arms around her, and drew her close to her heart. "If you had enough courage to risk your life and save another at the age of eight, sugar, you could move mountains now. There's nothing you can't do!"

"Thank you, Savannah. I love you. Always have."

"Same here, sweetpea. Same here. Now, let's go grab some more of those amazing cream cheese swirl brownies you made before that new fella of yours makes every one of them disappear!"

After a few more brownies, after a few more dances, and after saying good night to Mary, Ryan, and John, Waycross the DJ announced that he was about to play the last song of the evening.

Ethan just about overturned the picnic table, jumping up and running over to ask Alma for the pleasure.

On the other side of the table, sitting next to Savannah, Dirk snickered. "Man, that guy's a goner."

"He is, isn't he!"

They watched as Ethan and Alma practically ran to the dance area and melted into each other's arms.

"They'd better watch out or Granny'll be after them," Dirk said.

"I know. I don't think you could slide a potato chip between them right now." She watched a bit longer, then said, "I know women do, but do men ever fall in love that quickly? Love at first sight, and all that?"

"I did. But it might need to be a Reid woman."

"Aw, the perfect answer."

"Wanna go see if anybody can wedge a chip between us?"

"Sure! We'll show the kids how it's done."

Fortunately, the last song of the night was a waltz, so they were able to show off their Fred and Ginger routine.

One of the nicest surprises Savannah had discovered about her husband was that he had a passion for ballroom dancing. Even less predictable, he was actually good at it.

He pulled her into his arms and they began to glide, turn, and slide across the grass, using the full expanse of the lawn.

"Hey, we haven't forgotten how," she said.

"Never. But I think we should do this more often, just to make sure we don't."

After a few more turns, he bent his head down to hers and said, "I was going to tell you this later, but now's as good a time as any."

"What's that?"

"The phone call we've been waiting for, the one about our foster parent status for that mini ruffian we've been feeding and watering . . ."

"Yes?" she asked, her heart in her throat.

"It came through about an hour ago. I was inside the house, taking a leak upstairs, and I thought I heard the phone ringing, but I wasn't sure so—"

"Are you gonna tell me what they said, or am I gonna have to slap you nekkid and hide your clothes?"

"Yes."

"What? Yes? You're gonna tell me?"

"Yes."

"You are living dangerously, boy."

"They said *yes*. That CPS gal rushed the paperwork through, and the state of California has declared that me and you are able and fit foster parents. Officially. Done deal."

"Oh, Dirk!" She stopped dancing in midstride, and if he hadn't caught her, she would have fallen. Then she burst into tears.

He laughed, but when she continued to cry, he got concerned. "Um, you're happy about this, right?"

"Yes!"

"Just asking, 'cause you Reid women cry when you're mad, sad, or happy."

"We've been told that before."

"Sometimes, it's really hard to tell."

"Sh-h-h. Don't ruin the moment."

He grabbed her around the waist, picked her up off her feet, and swung her around several times.

"How was that?" he asked, setting her down.

"Much better. Thank you!" She turned and glanced around the yard, looking for Brody. Finally, she spotted him. He was lying on the grass near the rose garden, his head on the Colonel's shoulder. Both were sound asleep, obviously exhausted from the day's activities.

She started to cry again. She couldn't help it. Her heart was overflowing with happiness, and it was streaming from her eyes. Looking up at Dirk she said, "Then we can really keep him? At least for a while?"

"I asked about that. The CPS gal told me that his mom wants nothing to do with him, said it's his fault that she got nabbed leaving the drug house, and if it wasn't for him, she wouldn't've been charged with felony child abuse."

"What? I guess he whipped himself with that belt and burned his own butt with her cigarettes."

"Believe it or not, that's her defense."

"She's mean *and* crazy. She'll be going away for a long, long time."

"No kidding. So, I asked the CPS woman if she thought there was a chance, even a small chance in hell, that we might be able to actually adopt him."

"Adopt?" The very word sent a thrill through her that nearly caused her knees to buckle again. "*Adopt* him? Like *forever* adopt?"

"I know, I know. I should have asked you first, but when she told me about his mother I got all excited and thought, maybe we could. Maybe we had a chance. Then I asked her, and she said we had an excellent chance! *Excellent*, Van!"

He paused for a moment to catch his breath, and Savannah saw that he, too, had tears in his eyes. He sniffed, then continued, "But only if you really, really want to. It's a super big deal, I know, and you shouldn't do it just for me. I wouldn't want that. It's gotta be something that you want as bad as I do because—"

He couldn't say any more because she was kissing him, crying, and kissing him again.

"You *are happy*, right?" he managed to gasp when they finally came up for air.

"Ye-e-e-e-s! Ye-e-e-e-s! I'm so dadgum happy I can't stand it!"

"Oh. Good! Then me too!"